# DARK MEMENTO

## VERONA BAY

Katie Reus

Cover art: Jaycee of Sweet 'N Spicy Designs
Editor: Julia Ganis
Author website: https://www.katiereus.com

Publisher's Note: This is a work of fiction. Names, characters, places, and incidents are either the products of the author's imagination or used fictitiously, and any resemblance to actual persons, living or dead, or business establishments, organizations or locales is completely coincidental.

Dark Memento /Katie Reus. -- 1st ed.
KR Press, LLC

ISBN-13: 9781635560534
ISBN-10: 1635560535

*For all my wonderful readers.*

# PROLOGUE

Shards of agony ripped through her as she yanked against her bonds. The rope had rubbed her wrists and ankles raw enough that she'd lost a lot of blood and skin. But the pain reminded Serenity that she was still alive—and it kept her *awake*. She couldn't fall asleep, couldn't lose any time no matter how much it hurt or how exhausted she was. Not when her sister needed her. Not when she needed to stay alive.

"Savannah," she rasped out, turning her head to where her twin was strapped down on a makeshift wooden table less than ten feet from her in the semi-darkened room of the one-bedroom cabin. Flashes from the lightning outside illuminated her sister nearly every half minute, but she could still see her because of the lone oil lamp on the floor flickering between them.

Even though she could see Savannah, she might as well have been on another planet for how far away it seemed. They were both trapped in a horror movie come to life. The horror was almost too much to bear, too much to accept. But she wasn't going to let them get killed by a psychopath.

"Too cold," Savannah murmured, her body trembling slightly against her own restraints as thunder rumbled in the distance. Her voice was too weak, too thready. "Just want to…sleep."

Ice slid through Serenity at her sister's words. Serenity was naked, in pain and freezing from the lack of warmth in the run-down cabin, but that tone terrified her. Because it was filled with defeat. She knew her twin better than anyone, and Savannah was giving up.

"No." Her own voice was ragged, filled with a sort of manic desperation she recognized as the worst kind of fear. Worse than the thought of dying or being tortured, or even being raped—the thought of a world without her sister in it. She could not accept that reality.

She *would* not. "Keep your eyes open, look at me. *Look* at me!" she screamed as lightning flashed again.

Savannah's head rolled to the side, her eyes already glassy. "Get free…" Her voice trailed off into a whisper, lost as the rain picked up outside, beating against the roof even harder.

"You won't give up, I won't let you! We don't give up on anything, we fight!" she shouted, then jumped at a scraping sound.

She whipped her head around and immediately regretted it. A dull throb ricocheted through her skull and her heart careened until she discerned the source of the sound. Just a tree branch clawing at a window. The rain was torrential, the downpour thundering against the tin roof.

Their tormentor had left, but she knew he wouldn't be gone long. He had hit her in the jaw earlier as he'd stomped out of the cabin muttering to himself. When he'd struck her, it had been almost like an afterthought. He'd told her to shut the hell up, that she was next, that he was going to cleanse her, prepare her for her ascension—whatever the hell that meant. Freak. He just liked to hurt women, no matter what he said. He'd cut her sister up, letting her bleed out onto the dirty floor beneath them.

God, she wished he'd just hurt her instead of going after her sister. Hearing and seeing her twin in pain was worse than anything. She'd screamed at him to stop hurting Savannah, to stop cutting her. She'd begged him to hurt her instead, but he'd just continued humming some creepy song under his breath that sounded a lot like a hymn. While Savannah screamed until her throat was raw, until she passed out briefly.

Serenity knew who he was, or at least his moniker. Some asshole reporter had nicknamed him the Shepherd because of a message he'd left with one of his previous victims, taking credit for the killings.

Four women had been kidnapped from her college campus over the past year. Kidnapped, tortured, killed by strangulation and dumped on campus. It didn't matter that security had been beefed up, that there was a curfew and that she and her sister had been so careful—somehow he'd gotten them and they'd ended up *here*.

Wherever here was. She wished she could remember how they'd arrived here. The last thing she remembered was falling asleep in her dorm room. Then waking up in hell.

"Savannah, please say something." Tears rolled down her face as she looked at her sister again. Lightning flashed, brightening the room even as the rain abated.

Shadows stretched over everything, but she had enough visibility to see Savannah's face as everything else around them seemed to fade.

*Drip, drip, drip.*

Even with the pelting of rain, she could hear the drips of blood rolling from her sister's bound wrists and hitting the floor, one after the other, a macabre rhythm.

There was so much blood pooling on the rough wooden floor beneath Savannah. Too much.

It didn't matter that her brain was telling her one thing—Serenity's mind refused to accept what she was seeing. Savannah's jet-black hair fell limply off the makeshift table, her head lolled to the side. Her eyes, which had been a bright, electric blue, now stared sightlessly, their focus starting to cloud. And she wasn't blinking, wasn't breathing.

*Drip, drip, drip.*

Serenity held her breath and prayed as she stared at her sister. But there was no telltale rise and fall of Savannah's chest. Just the dripping.

*No.*

The cry of a wounded animal tore through the cabin. Another bolt of terror forked through her until she realized it was coming from her.

Serenity clamped her jaw shut and forced herself to stop screaming, knowing it was useless. If there was anyone nearby to hear their screams, that monster would have gagged them. He hadn't cared that they'd screamed, had seemed to get off on it. She needed a calm head, to think, but the searing agony of losing her twin was too much.

The rain picked up, harsh and pounding against the roof. Groaning, she struggled again, twisting back and forth like a woman possessed. Her wrists burned like her skin was on fire, but it was nothing compared to what he would do to her when he came back. He would cut her up and watch her bleed out too.

She had to get free. Get help. Get her sister out of here.

As she writhed back and forth, the board creaked and groaned under her weight. Savannah's board was supported by a crude-looking worktable. Serenity couldn't see hers, but the rough texture abraded her bare skin.

When the tabletop tilted a fraction under her weight, hope shot through her like a cannon blast. She didn't know if doing this would make her situation better or worse, but she had to get free. She started rolling back and forth as best she could with her limited range of motion, using her body as a weight.

Adrenaline punched through her as she gained more momentum but she didn't let up. Like a pendulum, she swung the board underneath her body until it started to fall, fall— She grunted as it crashed to the floor.

She heard more than felt the snap of bone. A split second later her brain received the message of pain. Another burst of agony ripped through her right hand. Her ring finger was bent at an odd angle.

A wave of nausea swept through her, but she didn't care because her wrists were free. Tears tracked down her face as she rolled onto her stomach. The ropes that had been holding her ankles fell loose, having slackened when the board fell off its frame. Using her good hand, she shoved up until she was on her knees.

Untangling her legs, she pushed to her feet, swayed once, twice, as she stumbled toward Savannah. "We're getting out of here," she said, her heart a staccato beat in her chest as she bent over her sister.

With a trembling hand she checked Savannah's pulse. *Nothing.*

That iciness pulsed through her veins again, this time threatening to take Serenity under. The only thing pushing her forward was that she needed to get her sister out of here. To survive.

Moving quickly, she crossed one palm over the other and started chest compressions. Then she lifted Savannah's chin up and breathed into her mouth twice. Then she started compressions again, over and over. It was difficult with her broken finger, but she forced her mind off the pain. Savannah's heart had stopped. She needed to get blood flow and oxygen circulating in her body again.

That was the immediate goal.

"One, two, three, four, five…" she counted out loud. With each second that passed with no results, sharp talons dug into her own chest, reminding her that time was running out.

She needed to get Savannah out of here even if she was gone, but their tormentor could be back any second and she was weaponless.

After the second set of chest compressions she tried to tear the ropes around her twin free. Savannah still wasn't breathing, wasn't moving. In her head Serenity knew what that meant, but she refused to accept it. In the recesses of her mind she realized she was going into shock as she frantically scanned the cabin, looking for something to cut her sister free with. They were in a sort of living room, though it had no couches.

She raced across the room, her bare feet slapping against the floor as she stepped into the attached kitchen. She started yanking open drawers. He'd taken his torture tools with him when he'd left. She'd been glad not to have to look at them as a taunting reminder that he'd be back, but now she wished they were still there— Serenity nearly shouted in triumph when she opened a drawer of mismatched cutlery.

She grabbed the biggest knife by its peeling rubber handle. She barely remembered moving back across the room, cutting through her sister's bindings, but when the second rope fell free of Savannah's wrist, the two around her ankles loosened as well. Serenity wasn't sure how he'd secured her twin, but the rope must be one long piece.

With shaky hands, she shoved the bindings off Savannah's ankles. She moved to the head of Savannah's table, looped her arms under her sister's and pulled her free. She was close, so close to getting her sister free.

The flash of lights—headlights—swept over the dimly lit living room. Like a starter pistol at a race, the brief illumination sent a rush of adrenaline punching through her.

Still clutching the knife, she dragged Savannah away from the front door and toward another near the back of the cabin. She wasn't sure how she was even carrying Savannah, given how weak she felt, but she pushed on. When Serenity shoved open the door the headlights from outside went off.

*Ohgodohgodohgod.*

She cast a frantic look around. The room had a small twin bed and two windows. No curtains. She dropped Savannah onto the bed and set the knife down to shove open one of the windows. Blood rushed so loudly in her ears it drowned out everything else.

Until the window creaked as she lifted it. The sound seemed like a gunshot going off. White paint flecks and dust covered her as she worked it upward. She peeked outside, only to be pelted in the face with a gust of rain and wind. The forest was thick behind the cabin, the trees beckoning to her.

She looked back at the bed. In her heart she knew her sister was... God, she wouldn't think the word. She still wasn't leaving Savannah behind. Hoisting her sister up, she choked back tears and shoved her out the window. When Savannah's body hit the wraparound porch with a sickening thud, Serenity grabbed the knife and followed.

Something slammed loudly inside—the front door against the wall.

"No!" he shouted, his awful voice carrying even over the storm raging outside.

Heart slamming, Serenity rolled Savannah off the porch, jumping after her into the mud and water. She only had seconds now before he figured out which way she'd gone. She couldn't escape carrying her sister.

So she did something she never could have imagined doing. "I love you," she choked out in a whisper. "I'm going to make him pay."

Then she ran, leaving Savannah's body behind. It was the only way her sister would get justice; that all the murdered women would. She could stay and attempt to fight him, but the man was huge and muscular and she was weak from shock and blood loss. And her sister was dead.

*Dead.*

Tears clogged Serenity's throat as she jumped over a jutting tree root. Her bare feet sank into mud and marsh as she raced through the dense forest. Chills racked her body, but nothing could stop her now.

She had no idea where she was, but she wasn't going to let that monster hurt anyone else, ruin any more lives. She didn't care what she had to do—she wasn't going to be his next victim.

She was going to make him pay.

Serenity hitched in a sob and kept running. If she had to run a thousand miles, she wasn't stopping until she found help. She didn't know much about the law, but his DNA was at that cabin and she'd *seen* his face. It was etched into her memory. He was...normal looking. Might even be handsome under the right circumstances.

But not to her. *Never.* The evil in his dark blue eyes was like looking into an abyss of rage and madness that wanted to see the world burn, wanted to hurt more women.

Rain slapped her face as she raced deeper into the woods. Adrenaline was her only fuel right now, keeping her going when it would be easier to collapse and give in to her heartbreak. She was on the cusp of breaking down, could feel it bone deep.

She thought she heard him behind her, turned to look. A dark, hooded figure like something out of her worst nightmare was lumbering toward her. He batted a branch out of the way, the movement angry.

She dodged to the left instead of continuing straight. With no idea where she was, she was running blind but at least the rain was hiding her tracks and covering most of her sound. It picked up again, lightning flashing in the distance.

Her thigh muscles strained as she pushed herself harder. Something sharp pierced her foot, but it barely registered. Almost as if she was sleepwalking, she continued on, slapping at foliage until she stumbled into a clearing.

*Oh God, no.* She needed the cover of woods. It was the only thing keeping her alive...

A flash of lights skated over the clearing, highlighting what she now realized were benches and tables.

Blinking, she saw that she was in a park of sorts and those lights were from a vehicle. *A parking lot.*

Knife clutched tightly in her hand, she sprinted straight toward where the headlights had been. As she moved, a blur of motion appeared from her right. Her reaction time was off as the hulking figure tackled her to the ground.

Screaming, she slashed out with her knife, slicing at anything she could hit.

He grunted and reared back. "Bitch!"

A kaleidoscope of colors exploded behind her eyes as he backhanded her across the face. She rolled to the side, grasping blindly for her knife, but clawed up nothing but grass and mud.

He pinned her down, his big body trembling with rage. "You're going to pay for this," he snarled.

"Hands in the air, now!" a male voice boomed through the air.

The man above her froze.

"Now, or I put a bullet in your head!" It was the same commanding voice.

*Do it!* she inwardly screamed. *Shoot him!*

When the man moved off her, she immediately scrambled, diving for her knife before turning to face the newcomer.

A man in a dark green uniform with a matching parka and heavy-duty rain boots had his weapon pinned on the monster who'd killed her sister. The knowledge that he was some sort of law enforcement pierced through the haze filling her mind as she watched him slam the psychopath to the ground and handcuff him.

When her savior turned to look at her there was a chilling mixture of horror and relief in his gaze. She was vaguely aware of him talking to her, but she couldn't make out any of his words. She just saw his mouth moving, and his tone was soothing as he took her knife away. She didn't fight him. He wasn't the enemy. Her numbed brain knew that much.

And as he slipped his parka around her, she forced herself to talk through chattering teeth. "She's dead. My sister's dead. He killed her."

And she would never be whole again.

## CHAPTER ONE

*Eight years later*

"Bye, Adeline," Serenity called over her shoulder as she left Tailwaggers Grooming.

The bell jingled overhead as she stepped out into the chilly afternoon air. In just three weeks the annual Verona Bay art festival would be here and the town was already getting prepared for it. Banners lined every light pole, brightly announcing the big event that brought a lot of tourism to the small, coastal Florida town.

Shivering in the coolness, she hurried down the sidewalk, past a coffee shop, an antique store, two clothing shops, and a tapas bar that wouldn't be open for a couple hours yet. She had two stops to make before she needed to pick up her daughter from school.

"Serenity."

Everything inside her went still at the sound of that deliciously deep voice. One she'd know anywhere.

Lucas Jordan.

Despite the chilly afternoon, heat bloomed inside her because of one single word from him. She was a grown woman with a young daughter, but around Lucas she felt tongue-tied and vividly aware of him in ways she'd been trying to ignore for months. Trying and failing. She didn't believe in fairy tales and happy endings anymore—

life had taught her to be too smart for that—but the man made her question everything.

Shutting the hatch of her SUV, she turned to find him standing on the curb looking just as sexy as always. He just exuded it without even trying. "Hey, what are you doing here?"

He shoved his hands in his pockets as she stepped up onto the sidewalk. Tall, dark and handsome didn't even begin to cover it with him. His dark brown hair was cut military short and only served to show off his too-handsome face. "Took a late lunch and saw you headed out. You picking up Harper from school?"

"Yeah, I've got a couple errands to run first though."

He gave her one of those sexy half-smiles she looked forward to far too much. With broad, muscular shoulders, Lucas was about six feet two and had twin dimples. So whenever he smiled she got a perfect view of them—and her insides melted. "How is she?"

"Good. It's music week so it's been very loud at our house. She got to bring home a mini-drum set yesterday, so that's been fun."

Lucas let out a short laugh, the action relaxing his entire body and making her want to dissolve into a puddle at his feet. It was seriously wrong how much he affected her when she'd been half dead inside for nearly a decade. "How did she like the stuffed butterfly?"

Last week he'd bought Harper a gift, which had surprised her. They'd been friends for six months—ever since he'd brought his dog Daisy in for grooming. But they usually just met up for coffee and occasionally lunch. With her schedule it was hard to do much else. And the truth was, she wasn't willing to make time for anything else. After her husband had died overseas in an ambush only two weeks before his deployment ended, she'd had to step up and take care of everything in her and her daughter's life—and discovered that she was more than capable of standing on her own two feet. She couldn't go back to that woman she'd been before, and a relationship with anyone simply wasn't going to happen. Not even with someone as wonderful as Lucas.

"She loved it, thanks. She showed it to all her friends—proudly. And she's even more excited for spring to come now so we can make a butterfly garden." Something told Serenity it was more the giver than the actual gift that meant something to Harper. Serenity wasn't sure how she felt about that, but there wasn't much she could do at this point.

"I'm glad." Clearing his throat, Lucas rubbed a hand against the back of his neck, looking almost nervous. His bright emerald green eyes flashed with something she couldn't quite put her finger on. "Listen—"

"Come on, slacker!"

Serenity turned to see Easton, Lucas's older brother by barely one year, stepping out of Momma's Kitchen and zipping his jacket up. At thirty-five, Easton looked younger than both his brothers, probably because of his easygoing attitude and slightly longer, shaggy hair. He smiled and gave Serenity a half-wave. He'd been a Marine years ago, just like Lucas. Now he was a firefighter in Verona Bay.

"Easton had the day off so we grabbed lunch, but it's the end of a project so I better get out of here." Lucas owned Jordan Construction with one of his cousins. The company had been passed on to them by their fathers and it was one of the most successful in the region. They did good, quality work and didn't try to screw people on prices. Plus they were diversified, doing both commercial and residential projects.

"Are you still coming by the shop tomorrow with Daisy?" God, did she have to sound so hopeful? She inwardly winced, wanting to snatch the question back. But six months of wanting him had apparently removed her filter. Even though she'd always known who the Jordan family was, Lucas was four years older than her and they'd never run in the same circles when she was younger.

She'd met him almost the first week she'd moved back to Verona Bay, and for her at least, the attraction had been instantaneous—and completely unexpected. Her husband had been gone for two years and even though things hadn't been great between them before he died, she still hadn't expected to want someone else to such distraction. She'd thought that part of her had died.

Lucas gave her one of those wicked smiles that had butterflies taking flight inside her. "Yeah, she needs a haircut pretty bad."

Daisy was a shepherd mix, and beyond adorable. Lucas had gotten her from an animal rescue shelter over a year ago, and seeing how wonderful she was made Serenity want to get another dog.

"See you then." And she'd definitely be looking forward to it. More than she should. They were just friends, something she seemed to be reminding herself of more and more. But even if she had been looking for a relationship, she and Harper were a package deal. She couldn't see Lucas wanting to take on a ready-made family anyway.

He nodded and gave her an intense, unreadable look before he turned and headed toward his waiting brother. She shouldn't watch him walk away. She *ordered* herself not to. But she was weak when it came to Lucas. So, so weak.

He wore worn jeans and a jacket over his work shirt, but nothing could hide the raw power of the man. He and his cousin took an active role in the day-to-day business and he definitely wasn't afraid to get his hands dirty. His body had been honed to perfection from hard labor. She'd had way too many fantasies about what he'd look like without his clothes on. And on that note, she needed to get out of here or she'd be late.

It didn't take long to stop by the local bakery and pick up her order. By the time she was on the road again, the scents of cinnamon, peanut butter and chocolate teased her as she made the short drive to the sheriff's station. She stopped by occasionally to drop off baked goods to the local law enforcement. It was partially a thank-you for the men and women who put their lives on the line every day.

If it hadn't been for a game warden pulling in overtime eight years ago, she'd be dead. But she also did it because she was friends with some of the staff, including Sheriff Lincoln Jordan—Lucas's brother. They'd gone to college together and he'd known Savannah, had been there for her after...everything. He was one of the few people she'd stayed in contact with after she'd moved away. Linc was one of those solid people you could just depend on. And that was another reason she couldn't get involved with Lucas: too many messy complications.

She'd finally gotten to a place where she felt almost normal. Since she'd moved back to Verona Bay, people no longer gave her pitying looks. She was now just known as Serenity Washington, single mom and pet grooming shop owner—not Serenity Washington, widow and sole survivor of a serial killer.

She might have adapted and survived, but there would always be a part of her missing. Losing her twin that terrible night had been like losing part of herself in some ways. Some days, when she was feeling extra sorry for herself, the pain thrived inside her, clawing at the memories she'd buried deep.

*Drip, drip, drip.*

She gritted her teeth, locking down that particular thought, and turned up the radio. But she frowned when the same black sedan stayed behind her for the ten-minute drive. Verona Bay wasn't so big that she wouldn't notice someone following her, but she tried not to let her paranoia get the better of her. Not when she knew it could become all-consuming. The driver was likely just headed in the same direction she was, that was all.

The man who'd killed her sister was in jail. Not everyone was a killer out to get her.

## CHAPTER TWO

Her fingers tightened around the steering wheel as she followed Serenity in her car.

Everyone thought Serenity was so perfect. But she should have died just like her twin eight years ago. Everything would be better if she was gone.

She'd been dealing with her anger—dealing with that stupid bitch living back in her town again—for too long now. She'd thought she could handle having to see Serenity's face, but Serenity had pushed her too far.

*She wants to take what's yours,* the voice always lurking in her mind whispered.

If Serenity was out of the way, her life would be better. Ever since the golden girl had moved back to town she'd ruined *everything.*

That dark voice inside her whispered to just end it today. Just kill Serenity. She'd never see it coming.

Then she could have everything she wanted. The woman just had to get in her way. Stupid cow still didn't realize the Shepherd hadn't worked solo all those years ago. No one knew. Not even the Feds. It was because of her that Serenity, Savannah and all the others had been taken. No one knew the part she'd played in everything.

All those girls had gotten what they'd deserved. They'd all had perfect lives, come from perfect families who were proud of them. They'd had the right clothes, right boyfriends, everything. While she'd been on the fringe. Always on the outside. A dirty, shameful little secret.

Not anymore. She was finally accepted, had made a life for herself as a normal, respectable member of society.

At least on the outside.

So what if she still had contact with the Shepherd? There was no way she could cut him out of her life. It would be like cutting out a part of her soul.

In him she saw the same darkness that lived inside her, had from the moment they'd finally met. That day was etched in her memory forever. But he'd be livid if she went after Serenity now. Before, he'd wanted to cleanse Serenity—and all the others—to do God's work. Only now...Serenity was a mother. The Shepherd never killed mothers. The very idea repulsed him.

*Who cares what he thinks?* that seductive voice whispered again. *This is your life. Take what you want. Make that bitch suffer.*

God, why had Serenity moved back to Verona Bay? She should have just stayed away. And since she'd returned she'd made friends with everyone—including her.

Poor little Serenity, who'd been through so much. Single mom Serenity, who'd had so much tragedy, but was so strong and giving. *Ugh.* "Give me a break," she muttered.

*The Shepherd was weak. He couldn't have done anything without you and you know it. Kill her. It'll be so easy.*

She swallowed hard as she listened to her voice, to her truest desires. She rolled her shoulders as she followed after Serenity, trying to ease the growing tension. She'd been fine for years, but now the voice in her head was stronger, more insistent. Always whispering what she needed to do. It was all Serenity's fault.

Disgust slithered through her as she saw Serenity turning off into the parking lot of the sheriff's department.

Little do-gooder dropping off baked goods like Mary freaking Poppins. Everything about her was fake. It was so obvious. But the people in Verona Bay couldn't seem to see past her façade.

She continued past the sheriff's department, keeping her speed steady. She hadn't planned to follow Serenity, it had just happened. She barely remembered getting in her car, but when she'd seen Serenity this afternoon talking to Lucas something inside her had taken over.

At the next turnoff, she steered into a gas station parking lot and pulled her purse into her lap. Her fingers trembled as she thought about what she was going to do. She knew this place didn't have a working security camera. The cheap owner had just drilled two fake cameras into place. Even so, she still parked around the back. After carefully scanning to make sure she was alone, she reached into her purse with trembling hands.

She'd been carrying this trophy around for months. Deep down she'd known this day would come, that she'd make Serenity pay for surviving. For taking the Shepherd from her. If she'd just gone away like all the others, this wouldn't be necessary now. Serenity deserved this, really.

*She's just jealous of you.* The softly spoken words in her mind wrapped around her, embracing her. Giving her strength. *She pretends to like you, to be nice to you, but she thinks you're garbage.* The whispering in her mind continued.

She slammed her fist against the steering wheel. The trophy wouldn't be enough—she needed to leave a note as well. Serenity needed to suffer, to know what was coming and fear it. Because *she* was the one who was trash.

And her time was almost up. It didn't matter that the Shepherd would be angry. He was in jail. There was nothing he could do about it when she killed that bitch. But simply killing her wouldn't be enough. She had to take everything from her first.

*Tick-tock, tick-tock.* The voice was louder now. A countdown. Serenity's time was coming to an end.

# CHAPTER THREE

Serenity adjusted her scarf tighter around her neck as she made her way across the parking lot. Her breath curled in front of her like soft, white smoke. She loved the winter and everything about the season, but she'd be ready for spring soon. The longer days, blooming of flowers, and metaphorical rebirth of everything soothed her soul.

Her boots crunched over the gravel as she weaved her way through the vehicles of the Verona Bay SD parking lot. The two-story building wasn't large, but the town wasn't either.

It had been good to see Lincoln, but now she needed to pick up her daughter. Even though her marriage hadn't been the best, the one thing she and her deceased husband had cared about was making sure Harper had a normal, safe life. As safe as any parent could make it, because she knew more than most what kind of freaks were out there.

When she reached her SUV there was a plain white envelope tucked under one of the windshield wipers. Frowning, she glanced around the quiet parking lot. One of the deputies who'd been inside was trudging to his car, saw her and waved. Smiling, she waved back before tugging the envelope free.

31

She slid into her SUV and ripped it open with cold fingers—and felt her entire world tilt on its axis.

Blinking, she slid the icy silver charm bracelet into her open palm. Fear crawled through her like thick, slow molasses as she stared at it. The angel wing charm was familiar; she'd worn one like it on her wrist from age fifteen to twenty.

Back before she and her twin sister had been kidnapped and tortured by infamous serial killer Michael Black.

He'd taken all their jewelry, and it had never been recovered by the FBI when they'd searched his residence and that horrible cabin. This wasn't hers though. It was a replica of Savannah's. It...couldn't be the real thing. No way.

What kind of sick person would leave something like this for her? She closed her eyes and regretted it the instant she did. *Blood trickled onto the rough wood flooring. Drip, drip, drip. Her sister's lifeless eyes staring back at her.*

Someone knocked on the window.

Serenity let out a short scream until she realized it was her friend and former elementary school teacher Maris Carson standing outside the driver's side window. It took her fumbling hands two tries to get the door open. "Hey, what are you doing here?" She couldn't keep her voice from trembling.

Maris watched her with sharp, brown eyes. The former teacher now ran a shelter for abused women. Today she wore what Serenity thought of as her standard "uniform"—dark jeans, a white T-shirt and a thick, button-down sweater with tap-dancing moose covering it. Normally the sight of the sweater would have made her smile, but Serenity couldn't force one out. She could barely draw in a steady breath.

"Just making a report. Had a problem down at the shelter, but that's not what's worrying me now. What's wrong?"

Wordlessly Serenity held out the bracelet. Maris frowned at it then raised her eyebrows as she took it. The angel charm flipped over and that was when Serenity saw the S-1 engraved on the back. Was this actually Savannah's bracelet? No...it couldn't be.

Bile rose in her throat. Shoving Maris out of the way she jumped from the SUV and retched onto the asphalt, losing what little contents her stomach had. All her muscles tightened as she continued to dry heave until it registered that Maris was rubbing her hand up and down Serenity's spine.

God, she needed to get it together. It was just a physical object, she reminded herself. It couldn't hurt her... Except it could. Someone had sent this to terrify her and it had worked.

Blinking away tears, she used her scarf to wipe her mouth before taking it off. She tossed it into her vehicle then leaned against the side of it. "It was Savannah's. It was taken when we were... Someone left it on my windshield." And she couldn't even think of what that meant. Black had taken their jewelry when they'd been drugged and unconscious. Even though none of it had ever been recovered, there had been enough crime specials on

Black years ago—and books written about him—that it wasn't a secret that he'd taken all his victims' jewelry.

Maris's face went hard. "You just found this?"

"Yeah. In an envelope." Her throat was dry and scratchy.

Maris looked inside and pulled the envelope out by the edges in case there were fingerprints on it. When she did, a small piece of paper fluttered out. Feeling about a thousand years old, Serenity bent to pick it up but Maris was faster.

"Tick-tock, tick-tock," she read aloud. Her jaw tightened even more as she scanned the parking lot. "Grab your keys. We're heading back inside."

Fear punched through her at the note and the bracelet, but she shoved it back down. Someone wanted to scare her but she wasn't going to lose control. She started to nod in agreement, but stopped. "Give me a sec. I need to make a call and make sure someone can pick up Harper." Because she wasn't sure how long this would take. And right about now, Serenity didn't even trust herself to be behind the wheel of a vehicle.

Maris nodded, glancing around the lot. Keeping watch. "Take your time."

With trembling fingers Serenity called Carol Rose, her next-door neighbor and friend. The woman had lost her own husband years ago, before Serenity had moved back to Verona Bay, and was one of the sweetest people Serenity knew. If she had grandparents still alive, she'd want a grandmother just like Carol. When her friend didn't answer, she frowned. As anxious as she was feeling, there weren't many people she trusted with Harper.

Thankfully, when she called Lucas he picked up on the second ring. Male voices murmured lightly in the background. "Hey, Serenity."

"Hey, I have a huge favor to ask, and I know it's an imposition, but can you pick Harper up from school?" She glanced at her watch. She'd never asked him for anything like this before, but right now she was feeling way too raw. She needed to know Harper was in safe hands after this little "gift" and Lucas was one of the most responsible people she knew. If he couldn't do it she'd head to the school herself. Even though she didn't want to drag her daughter to the sheriff's department, she wasn't letting Harper get sent to afterschool care.

"Ah, sure. Everything okay?"

*No.* "Yeah, just..." She cleared her throat, not wanting to get into the whole thing. "I need to talk to the sheriff about something. It's no big deal," she rushed on.

"Are you okay? What happened?" She could hear keys jingling, then the sound of a door opening and shutting.

"I'm fine, I promise. I just...have to deal with something and I'd rather not take Harper with me." The last place her daughter needed to be was at a sheriff department. "I tried Carol, but—"

"It's no problem. I'm on my way to the school. Will they let me pick her up?"

"I'll call and let them know there's a special circumstance. Harper has a key to the house and I'll text you the code to disarm the alarm. She'll be hungry when she gets in but she can tell you what kind of snacks she likes." Her daughter was very vocal about what she wanted. Serenity had taught her to "use your words." She never wanted Harper to think she couldn't speak up for herself.

"I'll call if there's an issue. You sure everything's okay? I can have Easton or my mom pick her up and I'll meet you at the station."

That little pitter-patter in her chest beat even faster at his offer. Lucas was making it really hard for her to remember that she didn't want a relationship. It was especially hard when he was always so thoughtful. Though none of that mattered, because nothing was going to happen between them. They were just friends. If she reminded herself of that enough, maybe she'd start to believe it. She'd already had one man take over every aspect of her life because he'd wanted to take care of her—she couldn't handle that again. She couldn't handle a relationship, period. She was too broken inside and it wouldn't be fair to someone like Lucas to saddle him with all that.

"I'd really prefer you to pick her up and stay with her. I need to know she's with someone I trust." And she knew Lucas was not only trustworthy, but capable of handling any potential threats. Her daughter would be safe with him.

A short pause. "I'll text you once I've got her."

"Thanks. I really appreciate it."

He made a grunting sound, something he always did whenever she thanked him for anything. They spoke for a few more moments, and when they disconnected she allowed the smallest sliver of relief to slide through her. If Harper was in safe hands, she could deal with anything.

"Everything good?" Maris asked.

"Yeah." Feeling as if she was on autopilot, she headed back into the station and tried not to look at what Maris held in her hand.

Maris had slid the bracelet back in the envelope, probably because she didn't want to smudge any fingerprints, Serenity belatedly realized. She couldn't know for sure if it was even her sister's bracelet, but it looked the exact same, and it wasn't polished, as if it had been tarnished with age.

How had someone even gotten this bracelet? Because the man who'd carved up and killed her sister—and would have done the same to Serenity—was in prison, awaiting his death.

\* \* \*

"It could be a prank." A really sick one. But even as Serenity murmured the words, her instinct told her otherwise. She'd dealt with enough weirdos over the years sending her stupid messages to be able to sift out the garbage. And this felt menacing.

She held the cup of coffee the sheriff had given her but wasn't drinking it. She soaked up the warmth, however, needing it to ground her right now.

"I'm running it for prints, and the prison has confirmed Black is still locked up and has had almost no contact with the outside world in years. He gets letters, but never writes anyone back." Lincoln leaned back, his chair squeaking slightly under the pressure. "How similar does it look to Savannah's?"

Hearing Savannah's name made her wince, at least internally. Serenity had learned to put on a mask years ago, not wanting the outside world to see her pain and anger. She'd lost everything because of that bastard. First her sister, then her mom had died months later of heart failure.

Serenity knew better though. Savannah's murder had broken her mother. Still, talking about this with Lincoln was easier than with some stranger. Lincoln was a year older, but he'd gone to college with her and Savannah. After everything that'd happened, he'd switched to a criminal justice major. She looked at the bracelet, now in a plastic evidence bag on his desk.

"It's the same. The charms are the same at least, and the engraving on the back of the angel wing is as well." S-1 was for Savannah, since she'd been born a few minutes before Serenity. Serenity's had S-2 engraved on hers.

She resisted the urge to reach out and touch it through the plastic. When she and Savannah had turned fifteen their parents had given them charm bracelets. Savannah's had ballet slippers, an owl, a surfboard, a graduation cap, and an angel wing on it. Serenity's had also had the angel wing and graduation cap, but her other charms had been different.

"And they were taken when..."

She cleared her throat, forcing the words out. "When *we* were taken. All our jewelry. Our earrings, necklaces and bracelets. I don't even remember the other jewelry I had on but these bracelets mattered to us." When Black had been caught, the jewelry hadn't been found. It was the same with his other victims. Something Lincoln would already know—everyone around Verona Bay and anyone who'd watched the primetime TV specials would know that fact.

She set the mug on his desk, feeling slightly more grounded as she talked. Still, she was worried about what that note meant. *Tick-tock, tick-tock* was a threat. A clock counting down. But to what? Obviously nothing good.

A shiver snaked down her spine with vicious, scraping talons. Some days she was terrified of her own mortality. If something happened to her, her daughter would have no one.

"You're sure you haven't had any strange calls lately? No one harassing you at work or at home?"

He'd already asked her these same questions twice. She understood he was just doing his job, but she didn't want to go through all of them again. Maris had left half an hour ago and Serenity just wanted to get home to her daughter. It didn't matter that she'd checked in with Lucas and that she knew Harper was in more than capable hands. She still needed to see and hold her little girl.

"No. And like I said, I'm very aware of my surroundings. I pay attention." That had been burned into her psyche eight years ago. Everything in her life had changed in an instant and the effects had trickled down into every facet of her life. She took self-defense classes now and looked over her shoulder more than most people did when out in public.

Sighing, he scrubbed a hand over his face and stood. "I'm going to put in a call to the FBI tonight just to touch base about this, and we'll be looking into it as much as we can. It could be a prank but I don't like it." His expression was as dark as her mood.

She stood as well, glad he'd be contacting the Feds. She knew she could too—the agent who'd been in charge of the Black case reached out to her at least once a year. But she'd let this go through official channels. It would mean more. "Thank you."

"I'm going to follow you home just as a precaution."

She wanted to tell him he didn't have to bother, but she wasn't too proud to admit that she was scared and wouldn't mind an escort. "Thanks."

## CHAPTER FOUR

"It smells good," Harper said, carefully watching as Lucas pulled the glass pan from the oven.

Serenity hadn't asked him to do anything other than bring Harper home and keep an eye on her, but he'd wanted Serenity to have dinner when she got back. Especially after the call he'd received from the sheriff—who was also his younger brother. Lucas couldn't believe Serenity hadn't told him she'd gotten something that might have been her dead sister's—something taken by that sick freak who'd killed so many women and damaged so many families.

He locked that thought down tight, not wanting Harper to suspect anything was wrong. "It'll taste good too, trust me."

The King Ranch casserole didn't look like much and was basically layered cheese, chicken, tortillas and sour cream with a bunch of spices tossed in. Not healthy, but it was easy comfort food, something he figured Serenity would need. And it was one of the meals he could make without a recipe. His mom had made sure her boys could make five meals by the time they were eighteen. She'd told them that once they were grown, they needed to take care of themselves and not depend on a partner to cook for them.

"How's your homework?"

"Good. I'm done." Harper closed her yellow folder a little too quickly and slid it across the kitchen table.

Lucas grabbed three plates from one of the glass-front cabinets. He'd never been in Serenity's house before, but it fit her. The kitchen was a mix of modern and traditional. It must have been recently updated with new white cabinets, stainless steel appliances and flooring that looked like wood but was the new tough vinyl that could withstand pets, kids and was basically waterproof.

The center light fixture doubled as a pot rack and the kitchen island had a prep sink, a nice addition. If he had to guess, it was probably one of the draws for why she'd bought the place. Whoever had done the work, the craftsmanship was solid. After he'd gotten out of the Marines, he'd started working for his family's construction business so some things he couldn't help but notice.

"You sure about that?" he asked, not looking over as he searched for napkins and silverware.

"Maybe I still need to finish a reading assignment."

"Maybe?" Yeah, he knew what that meant. He had enough young cousins to read her tone.

"Yeah, okay, I need to. Maybe you could help me after dinner?" Her voice was hopeful.

Lucas looked up, grinned at Harper. "You got it." The six-year-old was a miniature version of Serenity with jet-black hair and bright blue eyes. He had a soft spot for her, just like he did for Serenity. "What do you want to drink?"

"Milk."

After getting a drink and small plate ready for Harper, he sat at the table with her while she ate. He wasn't sure what time Serenity would get back but he wanted to eat with her. Not exactly the date he'd been envisioning, but any time he could spend with her, he'd take.

From practically the moment Lucas had met her, he'd been struck by that clichéd lightning bolt. It had taken him off guard too. After getting out of the Corps two years ago he'd moved back to Verona Bay and started to settle into civilian life, which was a feat in itself. Getting involved with a woman, much less a single mother, hadn't been on his radar.

Then six months ago he'd met her at her shop when he'd brought Daisy in for a grooming appointment, and he hadn't been able to get Serenity out of his mind since. But she was a widow, a single mom who'd gone through horrific trauma, and clearly wasn't looking for anything more than friendship. At least not yet.

He could be patient. He knew all about battle tactics. And as far as he was concerned, once a Marine, always one—and he was in this for the long haul. He knew she wanted him, could see flickers of interest every once in a while before she closed herself off. She was fighting the attraction for some reason.

But this, asking him to pick up Harper, was a big step. The circumstances might suck, but he was going to show her that they would be good together, that she could depend on him. He wanted to protect both her and Harper. Hell, he simply wanted to be in their lives.

"So, you like my mom?" Harper scooped up the chicken and cheese mixture on her fork and looked at him.

The question threw him, but he answered all the same. "Yeah, I do." That was a generic enough answer— and this wasn't exactly the conversation he wanted to have with a kid.

"Good. She likes you too. Hey, you want to hear me play the drums later?"

Smiling, he nodded. "That sounds like a plan. I hear it's music week."

"Yeah! I got to pick the drums for my instrument. My best friend Carson wants to start a band," she said around a mouthful of food.

"Is that right?"

"Yep. He wants to rock and roll."

Lucas stifled a laugh and just nodded. "What does your mom say about that?"

"She says as long as I do my homework first I can rock and roll all I want."

Before he could say anything else, the front door opened, accompanied by the soft chime from the alarm system.

Harper was off her seat and racing out of the room before Lucas had stood.

"Mommy! Lucas made dinner and he's going to listen to me play drums and help with my reading homework."

"Yeah?" Serenity was holding Harper tight in her arms, her face unnaturally pale. Lincoln stood behind her, his expression grim.

Lucas's combat instinct sharpened. He knew what his brother had told him, but a sheriff's escort meant Lincoln was taking this seriously—and thought there might be merit to whatever had been left on Serenity's vehicle.

"Yep. Dinner's really good too..." Harper continued, talking at warp speed, replaying her day until Serenity kissed her on the forehead.

"Sweetheart, I need to talk to Lucas for a second. Can you wait for us in the kitchen?"

It was clear Harper was going to protest until Lincoln stepped forward, slightly shaking his head. "I can't believe my brother actually cooked dinner. This I've gotta see."

Harper nodded enthusiastically. "He did. I'll show you. Can I see your badge? Do you have a gun? Have you ever arrested bad guys?" she asked, firing off even more questions as they headed into the kitchen.

As soon as they were out of sight and earshot, Serenity wrapped her arms around herself. He wished they were his arms instead. Stress lines bracketed her mouth, her blue eyes filled with something he'd seen more than enough times on the battlefield. Raw fear.

Lucas took a step forward, and without thinking pulled her into his arms. It was clear she needed comfort, and even if they weren't where he wanted them to be relationship-wise, she was still his friend. No matter what, he'd always be her friend and look out for her.

Shuddering, she leaned into his embrace and wrapped her arms tight around him. "Thank you so much for picking her up."

"You don't ever have to thank me for something like that." He inhaled her sweet scent, a vanilla and raspberry combination that was probably just her shampoo. Whatever it was, it was now embedded in his brain. Anytime he smelled either scent he thought of Serenity. Hell, pretty much anything made him think of Serenity. The woman had gotten deep under his skin and clearly wasn't going anywhere.

"Yeah, I do. God, Lucas..." Her grip tightened as she laid her cheek against his chest.

When she didn't continue, he leaned back to look at her. "Lincoln told me someone left something on your car. A prank, potentially more?" And even though he knew right now wasn't about him, he was pissed she hadn't told him herself.

She swallowed hard, that pop of fear visible in her expression again. "Oh God, I don't even know how to say it. When my sister and I were taken, that monster took all our jewelry."

He stiffened at her words. She'd never talked about what happened to her and he'd never asked. He hadn't known her when she was younger—he'd been overseas trying to stay alive—but he'd heard some details from his family about the Washington sisters and her being the sole survivor of a serial killer case that had rocked this entire region.

"After I was rescued the authorities never found our stuff—or any of the previous victims' belongings. And he would never tell the FBI where he'd stashed it all. But someone left my sister's bracelet on my windshield to-night."

A protectiveness like Lucas had never known swept through him. He tightened his hold on her. "You're sure it's hers?"

"Not one hundred percent. It could be a replica. But...it looks just like hers."

Even if it was a replica, it was creepy as hell that someone would have copied it in such detail. "What did they find on the security recordings at the station?"

"A hooded figure approached my vehicle but even when they zoomed in it was impossible to see any facial features or even body type."

Lucas planned to look at the video himself, but just nodded. He didn't care if he had a right to view it or not, he'd convince his brother to let him see it. "What—"

"I'll tell you everything later. I just need to be with Harper right now. I don't want her to have any idea that something is wrong." The desperation in her voice clawed at him.

"Fine, but I'm staying the night."

She stepped back fully from him, her hands dropping to her sides as she looked up at him with a mixture of shock and...something he couldn't quite define. "What?"

Ready for an argument, he crossed his arms over his chest. His mom had already picked Daisy up, so if Seren-ity brought that up, he was covered. "I'm staying." Be-cause there was no way in hell he was leaving her alone tonight.

## CHAPTER FIVE

"**B**ut Daisy—"
          "Is with my mom."

Serenity watched Lucas for a long moment and realized that any argument she had was going to be pointless. "So...you're staying." She couldn't even phrase it as a question because the answer was clear.

"Yep."

She hadn't realized how stubborn he could be, but watching that far too handsome face, she could see raw determination in his green eyes. "I don't have the energy to argue." And okay, she was unnerved by what had happened. Having a military-trained man in the house was definitely a good thing. Even if she had a security system, Lucas offered far more safety.

The tense line of his shoulders loosened and he half-smiled. "Good."

And that was that.

Lucas took over things shockingly fast, so subtly it surprised her. Once his brother left, he served both of them dinner, scooping out the cheesy goodness onto plates as he basically ordered her to sit and eat while Harper read to them.

The warmth of the food spread through her, mingling with the warmth that came from watching Harper and Lucas. Harper had adjusted incredibly well to her dad dying, maybe because Serenity had. Or more likely because she was a kid and they simply adapted to life in a way that was much harder for adults. She hated that her daughter had known loss so young but she was glad for her resilience.

"How was that, Mommy?" Harper asked as she shut her book.

Serenity grinned as she set her fork down. "Perfect. You're getting better and better."

"No one is perfect," Harper said primly, a mischievous glint in her eyes.

Serenity snorted. "Well, your reading was close to it."

Harper simply grinned and reached for an apple from the bowl in the middle of the table. She had to be going through a growth spurt because all she did lately was eat.

"Thank you for cooking dinner." Serenity focused on Lucas as she pushed her plate away. She'd barely eaten half of it, and even though it was delicious, her stomach was too tight to eat any more. The day's events had put a black cloud over everything and it would take her time to re-center herself.

Lucas looked at her plate and for a moment it appeared as if he wanted to say more, but he simply nodded. "I know you need to get Harper ready for bed, so I'll take care of the dishes."

"It's shower time!" Harper shouted, jumping off her chair, apple forgotten.

As of a week ago, Harper had decided that she wanted to take showers instead of baths. It was such a small thing but she was showing her independence. Which made

Serenity happy, but at the same time it reminded her how fast her little girl was growing up.

"You can just leave this," Serenity said to Lucas. "I'll get it when we're done."

He lifted an eyebrow. "So I'm just going to sit on my a...butt and do nothing?" He shook his head and picked up her plate.

Okay, when he put it that way, she was fine with him doing the dishes. Still, it felt weird that he was helping out and being all domestic in her home. Weird and good. Part of her really liked having a partner to help out, but the other part of her—the one who had let her husband take over everything—instinctively pushed back. She'd gotten so used to doing everything by herself and she wasn't sure she was ready to give up any of her control.

"All right, Harper, let's go get ready for bed."

"I want four stories after shower time," Harper said as they left the room, automatically grabbing Serenity's hand in hers.

She never got tired of feeling that little hand in her own. "One."

"Three."

"Two," Serenity said as part of the game they played every single night.

Harper giggled. "Two is good."

Serenity knew her daughter would pick the longest books she had, of course. But she didn't mind.

"Is Mr. Lucas staying tonight?" Harper asked.

Serenity was surprised by Harper's perceptiveness, but he was here pretty late and he'd cooked them dinner.

Which was a far cry from their ordinary nights. "Yes. In the guest room."

"Kind of like a sleepover, huh?"

"Exactly like a sleepover. He won't stay over all the time, just tonight." She felt she needed to stress that.

"What about Daisy?"

"She's with his mom right now."

"I love Mrs. Jordan. She always gives me treats when I see her."

Serenity nodded because she was well aware of that. Louise Jordan was definitely a force of nature. And considering she'd raised three boys, that was to be expected.

Serenity and Harper quickly went through their routine of shower time, her brushing out her daughter's hair and braiding it, then story time. By the time Serenity was done, she found Lucas sitting at her kitchen table, his laptop open. And the kitchen looked pristine.

Okay, she could admit that coming into a clean kitchen was pretty sweet. "Hey, thanks for cooking and cleaning."

His mouth lifted into a half-smile, revealing one of those damn dimples. "Gotta earn my keep."

Snorting, she crossed over to the table. "Seriously. Thank you. For everything. There aren't a lot of people I would trust to pick Harper up from school." She had a lot of friends, but she was very picky about who she would trust with her daughter. Experience had taught her to be careful about *everyone*. Lucas was one of those people her gut instinct told her she could trust with anything.

Just not her heart. She would never risk that again. She'd blindly given up control to Olsen—of their finances and pretty much everything else. When he'd died, it had been a wake-up call.

"Of course. I'm just sorry about the circumstances."

"Yeah, me too." Sighing, she rubbed the back of her neck as she felt a tension headache coming on. "The anniversary of Savannah's death is a month away," she found herself saying before she realized she'd planned to open up to him.

He paused for only a moment, then shut his laptop, giving her his full attention. "I didn't realize it was so soon."

She nodded once. "Yeah. I always think it will get easier, but every year it's just as hard." Hell, it was hard every day but she'd learned to live with that dull ache in her chest. It was impossible to describe to someone who didn't have a twin what losing one was like. And especially the horrific way she'd lost hers. It truly was like she'd lost a part of herself.

"Do you want to talk about it?"

She paused and shook her head. "Maybe later. I'm exhausted. And I need a shower." She'd had a long day at the shop and she was pretty sure she smelled like wet dog.

"Go ahead. I've already grabbed my bag from the truck. You can set the alarm."

She paused as she stood. "You had a bag with you?"

"I always do. In case of emergency. It's my go bag."

"I bet you're one of those people who has a whole emergency kit in the back of their vehicle too?"

He grinned in confirmation.

She laughed lightly. "I actually do too." Because she knew better than anyone that tragedy could happen at any moment.

His smile faded as he watched her, the heat and electricity arcing between them almost tangible. So much so that she took a step back before she was completely sucked in. *Damn. This should not be happening.*

Serenity muttered something she hoped made sense before hurrying from the room. She had no business getting involved with Lucas Jordan. Especially not right now.

No good could come of that. Her life was safe, drama free—or it had been until today.

\* \* \*

*Drip. Drip. Drip.*

*Serenity struggled with the bindings and her rage as she toppled to the ground. She was still bound to the board. Pain split through her shoulder as she struggled with her bindings, finally getting free. Oh God, she was free. She had to get out of here, had to save Savannah.*

*The front door swung open and he was standing there.*
*No!*

*Black holes were where his eyes should be as he strode toward her, gripping a knife in his left hand. Her adrenaline spiked as she drew in a breath to scream for help she knew was never coming—*

Serenity jolted upright in bed, her breathing jagged.

It was a dream. Or a nightmare.

And it was always the same. He came back before she had a chance to get away.

Covered in a thin layer of sweat, she stripped off her pajama top and shorts and took a quick, cool shower, rinsing off before she tugged on a new pair of pajamas.

It was three thirty in the morning and she still needed a couple more hours of sleep, but she wasn't so sure she'd be getting them now. Sleep rarely came after a nightmare.

Sighing, she headed to the kitchen, ready to make some tea. But she stopped short when she found Lucas standing at one of the countertops, his back to her.

He glanced over his shoulder even though she didn't think she'd made a sound. "Hey," he said quietly, shifting enough that she realized he was making coffee.

"You're up early," she murmured, stepping into the room and trying not to notice that he was shirtless. Damn, the man was built.

He nodded and pulled down a mug for her. "Want some?"

"Yeah, thanks." She definitely wasn't going back to sleep now.

"Why are you up?"

She thought about lying, but Lucas had been pretty incredible. If he couldn't handle the truth, the reality of who she was, then there wasn't room for a relationship with him anyway... No, she didn't even want to go down that path. It wasn't like they had the chance at a relationship. Still, she would give him the truth. The man was former military—he could handle this. "I had a nightmare."

He nodded. "I understand. I have them too."

She paused as she pulled a bottle of creamer from the fridge, surprised he was being so up-front about something so personal. "Because of your time in Afghanistan?"

"Yeah." His jaw tightened slightly as he poured a mug for her.

"Want to talk about it?" she asked.

"Not now."

She could definitely appreciate that. "Did you ever talk to anybody about...your nightmares?"

"Yeah, at the VA. For a little while anyway. Then I started writing therapy."

"I've heard of that. Does it work?" Her own therapist had suggested it years ago but she'd never been able to put pen to paper.

"It does. At least it does for me. I don't see a therapist anymore. I didn't actually see one for long. I understand why some people go, but I just couldn't open up to someone on a constant basis. That's where the journaling works. It's cathartic."

She'd seen a therapist years ago, and she was grateful for it, but it hadn't been a long-term thing for her either. Maybe she should try the journaling as well. Writing down her nightmares just felt so daunting. "That's where you write about your dreams—or nightmares or memories—and then throw them away, right?"

"It's not just one thing, but yeah. I write about my nightmares in the present tense then burn them. It's supposed to sort of rewire the brain to file the trauma into the past—where it belongs. For me, it feels symbolic." He rubbed the back of his head once. "But yeah, that's the gist of it."

Surprised he'd opened up so much to her, she was quiet as she doctored her coffee the way she liked it and leaned against the countertop. It was weird to be here with him, getting intensely personal, and she wasn't exactly sure what to say. He was so capable and strong, she'd never thought of him as vulnerable or...traumatized. Whereas she felt as if she struggled every damn day to hide her pain. As if she was barely keeping a lid on the crap from her past.

He stood at the countertop next to her, his body language casual enough, but there was a palpable energy rolling off him. "What time does Harper normally wake up?"

"Six thirty on the dot. My little girl does not sleep in. Not even on weekends." Good thing Serenity didn't usually sleep in either.

He laughed lightly. "Yeah, my brothers and I were like that. My mom said she usually ran on three hours of sleep, though I think she was exaggerating."

"Or maybe not," Serenity murmured, taking a sip of her coffee. She could imagine how wild the Jordan boys had been.

"Yeah, maybe not," he conceded, that grin back in place.

"So what project are you working on now?" she asked, forcing her gaze to remain on his face and not on all that bare expanse of skin. It was like he didn't even realize he was shirtless and making her crazy. Right now she really wished that she'd had a normal life and that things between them were different. That he was in her kitchen because he'd stayed the night and...

She bit back a sigh. There was no sense wishing for something different. Because things weren't. If they were, Savannah would be alive.

"A new retirement center," he said, cutting into her thoughts. "A fairly small one compared to some of the other jobs we've done, but it's a great contract."

"Good." She paused, fighting the awkwardness stretching out between them. They had coffee together multiple times a week and she had no problem talking. But this was different. He'd stayed at her house and now they were sitting at her kitchen table drinking coffee while he was half naked. It was all too...weird. Too intimate. Too much. "I dream about that night all the time," she blurted, then inwardly chastised herself. What the hell was this diarrhea of the mouth?

He set his coffee down, all his attention on her.

"Sorry—"

He frowned. "Don't apologize."

She shoved out a breath. "Okay. I...I have different dreams. Nightmares, I mean. I often have the same one where I escape—which I did. But in this scenario, I get free of the bindings and instead of breaking out of that cabin, he shows up before I can get out. He's a disembodied version of himself and he's carrying a knife." The words poured out of her but it was freeing to get them out. "Then I wake up."

Wordlessly Lucas reached across the table, taking one of her hands in his, and the strength and warmth of it had her throat tightening. The steady presence of Lucas Jordan was almost too much to handle.

"Thanks for listening."

He nodded, his gaze unnerving enough that she looked down into her coffee mug.

"I see the faces of the men I couldn't save when I sleep. Not always, but they come. Usually after a hard day at work when I'm in a dead-to-the-world kind of sleep."

She squeezed his hand in return, sorry he had his own nightmares. "The world is a screwed-up place."

"Yes, it is." His voice was a deep rumble, soothing all her frayed edges.

She had to look away again because of what she saw in those green eyes—far too much understanding and more than a hint of what he felt for her. She wasn't sure what to do with the feelings he evoked inside her either. When she was with Lucas, she felt like he understood her in a way most people never could. They'd both survived shitty situations, even if they were wildly different.

Serenity cleared her throat. "I think I'm going to grab a quick workout and then shower." She wasn't going back to sleep any time soon and she needed to get some distance from him. For her sanity. And working out on her elliptical machine was the only way she could expend all this energy right now. Well...the only way she'd allow herself.

He looked as if he wanted to say something more but simply dropped his hand and nodded.

She wasn't sure if she felt relief or disappointment as she headed out of the kitchen. She desperately wished she was in the right headspace for a relationship because Lucas was the strongest, sweetest man she'd ever known.

# CHAPTER SIX

Slowly, she drove by Serenity's house, though it was almost six in the morning. She had an excuse for being out this early if she was stopped by the sheriffs. Not that she thought she'd need it. The budget in a town this small wouldn't be enough that law enforcement could watch her house full-time. Even if Serenity had run straight to the sheriff once she'd gotten her little present yesterday.

Good. She wanted that bitch off her game. Wanted her terrified. If she'd just died eight years ago, none of this would be happening. It was her fault!

When she saw Lucas's truck still parked in Serenity's driveway, she froze for a moment before the rage flowed, wild and hot. He'd never left. Had probably comforted her, screwed her. She jerked at the sharp bite of pain in her leg and realized she'd clawed at her thigh.

*She's taking what's yours*, that voice in her head whispered. It was growing stronger, louder. Angrier.

She shoved it back down. "Shut up!" she shouted to the empty car. Serenity would not take what belonged to her. She wouldn't.

No, she was in control now, no one else.

Tightening her fingers around the wheel, she dragged in a deep breath, then another, steadying herself.

She had a plan and she would stick to it. She didn't care what Black said. In fact, she wasn't asking for his opinion about any of this. Serenity would die, and soon. But not until she'd paid.

Serenity would pay for not dying. For having everything. For existing. She'd been married and had a kid. Then she had to come back to Verona Bay and set her sights on Lucas Jordan. Because of course she did. He was a wealthy man from a good family. And he'd fallen for Serenity's pitiful act.

As she turned out of the quiet neighborhood, she headed east, toward one of her targets. She would hurt those who Serenity loved, then kill her. She had an entire list of victims just waiting to die.

*He'll be angry*, the voice whispered.

"So what?" she muttered.

*You'll leave her daughter motherless*, the voice whispered again, the words insidious, mocking.

Again, so what? Her own mother had abandoned her when she was young, and good riddance. She didn't care what Black thought. He was in prison. He'd abandoned her too.

He'd left her because of his own foolishness. He never should have gotten caught. Never should have left her alone.

Then he tried to tell her what to do, how to live.

Her fingers tightened on the wheel, her knuckles turning white. This was her life. She was in charge. Not him. She ran her own business, depended on no one but herself. She screwed who she wanted, did what she wanted. Serenity surviving was on Black. Not her.

*He* let Serenity live.

This was all his fault too. She was going to stop living by his rules.

It was as if a weight lifted as she continued driving, the voice in her head going silent as she turned into another quiet neighborhood of townhomes.

One of her targets lived here. Someone who would never see her coming. She wouldn't kill her today. Not yet. She'd save her for later, when the timing was right.

She might have never killed before but she wasn't stupid. She could be invisible when necessary. That was how she would get away with this.

By being smarter than everyone else.

## CHAPTER SEVEN

Lucas followed Serenity in his truck as she left the school and headed into work. He didn't want her going into Tailwaggers at all but that wasn't his call and that wasn't how life worked. She had bills to pay like everyone else, no matter how alarming yesterday had been.

As he drove, he called his brother, not caring how early it was. Lincoln would be awake anyway.

"Hey," his brother answered on the first ring. "Everything okay?"

"Yeah. Following Serenity to her shop. Where are you at with the bracelet?" He wasn't going to bother making small talk.

"Called Special Agent Amy Lin and overnighted it to her. We don't have the resources to get fingerprints in a timely manner. And I trust her to make this a priority if she thinks it's important."

"Good." Lin was the FBI agent who'd been in charge of the Michael Black serial killer case years ago. It was the case that had apparently made her career, and she was very good at her job, according to Lincoln. "What about Serenity? You going to have patrols driving by her place?"

"Did I miss something where you're my boss now?" His brother's tone was dry.

"Shut up," he muttered.

"Look, I'm short-staffed and you know what our budget is like. I've got my people running patrols and spending extra time on Main Street now. Tonight I'll have one of my guys do extra sweeps down her street."

"Good... Thank you."

"Just doing my job. I care about Serenity as much as you."

Now Lucas snorted. Lincoln knew how much Lucas cared about Serenity and it wasn't in the same stratosphere.

"You know what I mean."

Yeah, he did. Lincoln had been friends with both Serenity and Savannah, and Lucas was grateful his brother was the sheriff now of all times. Otherwise he wouldn't be getting any sort of updates about this at all.

As they disconnected, Lucas parked next to Serenity on Main Street.

"Thank you for the escort," she said, a half-smile teasing her lips as she stepped onto the sidewalk. Her grooming shop was a few stores down but there was no parking out front this morning despite how early it was. Probably because everyone was packed into Momma's Kitchen.

"Want to grab breakfast?" he asked, nodding at the diner.

"I can't, but thanks. I need to prep before Adeline gets in."

"My mom should be bringing Daisy in later. If you need anything today, just call me and I'll be here."

She nodded and shoved her hands into her jeans as she stood there, slightly shivering. She'd worn a thick cardigan and a scarf but it was chilly this morning. Her dark hair was pulled up into a ponytail, and if she had on makeup, he couldn't tell. As always, she looked beautiful...but today she looked exhausted. No wonder. If she was his, he'd have exhausted her with pleasure.

She looked as if she wanted to say something but just nodded. "I will, thanks."

He watched her walk down the sidewalk and waited until she went into her shop. He knew it had a security system and that she would be locking herself inside until it was time to open.

He inwardly cursed himself as he headed inside the local bakery, Sweet Spot. Things between him and Serenity had shifted, he was sure of it. And he knew what he wanted, but he didn't want to move too fast and push her away.

This morning at her kitchen table things hadn't been strained exactly, but different between them. He felt as if they'd crossed some kind of invisible barrier, but maybe he was wrong. She'd certainly surprised him by opening up to him in a way he was fairly certain she didn't do often with others—if at all. And he sure as hell had told her things he'd never told anyone except his brothers.

Shoving those thoughts away, he smiled at Bianca who was working behind the counter. As the owner, she usually wasn't up front in the mornings because she was in the back baking and prepping for the day. They'd grown up together and she'd taken over the shop from the previous owner.

The petite woman smiled brightly at him. "Morning, Lucas."

He returned the greeting even as he eyed the menu behind her. "A couple blueberry muffins, a small quiche, one coffee black and a café au lait, please."

Bianca lifted an eyebrow as she started gathering the food together. There were six tables inside, four of which were already filled. The little bell on the door jingled and he glanced over his shoulder to see two more people strolling in.

"Blueberry muffins and a café au lait—Serenity's favorite."

Since Bianca wasn't asking a question so much as making an observation, Lucas gave her a neutral smile as he pulled out a twenty-dollar bill and waited for her to get the drinks together.

She wasn't deterred, however. "Not going to give me any gossip, huh? At least tell me if you're off the market?" Her smile was flirtatious, though he was certain that had nothing to do with him and everything to do with her wanting an answer for the small-town gossip mill. She'd asked him out once when he'd first moved back to town but he'd politely declined. And since then she'd been nothing but friendly, if flirty.

"You're very nosy this morning."

She snorted. "I'm nosy every morning. So you're not going to give me anything?"

He lifted a shoulder. "Nothing to tell."

"Fine. But I already heard through the grapevine that your truck was seen at Serenity's house early this morning. And that it was there all night." Her grin widened.

*Ah, hell.* He tightened his jaw, handed her cash as she read off the total. He wasn't going to respond one way or another. Small-town gossip was the worst, and he hadn't even thought about how last night would look for Serenity. She was single and her husband had been dead for two years, but still, people would talk.

He'd have to tell her, though she might already know. People assuming that they were sleeping together was better than them gossiping about why he'd really stayed over. "Thanks," he said, picking up the bag and heading out.

The walk to Serenity's shop took all of thirty seconds. She smiled when she saw him through the glass window front, but her eyes lit up when she saw the bag in his hands.

"Please tell me there are blueberry muffins in there," she said as she opened the door for him.

"There are, but I didn't say they were for you."

She let out a startled laugh. "Really? Well, I'm going to have to rethink our friendship, then."

"I also brought you a café au lait."

She laughed again as she took the cup from his hand. "I guess we're still friends, then. Thank you for this." Sighing, she continued. "I have a feeling today is going to be one of those long days."

The faint scent of dog filled the air, but she had a couple diffusers running with lemongrass oil. It seemed to keep everything smelling fresh enough so that the pet smell wasn't overwhelming. Soon enough the place would be full of dogs, including the six individual stalls at the front where people could wash their dogs on their own.

"Look, I feel weird saying this, but Bianca mentioned knowing that I stayed over last night. Apparently one of your neighbors saw my truck in the driveway. So if she knows, there's a good chance a lot of the town does." Bianca wasn't known for keeping things to herself.

Serenity groaned as she pulled a muffin out of the bag. She hadn't eaten this morning—just had coffee—so he was glad she was now. "I didn't even think about that, but I should have. Freaking small towns," she muttered. "Some days I miss being anonymous."

He lifted a shoulder, trying to get a read on her. He couldn't tell if she was actually annoyed. "I just wanted you to be prepared in case anyone says anything."

She bit her bottom lip, looking thoughtful. "What should I say? I don't want to tell people the truth."

"You can just tell people we're dating." He wanted to be, anyway. Okay, he wanted more than dating.

"I'm not going to do that to you."

"Do what to me? Have the town think I'm dating a smart, successful, beautiful woman? Oh no, the horror." He gave her a dry look.

She looked shocked by his words even as she let out a sort of snort laugh that softened her entire face. God, he loved that laugh. "You know what I mean."

"No, I don't know what you mean. Is it so awful for people to think you're dating me?"

"*Please.* You know it's not." She rolled her eyes, as if he was ridiculous.

Did he? "We have two options at this point. The truth, or to tell people we're dating."

"Or the third option, don't say anything at all."

"True enough. But you know how well that will go over," he said. Not saying anything would just get the town even more curious.

Sighing, she leaned against the front counter where she sold all sorts of dog treats. "Fine. If people ask questions, I'll just be vague."

"Same here. I'll tell my family the truth but keep everything else vague enough."

"I'm sorry to drag you into this," she said, taking a sip of her drink.

"You didn't drag me into anything. I volunteered. And I don't care if people think we're together." He wanted to ask her out on an official date, but restrained himself. She had enough on her plate right now. And if she wasn't interested in him, he didn't want things to be awkward between them. Right now she needed a friend more than anything else. A friend and a protector.

That was something he could definitely be even if he wanted more. Because he would do anything to keep her safe. She'd been through hell and come out stronger for it. And he respected the hell out of that.

"All right, I've got to get to work," he continued. "What time is Adeline coming in?"

She glanced at her watch. "About half an hour. We have a full day today."

He nodded once, wishing they actually were in a relationship so he could kiss her goodbye, but said, "I've got my phone on me. Let me know if you need anything."

"Will do. Thanks again for the treats. I'll be sharing with Adeline."

Laughing, he let himself out and waited until she locked the door behind her. The only reason he made himself leave was because he saw a patrol car across the street.

The deputy nodded once at Lucas and lifted his own cup of what Lucas assumed was coffee in greeting.

Okay, he could breathe again. Serenity had Adeline coming in soon and a deputy watching out for her. Not to mention Main Street would be bustling with activity soon.

She'd be as safe as anyone could be in today's world. Though it went against all his instincts, he left.

## CHAPTER EIGHT

Serenity stepped out of the small bathroom of her shop where she'd taken a quick shower to freshen up and change out of her fur-covered, dog-scented clothing, and picked up her duffel bag.

"Are you good for the rest of the day?" she asked Adeline, who had just finished blow-drying an adorable Labradoodle. The medium-sized guy had gone from complete, fuzzy furball to a trimmed-up handsome little prince ready to go home to his owner—who spoiled him. Most days she really missed having a dog. Soon enough they'd be getting another one.

"Yeah, I've got it. As long as Callie handles the register, I've got these guys, no problem." There were only three dogs left to groom, wash and dry.

Louise Jordan had long since dropped off and picked up Daisy—and Serenity had been disappointed that it hadn't been Lucas picking her up. "Thanks. As soon as you're done, close up. Don't wait around for any walk-ins."

"You sure?" Adeline looked surprised, her dark eyebrows raised slightly. Today she wore a skintight, bright purple shirt that popped against her brown skin. And of course she had on her sparkly sneakers. Silver today—and she had them in every color.

"Yeah, I'm sure. And make sure you and Callie walk each other to your vehicles. Don't walk alone."

Adeline frowned as she started cleaning her tools. "Is something going on?"

Serenity paused for a second. She'd been planning to tell her friend and probably should've done it earlier in the day. Normally she told Adeline everything.

Quickly, she relayed what had happened and the brief details. As she finished, she said, "I have no reason to believe this will affect anyone else but...it just freaks me out."

Adeline stared in shock. "I'll be careful. And if I see any weirdos hanging around, I'll definitely let you know. I've always got my pepper spray with me anyway," she said, patting her back pocket.

"Good. And I know this is a weird request, but maybe just text me when you get home today?" Yeah, maybe she was going overboard, but yesterday had really rattled her. It wasn't like whatever weirdo who had left the bracelet had threatened her friends but Serenity still felt uneasy.

"You got it. By the way, is that the real reason that Lucas stayed over last night?"

Serenity blinked in surprise. "You know about that?" Adeline hadn't said a word about it today.

Her friend nodded. "Yep. The whole town is whispering about it. I figured if you wanted to say anything, you would, but after this little bomb I'm guessing that's why he stayed over."

"Yes. I'm keeping what happened kind of low-key, so if anyone asks you—"

"If anyone asks me, I'll tell them to mind their own damn business. You should know me better than that." She looked almost offended as she leaned over to pick up a blow-dryer, her own dark curls bouncing with the movement.

"Yeah, I do know you." Trust didn't come easy for her, not anymore. "Speaking of, have you thought any more about becoming my partner?" She and Adeline were tight and she was looking to expand—which would mean taking on a partner. And Adeline was smart, driven and trustworthy.

"I have... I'm still pro/conning it but I'm pretty sure I'm in. I think I just need to wrap my head around taking on a new venture. And listen, don't worry about all the small-town gossip. It will blow over. I just hope they figure out who left that nasty surprise."

"Yeah, me too." She knew that Lincoln had forwarded it to the FBI, which gave her some peace of mind. If anyone could find a lead, it was the Feds. Special Agent Amy Lin was incredibly sharp and always checked in with Serenity at least once a year, usually more. She hadn't forgotten about her...and Serenity could have contacted Amy herself but she'd wanted it to go through official channels. It had more of an impact that way. Amy had been closing in on Black even before he'd taken Serenity and Savannah. It had only been a matter of time before they captured him. Her escape and survival had just moved that up.

After leaving work she quickly fell into her normal routine of picking Harper up from school, taking her home and starting to prepare dinner. She liked her life tidy and ordered. It was a coping mechanism, and she didn't care.

"I finished my homework early!" Harper bounced into the kitchen, a little ping-pong ball of energy. "Can I watch TV while I play with Legos?"

"Of course." She kissed the top of Harper's head before her daughter ran off to the living room. When Serenity heard a knock on the front door, she automatically tensed but when she saw Mrs. Rose—aka Carol—through the peephole, she smiled and opened the door.

"I'm sorry I didn't return your calls," Carol said as she stepped inside, her Chanel No. 5 wafting in with her. "My daughter had an emergency so I was out of town and I completely forgot to tell anyone I left."

Laughing lightly, Serenity stood back and let her neighbor inside. "That's fine. Are you in the mood for some tea?"

"Tea with a side of gossip, preferably. Earl Grey if you have it." There was a mischievous twinkle in her brown eyes as she followed Serenity into the kitchen.

So she must have heard about Lucas staying over. "Not you too?"

"Well, I got in about four this morning and I saw Lucas's truck outside. So...it wasn't hard to figure out he'd stayed over. What's going on with you two? Did he finally make his move?"

She blinked at the word *finally*, but shook her head before quickly recapping everything in much the same way she had with Adeline.

"Oh honey, that's awful," Carol said when she was finished. "I'm glad Lucas stayed over."

"Feel free to tell people Lucas and I are dating if anyone asks you."

The older woman rolled her eyes. "I'm not going to tell anybody anything. But I was curious. I'm sorry someone has decided to be so awful to you. I hope it's nothing more than a sick prank. Does Lincoln know anything yet?"

"No...the department has sent the bracelet to the FBI so I should find out soon enough if this is a serious threat."

"People can be such garbage sometimes."

Serenity nodded as she pulled the teapot off the stove and started pouring them mugs. "Let's not talk about me right now. What's going on with your daughter?" Carol's daughter lived two towns over and she got over to see her as much as possible. Serenity was pretty certain that in the next year she'd move there for good. She'd miss Carol, but knew it would be good for her to move closer to her family.

Her friend started talking, and hearing about Carol's last few days eased the tension inside her. It felt normal to be sitting here chatting about life. Normal and nice. And right now, that was what she needed.

\* \* \*

Serenity glanced at her buzzing cell phone as she stepped back into the kitchen. She'd gotten Harper to sleep and she was ready for a glass of wine. The last two days had been impossibly long. Fully expecting to see another message from Lucas or her neighbor, ice slithered up her spine as she stared at the message from an unknown number.

*Tick-tock. Tick-tock. Maybe you should check on your neighbor.*

Shit, whoever this person was had her phone number. Which was…beyond disconcerting. The house on the other side of her was for sale, and vacant, so she had little doubt who this text referred to.

Serenity didn't pause—she called Carol but it kept ringing. Over and over. She desperately wanted to go over there but this could be a trap and she would be leaving Harper unguarded. She dialed Lincoln's cell phone number instead of calling 911, knowing he'd help immediately.

He answered on the second ring. "Hey, is everything okay?"

"I don't know. I got a weird text from an unknown number telling me I should check on my neighbor, Carol…ah, Mrs. Rose. They used the same tick-tock phrase from before. It feels really threatening. And I can't get her on the phone." Her breathing was choppy as she relayed everything. She tried to remain calm, but her heart thudded wildly in her chest.

He cursed under his breath. "I'm on my way over there. Stay inside and keep your doors locked."

Though she hated doing it, she stayed inside, checking on her daughter. She swore it felt like an eternity, but only eight minutes passed before she saw the flashing blue lights of Lincoln's sheriff's truck as he pulled into Carol's driveway.

It took everything in her not to go next door, but she simply couldn't. Instead, she peered in on Harper and watched her daughter sleep. When she heard a siren in the distance, her stomach dropped and she hurried to the front of her house.

Peering through the curtains, she watched as Lincoln approached Carol's house, weapon drawn. Then he was out of her sight. Tension spread throughout her as she said a little prayer for Carol. She hoped this was just a sick prank, not something...worse.

The sirens grew closer and closer, an emergency vehicle tearing down her road and stopping in front of Carol's driveway. Less than sixty seconds later two more sheriffs cars showed up, lights flashing.

Serenity disabled the alarm and hurried outside but quickly locked the door and reset the alarm using her phone app. Harper would be safe and she'd be alerted if anyone tried to get inside. And that kid could sleep through anything, thankfully.

She hurried across her lawn and spotted Lincoln stepping out of the front door, his expression grim. *Oh, no.* She could read it in his face. The worst had happened.

He held up a finger to one of his deputies and met her where the two lawns connected.

"I'm sorry," he said. "She's gone."

It took a few moments for his words to register, even though she'd read the truth on his face. "Wait...gone?" Her words came out as a raspy whisper.

He nodded. "No sign of a struggle. I shouldn't even be telling you this but I'm going to. I think it might be poison. We're going to have the coroner run her toxicology."

Everything phased out in front of her for a moment as she tried to digest everything he was saying. She'd just sat with Carol at the kitchen table a few hours ago. "No sign of a struggle?"

He shook his head. "There's nothing good about this but at least she wasn't... It could've been worse. A lot worse."

Serenity closed her eyes and dragged in a deep breath. How could this be happening? "We need to tell her children."

"I'll make the calls. Just go back inside and keep your doors locked. I'll be over to talk to you in a little bit. I'll station someone in your backyard, so don't be alarmed. I need to take care of...this first."

She wanted to argue with him, but there was nothing she could realistically do. Feeling numb, she stumbled back toward her house, turning off the alarm and resetting it on autopilot as she locked the door behind her. Carol was dead?

Whoever had been taunting her had done this, she had no doubt.

This wasn't a sick prank. No, this was a very dangerous predator who had no problem going after an elderly woman who wanted to enjoy her retirement. And the bastard would have no issue coming after Serenity. Maybe even...Harper. *Oh, God.* Someone had hurt her neighbor just to get to her. They could do anything, be anyone.

Sick to her stomach and terrified, Serenity headed to her daughter's room and peeked inside, breathing a sigh of relief to see Harper sleeping soundly, her little unicorn twinkle lights creating a kaleidoscope of colors on the ceiling. All was right in Harper's little world and Serenity was going to make sure it stayed that way. Tears stung her eyes as anger pushed up, threatening to overwhelm her fear.

Whoever had done this, they were going to pay. She'd been a victim once. Never again.

Exhausted, she sank into the rocking chair next to Harper's bed and closed her eyes. She'd just rest for a bit. No way was she leaving Harper's side. Not yet.

Serenity nearly jumped out of her skin at the sound of her cell phone buzzing sometime later. Opening her eyes, she was disoriented until she saw the twinkle lights flashing around the ceiling of her daughter's room.

She must have dozed off. Preparing herself for the worst, she looked at the screen, but relaxed when she saw Lucas's name popped up.

*I'm outside. Open up.*

After she saw that it was indeed Lucas through the peephole, she quickly opened the door. She couldn't believe he was here, but was glad for his presence.

Wordlessly, he stepped inside and pulled her into his arms in a hug she desperately needed. He shut the door behind him with his foot as he held her tight.

Needing the contact, she returned his embrace, burying her face against his chest as she fought tears. Carol had been one of the first people to befriend her when she'd moved into the neighborhood. Then they'd started having weekly tea dates. She'd been a teacher for nearly thirty years, volunteered at the local soup kitchen and helped out with her church's bake sales. She was always giving her time to those who needed it.

And now she was gone.

It was too awful to think about. She understood loss but that didn't mean it got any easier, and she wasn't going to tell herself that it would be okay. Because death was final, and loss hurt.

"I'm so sorry," he murmured against the top of her head, still holding her close.

She couldn't find her voice so she hugged him back. She wasn't sure how long they stood there but when she stepped back he cupped her face gently with his big, callused hands, swiping away her tears with his thumbs.

She hitched in a breath at the contact, a weird energy simmering between them as he stared down at her. Undeniable longing flared in his eyes, so sharp that it surprised her.

Suddenly he looked away, jaw tight as he ran a hand through his military-short hair. "I'm really sorry about your friend."

Reality crashed back in on her, helping her to take another step back, away from Lucas and *that look*. "I am too. And thank you for coming over." Maybe if she pretended that they'd never shared that intense look, he would too. "Did Lincoln call you?" she asked, then chastised herself. Of course Lincoln had.

"Yeah. It's pretty clear that someone is targeting you. Lincoln has already let the FBI know about tonight. I'm guessing they'll try to figure out who texted you. They've got the resources."

"It's probably a burner phone." Unless someone was really stupid enough to text her from their own phone. She doubted it though. Whoever it was had been smart enough to get inside Carol's house undetected. Unless...Carol had let them in? The thought of that sent another jolt of fear down her spine.

"Probably, but the Feds have resources the Verona SD doesn't. Hopefully they'll be able to figure out who bought it or...something concrete."

"I know... I'm not really sure what to do at this point. I need to tell all my friends that they might be targets. Or I assume I should. Is Lincoln going to talk to me tonight?"

He nodded. "Yeah, I grabbed him for a second before heading over here. He'll be over as soon as... He'll be over soon. He's questioning the other neighbors first to see if they saw anything."

Of course he would. Ugh, this was all too awful and surreal. "Come on, let's go to the kitchen." He followed and sat across from her as she collapsed in a chair, feeling decades older. "I'll start making calls tonight, let everyone know to be careful." She dreaded making these calls, but knew it was necessary. She'd moved back to Verona Bay to reclaim her life and raise her daughter in safety. Now she wondered if that was even possible. If she should even be here.

"Listen...it appears as if Mrs. Rose turned off her security system," he said as she pulled out her phone. "Lincoln will go over everything with you, but unless someone poisoned her earlier, she let whoever it was inside."

Serenity blinked. "She let them inside?"

He nodded, his expression grim.

"She's an older woman living by herself. She wouldn't have let just anyone into her home." No way. Serenity knew that in her gut.

"Not unless she knew them."

*Oh, God.* The sick feeling intensified. Could she and Lucas know who had done this? The thought was unthinkable but...believable at the same time. Unfortunately Serenity knew people hid their evil behind a mask of civility. Normal-looking people walked around everyday hiding their dark deeds from the world. "This is a nightmare. I should just leave. Take Harper with me and go."

He frowned at her. "Running isn't the answer."

"Then what is?" she snapped. "Harper and I were fine before moving back here and now someone is targeting me. And clearly it's linked to that bastard, Black." Otherwise they wouldn't have left Savannah's bracelet for her to find. That taunt meant something.

"He's locked up and behind bars."

"Who's to say he didn't have an accomplice?"

Lucas shifted slightly, his back straightening. "Did you ever see one?"

"No. But the Feds never ruled out the possibility. I still don't understand how Savannah and I got from our dorm to that cabin. There's a huge blank in my memory. I remember going to sleep in my bed, then waking up in hell."

He let out a low curse. "Did they do a toxicology report on your blood?"

She nodded. "My hair, actually. I was drugged. And food and water bottles had been removed from our dorm room so...anyone could have taken them, getting rid of the evidence. Black himself or someone else."

"Lincoln is good at his job. And the FBI isn't going to sit back and not do anything. But you running with Harper isn't the answer," he reiterated.

"Maybe. I'm just scared and I hate not knowing who could be after me. That's even worse. It could be one of my friends. It could be one of my neighbors. It could be the freaking mailman." The truth was, she wasn't sure how she would afford to go on the run with her daughter anyway. She didn't have unlimited funds, and separating herself from her community would just make her more vulnerable. Even though she knew that, her flight instinct had kicked in and she was having a tough time fighting it.

"Whoever it is, he or she will make a mistake."

"How many people will get hurt before then?" she asked, even though she wasn't really looking for an answer. "Everyone in town is going to hate me now." She raked a trembling hand through her hair. Though that was the least of her worries.

"Why the hell would they hate you?"

"It's my fault that—"

"None of this is your fault. The person at fault is the monster who killed Mrs. Rose. And they will be caught." He had so much conviction in his voice that she wanted to believe him.

Wanted to believe that no one else would be hurt. Guilt already clawed at her because of Carol. Deep down she knew it wasn't her fault, but that didn't stop the wave of nausea sweeping through her as she thought about her sweet neighbor, always ready with a kind word, now gone.

No matter how much she wanted to cling to hope that whoever had done this would be caught, Serenity knew better than anyone that the world was full of monsters, and that bad things happened every day to good people. "I'm going to start making phone calls. You want anything to drink?"

"You just do what you need to do. I'll make myself at home."

It was pretty clear he wasn't going anywhere and she could admit that she didn't want him to leave.

Serenity hoped he planned on staying the night, even though she knew it would probably confuse Harper in the morning. But right now she needed to feel secure. And when Lucas was around, she felt safer at least.

She hated that he was putting himself in danger but of all people she knew, he could take care of himself. The man was a trained warrior. That had to count for a whole lot.

She only regretted that she couldn't be what he needed.

## CHAPTER NINE

*R*ain *slapped Serenity in the face as she raced through the woods.*

*He was getting closer. Run. Run. Run.*

*Escape. Find help.*

*Lightning cracked, illuminating the forest. She let out a scream as he stepped up from behind a tree, his eyes wild and manic, his face elongated like a werewolf.*

*A scream caught in her throat as she turned and ran. Her feet slipped in the mud, propelling her forward.*

*Pain ripped through her skull as he grabbed the back of her hair.*

*"No!" She tried to scream but the word got stuck in her throat. Every time she tried to shout for help it came out as a whisper.*

*She fought against the mud and grass with her feet but kept slipping as he continued dragging her backward.*

*She wouldn't go back there. She couldn't go back there.*

*No.*

*Everything in front of her morphed and suddenly they were in that wretched cabin again.*

*He tossed her onto the floor, her palms slamming against the wood. Pain splintered through her, her heart racing out of control.*

*"Not done with you yet," he growled, the sound inhuman.*

*Savannah sat on the table now, blood pouring from all of her wounds, her skin a grayish color.*

*"You should have run faster." Her sister's words were disembodied.*

*Serenity shook her head. This wasn't real. It couldn't be. She'd escaped. She wasn't still stuck here.*

*"Be careful," her sister whispered. "There is danger on the horizon."*

*"What?" She stared at her sister in horror. She couldn't seem to get up, couldn't seem to make her limbs obey her. To move. To run.*

*"Run!" her sister screamed.*

Her eyes opened with a start.

A nightmare. Just another nightmare. Though this one was different than before.

He'd never brought her *back* to the cabin.

Despite being soaked in sweat, a chill snaked through her, making her tremble. It was just a nightmare, she reminded herself. Nothing more.

She couldn't be back in that cabin, stuck in hell.

## CHAPTER TEN

She was dead. Carol Rose was actually gone. It was hard to believe it, but she'd actually killed her. Was it only last night she'd done it? It felt as if an eternity had passed already.

At first the adrenaline rush had been fierce, like a hurricane roaring through her as she'd watched the old woman drink her poisoned tea. But her death had been over far too quickly. She'd been there one moment, then had overdosed. Then...nothing.

And she'd had to be careful to clean up after herself, to make sure there were no traces of her presence left behind. Going after her last night had been a risk but she'd wanted to strike now. She'd been unable to stop herself, if she was being brutally honest. That need, that growing hunger to hurt others had urged her to take action.

At least it quieted down the voice in her head.

She'd needed to hurt Serenity and this had been the easiest, cleanest way to do it. She'd realized something about herself though—she wanted more time with her victims. She wanted them to suffer more. She wanted to watch the life drain out of them, slowly, painfully.

Mrs. Rose was just the beginning. Poisoning her had been quick, but it wouldn't be her method after today.

No, she had a much better idea.

At that thought, the joy was back, though not as strong as before. She'd expected to feel a rush for a lot longer but it was already fading into nothing. She hadn't even been able to stick around to wait for the old woman to grow cold.

She'd had to kill her and get out. Because she wasn't getting caught. She was too smart for law enforcement. Too smart for this stupid, pathetic little town. Everyone underestimated her, always had. It was her time to bloom.

She stepped inside Serenity's grooming shop and waved at the girl behind the counter. Callie something. The younger woman wasn't one of the groomers, just the girl who ran the cash register. Thankfully the woman was talking to another customer while she picked up a few things for a cat she didn't really have. But she needed a reason to be here. As she grabbed random toys, she tucked a gift into a pile of them, leaving it for Serenity. She doubted the bitch would find it so she'd have to let her know where to look.

Anticipation buzzed through her as she strode toward the cash register, hoping she looked normal and calm on the outside. Playing with Serenity was a lot more fun than she could have imagined. She should have done this *months* ago.

Now that she had no one to answer to, she felt free. She still loved her father, but he'd been holding her back.

If he'd told her how good this would feel, she could have been doing this long before now. Instead he'd lied to her, told her she needed to keep the voice in her head quiet so she wouldn't end up like him. Rotting in jail.

What a crock of shit.

This felt good. Killing was freeing.

And this was just the beginning.

She wasn't stopping.

## CHAPTER ELEVEN

Lucas wrapped his fingers tightly around his steering wheel as he turned onto Main Street.

"Thank you for taking Harper to school with me," Serenity said next to him, staring out the passenger window. "And you seriously don't have to hang out at the shop today." Her tone was tart, probably because they'd already had this conversation more than once.

He wasn't changing his mind. "I know, but I am."

"You have a job to do," she snapped. "And I don't like your bossiness."

He lifted a shoulder, ignoring her tone, even though he was surprised by it. "After last night I'm keeping a close eye on you. I'm not trying to control you, just keep you safe." Simple as that.

"Mrs. Rose was killed by poison. Whoever did it didn't get up close and personal with a weapon. They're a coward." Her voice vibrated with barely contained rage.

He noticed that she'd shifted from raw fear to burning anger overnight. She was still afraid, he knew, but she was pissed now. And anger was better than fear. Fear had a way of making you hole up, withdrawing and acting rashly. "I don't care."

"I'm going to be in the back of the shop the entire day grooming dogs. I won't be eating or drinking anything I didn't bring myself. You can't be lurking around the shop like a bodyguard. I need my business to succeed."

"I won't be lurking around." He kept his tone neutral, even though he was annoyed. He wasn't leaving her to her own defenses and he would do anything to keep her safe.

"So what I want doesn't matter? I had one man try to control my entire life. I won't let you do it too," she snapped again, her sharp tone out of character for the woman he knew.

He looked at her in surprise. "What?"

She opened her mouth as he pulled into a parking spot in front of her shop, then shook her head. "Never mind. I'm sorry for snapping at you. I'm mentally exhausted and sleep deprived right now. I didn't sleep well and I...actually appreciate what you're doing. I know it's the smart thing. I was just lashing out because apparently I'm a jackass when I'm sleep deprived." She winced, scrunching up her nose. "I truly am thankful for you... I just hate this whole situation and I'm taking it out on you when you certainly don't deserve it. I'm sorry."

He wanted to circle back to what she meant by having a man control her life. He'd assumed that Serenity and her husband had a perfect marriage, though he wasn't certain why. She never talked about her dead husband, and there were only a couple pictures of him in the house, he'd noticed. "Apology accepted. I'm cranky when I don't get sleep too so I get it. I'm going to head down and grab some coffee for you and the others at the shop. Any requests for food?" He knew she hadn't eaten that morning and he hadn't wanted to push her. She was wound up bowstring tight—not that he blamed her. But he wanted her to eat, to take care of herself.

"Surprise us," she said, sliding a twenty-dollar bill across the seat. "And...thank you, seriously. For everything."

He frowned at the money, but tucked it into his pocket. He would just put it back in her purse later. After walking her inside the shop and seeing how busy the place was with familiar customers, he made his way down to the local cafe. She might not like that he was going to be hanging around today but it was happening. He'd already called his cousin and let him know he'd be taking lighter duties for the foreseeable future. Not a long-term solution, but he didn't care.

People in small towns tended to take care of each other. But his need to take care of Serenity went far deeper than wanting to take care of a friend or neighbor.

He wanted more than friendship from her and he wasn't sure it would ever happen.

* * *

Adeline pulled Serenity into a big hug the second she stepped into the back room. The soft scent of her lemongrass diffuser filled the air, muting the damp puppy smell. A couple of the dogs barked at her entrance, but they were all regulars so they settled down almost immediately. Not having to see customers was a huge plus today. Hell, Serenity didn't even want to be here, but she needed to work for multiple reasons, including to stay busy. But she also needed to pay bills and keep a roof over Harper's head. Just because someone was stalking her didn't mean her bills stopped coming in.

"I'm sorry about everything," Adeline said, her grip tightening.

"Thanks. I really can't talk about it unless I want to start crying."

"Fair enough. We've got a busy day today anyway. Hopefully I'll take your mind off...everything." Her expression was one of pity, which was appreciated, but almost made things worse. Adeline hadn't known Carol so this wouldn't affect her as much, which was just as well. Both of them couldn't be caught up in grief.

Serenity simply nodded and forced herself to keep it together. She'd talked to Carol's daughter this morning and they would be having the funeral in just a few days. It was all she could think about. Lincoln had told her that the FBI was on the case now and looking into who had texted her, using all the technology they had, but at this point she simply wanted to pack up and run. Even though she knew that was futile. Whoever had done this could just follow her.

And she wasn't going to run from this threat. No, she'd face this bastard down just like she'd faced down Black in court. That had been the hardest thing she'd ever had to do—to look into the eyes of the monster who'd tortured and killed her twin. But she'd done it. She would get through this too.

Ten minutes later there was a knock on the door, making her entire body tense. She knew there was a deputy stationed right out front so she was worrying for nothing. Even so, all her muscles pulled tight until the door opened and Lucas stepped in, a white bag in one hand as he balanced a tray of drinks in the other.

He gave Adeline a quick smile, and had a long, lingering look for Serenity as he set everything on a nearby table. "I'll be hanging out if you need me, keeping an eye on things. I won't scare away customers," he said, ducking out before she could respond or even say thanks for the stuff.

Adeline let out a low whistle as the door clicked shut. "Please tell me we're going to talk about that look."

"What look?"

"Come on. It's okay to live your life," Adeline said, giving Serenity a pointed stare.

Serenity knew that Adeline had been through her own shit. Far more than anyone should have to. So she knew those words were from experience as well. "Fine." She shifted Pepper, the goldendoodle she was currently trimming, on the table. "We might have...shared a charged moment last night." It had happened so fast—the sharp, lingering look gone before it had even really formed. Because all she'd been able to think about had been Carol, and how she was going to keep Harper safe.

"Might have?" Adeline peered into the bag he'd left and pulled out a croissant.

"Fine. We *did*. But it was one of those intense things that just sort of happened. Last night was bad and... I don't know. Nothing will come of it. We're just friends."

"Oh yeah, that was *really* clear. There is definitely no attraction between you two." Adeline snorted as she hopped up onto one of the counters, already devouring her croissant.

"I'm a mom," she blurted.

"And? What the hell does that mean? Moms don't have sex?"

"No, of course we do. I didn't mean it like that. I just meant...I'm a widow and I have a daughter. He isn't going to want to deal with all that on top of this craziness."

Adeline made the sound of a buzzer Serenity recognized from a familiar game show even as she gave her a thumbs-down sign. "That's a dumb excuse and beyond weak. Come on, you're a widow, not dead." She winced. "Sorry, really wrong choice of words. Wow, really bad. You know what I mean though."

"I just don't think I'm ready for a relationship."

Adeline hopped off the countertop and wiped her hands on her pants. "If that's true, then I get it. If you're not ready, don't push yourself. But I think you're lying to yourself. You've been a widow for a couple years and I know things between you and Olsen weren't great at the end."

Adeline was one of the few people who knew that she and Olsen had been rocky even before he died. Serenity wasn't sure they would have lasted had he lived. Hell, she knew they wouldn't have. She'd already had one foot out the door. If it hadn't been for Harper, she'd have already been gone.

She pulled out the blow-dryer. "Lucas is a good friend and I don't want to lose him. And...I'm *scared*. I'm scared of a relationship, of change, of everything going on right now." And that was the truth.

"That I believe. It's okay to be scared. Just don't hide yourself away and live a muted life because of fear. You literally survived hell. You deserve to live your life in freaking Technicolor. That bastard took a lot from you. Don't let him take everything else." Adeline lifted a Maltese named Bailey out of one of the kennels and set him on the table. The little guy immediately started licking her face.

Serenity didn't respond as she started the blow-dryer, because there wasn't much to say. Her friend was right. But that didn't mean she was ready to let go of her fear. It had dug its fingers in tight.

Some days it felt like she was simply surviving. She'd sworn she would never be a victim again, but part of her wondered if she was still letting Michael Black control her life. Okay, she knew she was. It wasn't even a question. She wasn't sure how to let go, however. She wanted to be a good role model for her daughter, to protect her— to make sure Harper didn't grow up afraid of everything.

Shaking off those thoughts, she forced herself to focus on her job.

Someone out there was determined to hurt her and those she loved. She couldn't let that happen.

# CHAPTER TWELVE

Six hours later, Serenity hung her apron on the hook by the door. "I'm going to get out of here. Are you good?"

Adeline looked up from her current dog, a terrier mix. "Of course. I feel like I already know the answer, but are you going to quilting class tonight?"

"No. I want to stay close to home with Harper." Coming to work had helped her stay focused but she couldn't be out after last night. It felt wrong to go anywhere with Carol dead. And even if it didn't, she wouldn't be away from her daughter. Harper was the most important person in her life.

"I understand. I've already talked to everybody in the group and we'll all be heading to our cars with buddies after we're done. And you know me, I'm going to have double pepper spray."

Serenity snorted even as a trickle of fear slid through her veins. She couldn't tell her friends not to live their lives. She just wished she could keep them all safe. Quilting class was safe though. The parking lot was fully lit up outside the shop and everybody always walked to their vehicles together. "Okay, I'm still going to tell you to be safe anyway."

As she stepped into the main area of her shop, aware-ness jolted inside her to see Lucas waiting for her in one of the chairs.

"Hey." He immediately stood, tucking his phone away. "I texted you but—"

Her heart rate kicked up. "Crap." She fished her phone out of her back pocket, cursing herself for not hearing it. She'd been checking on and off all day but she must have missed it when she was blow-drying one of the dogs. And if she'd missed his text, she might have missed mes-sages from other people. Harper's teacher had told her she would check in periodically—the school knew what was going on and they were being proactive about keep-ing an extra eye on Harper.

As she looked at the screen, she let out a sigh of relief to see a message from Harper's teacher telling her that everything was normal at school. Part of her didn't want to even let Harper go to school at all, but she figured she was safer surrounded by classmates and people who cared for her.

The next text, however, had ice freezing in her veins.

"What is it?" Lucas was next to her in an instant, grabbing the phone from her fingers.

Before she could even move into action, he'd strode across the shop and started digging into a basket of dog toys.

He let out a curse even as she moved up beside him. She was aware of Callie's curious look from where she stood at the cash register but her employee didn't say an-ything.

"Do you know what this is?" he murmured.

Serenity stared at the necklace for a long moment and had started to say no when it registered exactly what it was. "Yeah. Put it down." She hurried to the countertop and pulled out a little baggie they used for dog treats. Grabbing it by the edges, she put the necklace inside with trembling fingers. She had no doubt that Carol's killer had been in here. Sometime today likely.

She closed her eyes for a long moment as she tried to steady herself against the raw fear that threatened to knock the breath out of her. "It's from one of Black's victims. I recognize it from one of the TV specials," she said, quietly enough for only him to hear.

After her sister's murder and Black's imprisonment, she'd followed stories about him on the news and read up about him and his other victims. She'd wanted to understand why he'd done what he'd done, but eventually she'd realized that you can't understand or rationalize the motives of evil. He'd gone after women who'd all looked the same—black hair, blue eyes, slender and in their late teens or early twenties, with twenty being the average age. It was the same age his own mother had been when she'd abandoned him to his grandparents. So the asshole had mommy issues. It wasn't an excuse to go on a killing spree.

"This necklace was never recovered," she continued. Just like all the other jewelry he'd taken. Maybe it wasn't real, but after last night, she believed that it must be. Soon the Feds should tell them if the bracelet left on her SUV had been real. She was betting yes on that one too.

He tucked the plastic baggie into his pocket. "I'm calling Lincoln—"

"No," she whispered. She did not want the sheriff down here. "I'll give him this and he can come in after hours and search for whatever he thinks might be helpful, but I don't want law enforcement at my shop. Please," she whispered.

He paused, but nodded sharply even though it was clear he wanted to argue.

"I need to pick up Harper from school. I don't want this garbage to taint her. I just... She lost her father, our dog, and then we moved here. I'm trying to give her a sense of normalcy." Soon she'd have to sit Harper down and explain a little bit about what was going on, though she'd leave out most of the details.

"Black has got to be communicating with someone on the outside and using them to send these...things," Lucas murmured.

Throat tight, she nodded. She agreed with him. She knew that serial killers often had fan clubs, which was disgusting. But there was a lot of evil in this world. Hell, if not someone from his fan club, it had to be someone who'd known about what he'd done. Someone who'd been involved. That thought made her stomach roil but she steeled herself. "I know."

"Look, I know you want to wait, but you need to call Lincoln. The deputy watching your shop had a call out he had to take. A domestic issue. So no one is watching your shop now. And Linc will want to talk to Callie," he said quietly. "Especially if she's been working all day."

*Damn it.* "You're right. And...I think I might tell her to take the rest of the week off. I can manage without her and I'd feel better if she wasn't here." Even if she and Callie weren't friends, but simply employee and employer, she could become a target.

"I'll cover the front of the shop."

In that moment she wanted to kiss him. Not in a romantic way, but she wanted to convey to him how grateful she was for his presence, for his strength. He'd stepped up in a way she never could have expected. And she wished she wasn't so broken. That she could deal with a relationship, because he was exactly the sort of man she would choose.

"I can have my mom pick up Harper. You know she'd love to. And then I'll man the front while you and Callie talk to Lincoln. He'll be discreet and talk to you guys in the back. This won't affect your business."

Except she knew that it would. If anything, she'd probably get more business if word of this got out. Which was gross on so many levels. But people, even well-meaning people, were drawn to trauma. It was a weird glitch of human nature. She closed her eyes for a long moment. "I'll call the school and let them know to expect your mom."

"And I'll call Lincoln right now."

She locked up then, and called Adeline out to the front so she could tell her and Callie everything at the same time.

At this point she wasn't sure if she should just close up her shop completely or what. She didn't know what the right answer was. This person could be anyone, anywhere.

She needed to make a living, but she didn't want to die because she'd made herself an easy target. At the same time, Adeline and Callie depended on her for their living as well.

There was no easy decision, she realized, dread settling low in her belly as she waited for Lincoln to arrive.

## CHAPTER THIRTEEN

"So I take it Serenity isn't coming tonight?" Bianca asked from across the table. Her blonde hair was pulled back in a perfect plait.

Adeline looked up from her own quilt that she was currently stitching a new square onto. There were eight of them here tonight for quilting class, something she'd only taken up this year. Class was every Thursday night and they had between eight and twelve quilters attend on average.

"She's not coming," Adeline said simply.

"Is anyone else going to talk about what's going on, then?" Bianca asked, looking around the group.

"Talk about what?" Adeline set her square down on the table, feeling her temper rise. She was protective of Serenity and wasn't going to sit here and let people gossip about her.

"Mrs. Rose was murdered. It's pretty clear from what Sheriff Jordan said that this person is targeting people who are friends with Serenity. How are we not talking about this?" She sounded exasperated.

"Not sure what you're worried about, since you're not her friend." Adeline normally kept a cool head, but Bianca's tone ramped up her anger.

Next to her, Chloe, another shop owner, snickered but quickly hid her face in her own quilt when Bianca shot her a glare.

Bianca narrowed her eyes at Adeline from across the table. "What the hell is wrong with you?"

"I don't like talking about Serenity—my friend—while she's not here. This group has never been about gossip and I don't want to start now." Most of the women who came to the class were local business owners or employees. They usually talked about tourism and ways to help promote each other. Mean-spirited gossip wouldn't be tolerated.

Bianca lifted an eyebrow. "I'm not gossiping about her. I'm simply talking about what's going on. You guys aren't scared?"

Paisley, who owned a clothing boutique that sold gently used items, nodded. "I'm scared. I think everyone is. I still can't believe Mrs. Rose was actually murdered."

Adeline nodded in commiseration because it was true. It *was* hard to believe. They hadn't had an actual murder in town in... She wasn't even sure. Well before she'd moved here. And part of the reason Adeline had moved to Verona Bay had been to start over, to get a fresh start as she escaped her own violent past. The low crime rate and mild winters here had helped make her decision.

"Look, I didn't mean to upset you," Bianca said. "I'm just scared. There's no other way to say it."

Some of her temper eased. "That's fair. I think we all are. But we also need to rally around Serenity, not ostracize her or make her feel like this is her fault."

"Of course it's not her fault," Chloe said, giving Bianca a pointed look.

Bianca shifted in her seat. "I never said it was."

Yeah well, she'd been heading in that direction, Adeline thought. But she held her tongue. Right now she didn't trust herself not to say something she couldn't take back.

By the time the night was winding down, Adeline had cooled down. Her mother had always told her that her temper would get her into trouble so it was something she worked on. Quilting—something she'd never imagined as an activity she would get into—calmed her on an epic level. Some people were now into coloring. Well, quilting did for her what coloring did for them, and she loved it. She'd never win any awards for it, but it soothed her.

"Are you about ready?" Bianca asked, setting her bag on the table.

Adeline had planned to leave with Chloe, but the shop owner had left with Paisley so now she was stuck with a woman she didn't care for. "Yep." She slid the last of her blocks into her bag.

"Look, I'm sorry about earlier," Bianca said as they stepped outside, a chilly breeze skating over them.

Adeline shrugged as she locked the door behind them. Norah, the owner, let them lock up after themselves, something that would have been unheard of in a bigger town. After locking up, she scanned the parking lot. Just their two cars were left but she didn't see anyone else. Still, she pulled out her pepper spray. "Your quilt is looking good," she said, aiming for civility. Better than her own.

Bianca's mouth tightened as she pulled out her key fob. "What is it about me that you don't like?" she asked bluntly.

Surprised by the question, Adeline decided for neutrality. "I don't not like you. I don't have any particular feelings toward you." She'd simply had enough of the Biancas of the world—the perfect, mean-girl types who more often than not put themselves before everyone else. She'd seen the way Bianca was with married men and it annoyed the hell out of her. There was just a certain type of woman who went after men who were taken, and Adeline didn't understand that. So yeah, she judged her a bit.

"Whatever," Bianca muttered, pressing the key fob to her car. "I have nothing against Serenity."

"No, but you *would* like to get Lucas Jordan into bed." It came out before she could stop herself.

Bianca paused as they reached the front of their two cars, which were unfortunately parked side by side. "So what if I do?"

"I just think it's gross how you go after men who are taken." Damn it, she hadn't meant to get into any of this, but the words just poured out.

Bianca blinked in clear surprise. "Is that what you think about me?"

"I know what I see." She pressed her own key fob and turned away from Bianca as she opened the driver's side door.

At a sharp intake of breath she started to turn toward Bianca, then all the muscles in her body pulled taut as a shock of pain punched through her.

Wave after wave of pain rolled through her before darkness engulfed her.

\* \* \*

Lincoln paused for only a moment at his next-door neighbor's door, then knocked. He wasn't sure what it was about Autumn Perez that had him twisted up inside, but whenever he was there he felt like a teenager. One who couldn't string coherent sentences together in the face of the sexiest woman he'd ever met.

He could hear movement inside and knew she was home because she rarely left, anyway that he knew of. There was a little sound behind the door, then she opened it, but not fully. Which was pretty much par for the course when it came to Autumn. She had no problem keeping him at arm's length.

"Hello, sheriff." Her tone was perfectly polite as she stepped out onto the porch. Her thick, wavy dark hair was pulled up into a ponytail and she eyed him carefully with brown, amber-flecked eyes. "Is everything okay?"

"That remains to be seen. Did you see the notice we sent out about Mrs. Rose?"

She nodded, her expression still neutral. "Serenity called me too. It's why I'm not at quilting class tonight. I decided to stay in just to be safe."

He hadn't even realized she was a part of the class, or that she was friends with Serenity, which reaffirmed exactly how much he knew about her: almost zero. But he wanted to know everything about the pretty woman with the mouthwatering curves and sharp eyes that seemed to see everything.

"I just wanted to check in and make sure you were taking precautions."

She looked confused for a moment. "Are you going around to all of our neighbors?"

"Yes. I'm doing a walkthrough of the neighborhood." He hadn't intended to but now he would so he wouldn't be a liar.

She seemed to relax at that and nodded, giving him a half-smile. That simple action had all his muscles pulling taut. "Thanks, sheriff."

"You can call me Lincoln." Something he'd told her more than once, but she insisted on referring to him as sheriff.

Her gaze flickered down to the sheriff insignia sewn onto the left breast of his work jacket. "Sure thing, sheriff." She gave him a smirk as she stepped back inside but didn't fully close the door on him. "You need anything else?"

"Nope. Just be careful," he said as he turned away.

Maybe it was because he was so used to women falling at his feet that he was intrigued by her stand-offish-
ness. No, there was something about her that simply
drew him in. But it was clear she wasn't interested. And
considering that he was the sheriff, he would never
abuse his power that way. Hell, he'd never abuse his
power regardless, but he had to walk a fine line.

Some women saw the badge and tended to throw
themselves at him, while others were turned off by it.
There didn't seem to be an in-between. It was part of the
reason he didn't date anyone in town. But if Autumn
were to show even a flicker of interest, that would be a
different story.

Shaking his head at his own foolishness, he headed
down the sidewalk, intending to speak to each of his
neighbors individually. It was a good idea anyway considering what had happened earlier at Serenity's shop.

He'd spoken to her, her employees and sent off the
necklace to the FBI for testing since they had a much bigger budget and had handled the Black serial killer case.
He'd also sent out an alert to the entire town but not everyone would have received it yet. He cared about his people, and he took their security and safety seriously. They
had petty crime here, but murder? There hadn't been
one since before he'd taken office. And if he could help
it, there wouldn't be another one. Which was why he'd
reached out to the FBI so quickly.

As he reached the sixth house on the street, his phone
buzzed in his pocket. Even though he was off duty, he
was never officially off. Hell, especially now. Which was

why he rarely drank alcohol. He never knew when he'd be called in.

When he saw Deputy Cole's name on his caller ID he answered right away. "Yeah?"

"You're going to want to get down to the parking lot of Norah's Quilts. Adeline Rodriguez has been kidnapped."

## CHAPTER FOURTEEN

Special Agent Amy Lin nodded once at the guard who unlocked the door for her. Michael Black wasn't going anywhere but this was a maximum-security prison in north Florida and they took all security precautions seriously.

His chains jingled against the table as he shifted in the seat when he saw her. His hair was still a dark brown, but now peppered with gray and thinning. His once almost handsome, charming facade had been stripped away, and deep lines bracketed his eyes and mouth. His blue eyes seemed faded as well. At six feet one inch, he should have seemed larger, more intimidating. Instead, he was a sad little man.

She gave him a cool look and set her briefcase on the ground as she sat.

He held her gaze, his expression stony. "What are you doing here?"

"I would think you'd be happy to have a break from the monotony. You've gotta get bored in that cell all by yourself." She casually leaned back in her seat as if she had all the time in the world. When he didn't respond—not that she'd expected him to—she continued. "I've heard you aren't even reading your letters anymore. And you have quite the fan club." Sad, desperate men and women reached out to Black for... Hell, Amy wasn't even sure why. Being sad and desperate was one thing. Reaching out to a psychotic serial killer? Nah.

He glanced away, his jaw tightening. "Whores. All of them."

Well, he definitely hadn't changed. Not that she'd thought he would. Black had always thought he was way smarter than he was. In reality, he was just another violent, misogynist asshole. He hated women and blamed his lot in life on his mother abandoning him. Boo freaking hoo.

Even if that hadn't happened, Amy had no doubt he would have found another reason to hate the opposite sex. Because he was human garbage who loved to play the victim card. Poor little Michael Black, abandoned by his mother and raised by his rich, loving grandparents who'd sent him to the best schools and provided everything for him. He'd been mediocre, however. He'd had no drive, had average grades and hadn't been able to hold a job—but he'd liked to hurt women. That, he'd been good at.

"You're communicating with someone, however." She tapped a crimson-painted fingernail on the metal table separating them.

His head whipped up as he finally looked her in the face, his eyes narrowing slightly. He'd lost a decent amount of weight in the last few years. She knew from the warden that he wasn't eating as much. But he wasn't starving himself so it didn't warrant a feeding tube. Not that she cared. Let the man starve. Her only regret was that she hadn't caught him sooner. Soon enough to save those girls, including Serenity's twin.

God, if only they'd been a little quicker. But she banished the thought. She'd played the "what if" game in her head far too many times. And she couldn't change the past no matter how much she wanted to build a damn time machine and do just that.

"I'm not talking to anyone." His tone was neutral.

She lifted an eyebrow. "Is that right?"

He simply stared at her, unmoving. She had nothing to offer him. Not when he was on death row. He'd fired his last attorney and had chosen not to appeal. Which was just as well, because it would fail, even if it would drag things out in court for years and waste everyone's time and money.

When he didn't say anything, she bent down and pulled out two little plastic baggies. Sheriff Jordan had couriered the last "gift" left for Serenity to a local FBI office and they'd made sure Amy got it. She wanted to see Black's reaction to the actual jewelry.

Telling him was one thing, but showing him something he'd taken during his sick crimes was quite another.

His entire body language changed, his spine straightening as he stared at the jewelry in surprise. His dark blue eyes widened in true shock. "Where did you get that?"

"Present, left for Serenity Washington. You remember her."

His eyes lit up with what she could only describe as manic glee before his expression turned very carefully neutral. He was good at that, hiding his emotions. Probably because he lacked basic human empathy. Even so, he never took his gaze off the jewelry. He wouldn't even look at her, simply stared at the necklace and bracelet.

"Someone left those for Serenity?" He said her name as if he knew her on a personal level. But he didn't, no matter what he thought. He only knew her as the young woman he'd taken, intending to torture and kill.

"Yes. And I guarantee you know who did it." She wasn't here to beat around the bush. She wanted answers.

He shifted slightly in his seat, finally flicking his gaze up to hers, though she could tell it strained him to do so. He liked seeing the jewelry. "Those must be fakes."

"They're not. They're the real deal. Which I'm guessing you know. I thought you didn't kill mothers."

"Of course I didn't! I would never." He sounded offended that she'd even suggest it.

Amy resisted the urge to snort. He acted as if having some bizarre moral code made him superior. "If you don't hurt mothers, then tell me who is targeting Serenity. She's a mom now. A widow. Her little girl depends on her."

Something in his expression changed but she couldn't get a read on him. That was the problem with Michael Black. He had narcissistic personality disorder—or NPD. He had brief flashes of compassion, though she was certain those were mostly fake. He looked out for number one. Always had, no matter how his multitude of attorneys had tried to paint him as a misunderstood, bullied youth.

"No one is targeting her," he said, sounding confident.

"They are," she said bluntly, leaving no room for argument. "Someone killed her neighbor. And they've left these for her as presents, telling her that her time is coming. Someone is systematically hunting her. If they weren't, I wouldn't be here. My time is worth more than that," she said, injecting anger into her words. "You know that."

For the briefest moment, Amy saw fear flicker in his gaze. It was there and then gone so fast she might have imagined it. She would review the security recordings later to be sure, but she knew what she'd seen. Fear for a man like Black was foreign—and it did not make sense. She mulled that over in her mind as she plucked the plastic bags back up and put them in her briefcase.

She could practically see the tension in his shoulders growing as she hid his prizes from his view. "Who is your partner?" she asked as she snapped her briefcase shut.

"I've told you multiple times that—"

"Yeah, yeah, you didn't have a partner. But I know you did. You weren't smart enough to pull that off by yourself." She leaned across the table, getting in his personal space.

She wasn't worried about him attacking her. If he tried, she could restrain him no problem. He was a weak, pathetic little man who'd had to hurt young, college-aged girls to assert his dominance. It didn't matter that he'd claimed he needed to cleanse them from their sins, to kill them before they became mothers and potentially ruined young lives. She'd never bought his shtick. He'd simply liked hurting women. Period.

"Whoever your partner is, they're going down. And I'm going to make sure they get the needle too," she whispered. In reality, she had no control over that, something he should know.

But her words struck home because fear popped wild in his gaze. He lunged at her, but she moved back, far quicker than him, and his chains jerked taut.

He raged, screaming obscenities as he tried to lift his hands higher than the few inches the chains allowed him. Spit flew out of his mouth, his eyes so wide she could see the whites all around them as he continued screaming that he was going to kill her.

Well, well, well. That was a very interesting reaction. Whoever his partner was, they mattered to him. This was somehow personal for him. And it gave her information she needed. She'd known he'd never give up the name of his partner, but he'd given her valuable information nonetheless. She picked up her briefcase and stepped outside, bypassing the guards who rushed in.

She waited until she and her partner were in the parking lot and completely alone before speaking. "I want information on every single guard who has contact with Black. He's getting messages out to someone."

"He didn't like that little threat you made," Frank said, pulling his cell phone out. His face was grim, but that was pretty much his resting expression. In his late forties, Frank had been assigned as her partner eight years ago when she'd been twenty-eight—and to everyone's surprise they'd worked out perfectly. He could be grumpy, but he had a good instinct.

"He's definitely covering for someone. My money is on it being a relative."

Frank straightened. "Are you serious?"

She paused, mulling over his reaction. "Maybe. My gut is telling me this is very personal. Otherwise why cover for a partner? Especially someone with NPD. No... It wouldn't be his parents. He hated them too. Lover, maybe."

Frank simply snorted, giving his opinion with that one sound.

"Yeah, I know," she muttered. "It definitely wouldn't be a lover. He would have no love for anyone. No...it's got to be blood. At least that's what my instinct says. But he never had a kid. Not that we know of anyway."

She had his dossier memorized. Michael Black had been her first big case. Stopping him had put her name on the map. Even if that game warden hadn't caught him, her team had already figured out who he was. They simply hadn't known where he was hiding out.

"There's something we aren't seeing right now. But we will." She always got her guy. And even though this case had made her career, it still felt unfinished. She'd *always* thought he had a partner—someone mentally weaker than him. Someone he could control.

But there had been no way to prove it and he hadn't admitted to anything. Her bosses had wanted everything closed up neat and tidy. His murders had rocked the Southeast. Since he'd been the one behind the actual murders, she'd been fine with nailing his ass to the wall, but if there was someone else out there... She wanted them too.

"This isn't a simple copycat case," she said, talking more to herself than Frank as she headed toward the private airport. "It feels personal, targeted toward Serenity specifically. But why now after all these years?" She wasn't looking for an answer, it was just easier to talk out loud. Thankfully she and Frank had been partners long enough that they were used to each other's quirks. He let her talk to herself and she didn't give him grief when he ate tuna casserole in the car.

Next to her, Frank was making calls, instructing their team to dig even deeper into all the guards who had access to Black.

She slipped her Bluetooth in her ear when she saw Oliver Baker, one of her people, on her caller ID. "We're almost to the airstrip."

"Good. There's been a kidnapping in Verona Bay. We're rolling out as soon as you get here."

"Shit."

## CHAPTER FIFTEEN

"Tell me what you think about this Bianca," Special Agent Amy Lin said to Serenity as she shoved her phone back in her pocket, done with whoever had called.

Wearing skinny jeans, a white button-down shirt and a loose black jacket, she looked much the same as she had all those years ago when Serenity had first met her. Her jet-black hair was pulled up into a ponytail, her dark eyes vivid against her pale skin, and she didn't seem to have aged at all. She was petite, probably about five feet even, but she had a presence that somehow made her seem taller, larger than life.

Serenity glanced around her shop, watching as one of Amy's agents worked. "What do you want to know?" Bianca Copeland had been bashed in the head, knocked unconscious, only to wake up and realize that Adeline had been taken. Her purse and all its belongings had been left behind with her car door still open. Thankfully Bianca hadn't been knocked out too long so she'd been able to call law enforcement almost immediately. But it was still too late because Adeline was gone.

"What kind of person is she? Could she be behind this?"

Serenity blinked in surprise. "I don't particularly care for her. We're not close, but no, I don't think she could have taken Adeline. She runs Sweet Spot... Which you already know." She forced herself to stop rambling and focus. "If I'm being brutally honest, she's not the type of woman to have a lot of girlfriends. She rubs people the wrong way. But she is great at business and runs her shop with efficiency. She has a fairly quick turnover, at least in retail terms. She keeps employees almost one year exactly before they get tired of her micromanaging. I have no clue if she has a boyfriend, or girlfriend for that matter. I assume she's heterosexual because of the way she interacts with men but...I don't know enough about her. I get together with the quilting group every Thursday, which I'm sure you already know. But usually those get-togethers are about businesses. All local owners and employees are welcome but it's usually the same group of us talking about tourism and ways to boost upcoming events or festivals."

Amy nodded, but it was clear she knew some of this already. Which made sense. She would have already talked to the sheriff and gotten as many details as possible since she'd arrived last night, right after Adeline's kidnapping.

Serenity tightened her jaw, forcing herself not to break down. Her friend had been taken and she needed to keep her shit together until Adeline was found. Freaking out would do no one any good. "I'm surprised you're able to spare so many agents," Serenity said as one of Amy's people finished installing another security camera inside her shop. There was a team of two working, one sweeping for any type of recording device and the other installing cameras. She had basic cameras she'd bought online but these were high-tech, tiny, and transmitted back to whatever command center the Feds had.

Amy gave her a curious look. "We're going to do everything we can until this person is caught. I always knew he had a partner. My bosses are backing me up on this."

Serenity simply nodded, exhausted and terrified for her friend. She hated that they were here installing cameras to help guard her when they should be out looking for Adeline.

As if she read her mind, Amy lifted an eyebrow. "My team is currently looking at every security camera downtown—the locals are being very helpful. We're also looking into other leads. We're going to find your friend."

Yeah, but would Adeline still be alive? For a sharp moment she remembered waking up in that cabin, tied to a board, her body restrained, her sister mere feet from her. She swallowed hard, hoping Adeline wasn't in the same agony. Could she be alive?

Again, the woman who had the uncanny ability to read her freaking mind said, "The fact that she was taken and not killed on site is a good thing, whether you want to believe it or not." She gave Serenity a pointed look. "I don't say this in a flippant way, but my profilers think your neighbor's murder was…interesting."

"Interesting how?" she demanded. She only knew that Carol had been poisoned, but didn't have any other details.

But Amy simply shook her head and pulled her buzzing phone out of her pocket. "Hold on."

Thoroughly dismissed, Serenity rubbed a hand over her face. She hated this, hated the not knowing, not being able to help. Harper was currently in school, which was being monitored on site by a federal agent. Amy definitely wasn't messing around, something she was grateful for. Now that Amy had made a name for herself and had the capital to back it up, she was apparently using all of it for this case. Because Serenity knew that if this hadn't been linked to Michael Black, the Feds wouldn't have been called in so quickly. Or at all.

Even though she didn't want to be here, she was going to keep the shop open at the Feds' urging. They didn't think it was likely the person would strike out at her here—somewhere so public—but they wanted all options covered. And at least they could control this area. So for now one of Amy's agents would be working the cash register, though Serenity would still be paying her other employee. It didn't feel like enough. Nothing did.

Finding Adeline before it was too late was the only thing that mattered.

"Can I get out of here?" she asked as Amy ended her call. She'd closed for the day so that the agents could do their job and she wasn't in the mood for walk-ins anyway. She couldn't deal with people in general right now, not when her best friend was missing. "I need to pick up Harper soon anyway."

"Yeah. But I still want an agent staying inside your house."

Serenity shook her head. "We've been over this. I've got a security system and cameras—which your team now has access to. You said yourself someone will be keeping watch in my driveway and if the alarm is triggered, they'll get an alert. I don't want some stranger in my house." Whoever was taunting her wasn't invincible. If for some reason they got past the Feds, Serenity had a security system and a gun. Not that she wanted to use it, but her house was protected. The person doing all of this wasn't a ghost or some supernatural entity who could walk through walls.

Amy's jaw tightened but she nodded. "I know you're careful about security. More so than most of the population. And I seriously doubt that whoever this is, is going to target your house anyway. Hey…what's changed in your life recently? Anything big?" she asked as Serenity picked up her purse.

"Nothing. I mean, I haven't even been back a full year. The move home itself has been pretty big." At the time she'd been so sure it was the right decision. Now? Hell, now she didn't know what to think. Harper had adjusted so well to small-town life and was thriving. But someone clearly didn't want Serenity here.

Amy tapped her finger against the countertop. "I know. I'm just trying to get a feel for what's going on, if something happened to trigger whoever is doing this."

"What, like I caused this?" she asked dryly.

"Hell no." Amy's dark eyes flashed. "I'm just trying to get in this perp's head. Did you start dating anyone? Or sleeping with anyone? Multiple someones?"

Serenity paused for a moment. "No. There's no one."

Amy's gaze narrowed ever so slightly. "What was that pause?"

"There was no pause."

"Bullshit."

Serenity inwardly smiled, despite the situation. Amy had always been blunt, and while she had been incredible after Serenity had been found, she'd never treated Serenity like a victim. In the very beginning, sure, Amy had treated her with kid gloves, which Serenity had appreciated. But after that, Amy had simply treated her like a person. "I'm not dating anyone."

"What about the sheriff's brother, Lucas Jordan? I know he's been staying with you."

*Oh damn, bull's-eye.* She turned away from Amy and moved to one of the shelves, straightening little baskets of dog treats. "We're not dating or anything. We're just friends."

"Could it appear as if you're more than friends?" Amy's tone was neutral.

"Yes. Rumors have been flying about us."

Amy simply nodded, her expression taking on that slight haze that said the federal agent was deep in her own head.

Which was her cue to go. "Well I'm gone, then. You know where I'll be if you have more questions." And she also knew that Amy had an agent who'd be tailing her around. Which was fine with her. Having a private escort who was fully armed? She'd take it.

When she headed down Main Street to where she'd parked her vehicle, she felt as if there were hundreds of eyes watching her. It wasn't true, but she couldn't shake the feeling of being watched regardless. Most of the shop owners downtown already knew about the FBI's presence. It wasn't exactly a secret, even if they were being very subtle about installing cameras at her place. After Adeline's kidnapping, everyone in town knew something was up. This was a small town and outsiders stood out.

As she slid into the front seat of her car, she wanted to cry in frustration. But she kept it together, frowning when she heard an unfamiliar ring tone coming from...somewhere inside the vehicle.

Her frown deepening, she glanced around her SUV. There was a phone tucked into the center console and it wasn't hers. It was one of those Tracfones.

Invisible talons of fear scraped down her spine as she grabbed her own cell phone and dialed Amy's number even as she picked up the cell phone from the console. "Who is this?"

She could faintly hear Amy's voice on the other end of her phone, but couldn't talk directly to her as a modulated voice said, "Hello, Serenity. I have something you want."

"Where's Adeline?" she shouted, knowing that Amy would hear her. The other woman was smart and trained enough to pick up that something was going on.

"If I told you, that wouldn't be any fun. But she is alive. If you want to see her again, go to the Little Children's Park in Bishop's Creek."

Bishop's Creek was one town over and only a half-hour drive. She kicked her vehicle into gear. "Bishop's Creek?" she asked.

"No calling in your Fed friends or the sheriff. I'm watching your every move." The sound of the machine-like voice sent chills down her spine.

"How do I know Adeline is alive?" She glanced at the vehicle pulling up behind her—being driven by one of Amy's people.

"You don't. Now toss your cell phone out the window—and you better ditch your Fed friend. Tick-tock."

*Tick-tock.* God, this sick asshole had done all of this to get to her. "I'm throwing my phone out the window now," she said, hoping Amy could hear her. She didn't actually believe this caller was going to let Adeline go but she couldn't not follow these instructions. Because what if Adeline's life was depending on her doing this?

Knowing the agent was behind her eased some of her fear. But not much of it as she rolled down the window and tossed her cell phone out.

"Good girl. Now you better hurry or I might get impatient and kill Adeline." The line went dead.

Her heart rate kicked up as she pressed on the gas. It was far too much to hope that Adeline was alive and waiting at the park for her. But she sped up regardless.

She made it there in record time, and when she pulled into the nearly deserted parking lot, she wasn't surprised when the agent pulled in next to her.

A text popped up. *Told you to lose the friend.*

*It's the FBI,* she texted back. *I don't control them and you didn't give me a chance to lose them.*

There was a long pause, then another text came through. A video. It took a moment for it to load, but when it did, all the air left her lungs.

She ignored the knock on her driver's window as the video played. Adeline's dark, curly hair was limp against her face, her wrists chained to a radiator and she was— Oh, God. No, she wasn't dead. Serenity could see the rise and fall of Adeline's chest. She was just sleeping.

The door was yanked open so she held out the phone for the agent to see. He was silent as the video continued, zooming out to show Adeline's signature sparkly sneakers and the day's newspaper. So she had been alive at least this morning. Which was something.

Serenity wiped her damp palms on her pants as the phone buzzed again. *Tick-tock, tick-tock. Find your friend before she dies of starvation. Not a pretty way to go.*

Bile rose in Serenity's throat as the video ended.

"Do you know the identity of the caller?" the agent asked, taking the Tracfone from her. Clearly Amy had picked up on her conversation.

She quickly relayed everything and he simply nodded. "Smart thinking, calling Amy. She picked your phone up from the road. She should be here in—" The burner phone dinged in his hands. A text.

*Go look behind the little swing set. The one with the blue-colored baby swings.*

The agent looked around, weapon up. It was too cold for parents to be here with their kids so at least the place was deserted. Serenity's breath was visible in the air, little wisps of smoke curling up against the gray background of the park and sky.

"Amy's almost here," he said, glancing down at his phone once.

Serenity looked over her shoulder when she heard the sound of tires rolling over gravel. It was Amy, her partner in the passenger seat.

The two of them jumped out together, practically in unison as if they'd choreographed it.

"It was smart to call me," Amy said as she approached, her weapon also drawn.

"I didn't know if I should follow the instructions or not, but I did." For all she knew she could've made herself a target. Her stomach was twisted up in vicious knots as she thought about what Adeline must be going through.

"We'll talk about that later—I don't want you going off without us again, even if you knew we were following you."

Her partner Frank had already broken off from them and had disappeared into the woods surrounding the park.

The other agent held out the phone to Amy so she could read.

After she looked at the screen, she glanced around, weapon still up. "I don't like any of this."

*Yeah, no shit.* A chill snaked down Serenity's spine as she looked at the trees surrounding the park. Green still dotted some of them but they were mostly bare as they rustled in the wind. She followed after Amy, her heart pounding a staccato beat in her chest.

By the time they reached the swing set, Frank and two more agents she hadn't even known were here filtered out of the woods nearby like freaking ghosts.

"No sign of anyone," one of the agents said. "But I found this," the woman continued, holding up a small camera. "It was secured to one of the trees. Gonna bag it for the techs."

Amy tucked her weapon away as they all began searching around the swing set area.

"There." Serenity pointed to a piece of plastic peeking out of the sand by one of the poles.

Amy moved closer and gingerly pulled it out. "It's another bracelet and...a photograph." She slid gloves on, then opened the bag. "It looks like you."

When she held out the Polaroid to Serenity, she felt all the blood leave her face as she stared at the picture of her sister asleep in their dorm room. It was from the night they'd been taken.

"Not me," she rasped out. "Savannah. I think it's from...that night." Her throat constricted as she forced the words out. "She's wearing the same pajamas from that night."

Frowning, Amy flipped the Polaroid over and let out a curse. "It's dated the day you guys were taken."

Someone had taken a picture of them the night they'd been taken. A shudder snaked through her, revulsion settling in her gut. She'd always known that but she'd never understood how it had happened. Obviously they'd been drugged but—

"Excuse me," she blurted, turning away and promptly throwing up.

## CHAPTER SIXTEEN

"Thank you again for picking up Harper," Serenity said, collapsing onto the couch opposite Lucas.

"You don't ever have to thank me. Are you going to tell me what happened?" Lucas had been surprisingly patient, waiting until she'd gotten Harper bathed and in bed before asking questions.

He definitely deserved an answer. She quickly ran through everything that had happened that afternoon. Thankfully Amy had called Lucas's brother and told him that someone would need to pick Harper up from school—because she'd been thinking clearly. And Lincoln had of course called Lucas, who'd stepped up once again. He knew that Adeline had been kidnapped—everyone did—and that this afternoon something had happened related to it, but he didn't have any other details.

Lucas's expression was tight by the time she finished about the Polaroid. "Someone close to you had to have drugged you back then."

"I know. And Amy agrees as well. We always thought he had a partner." She'd already told him as much earlier, so he didn't look surprised. "But there was no way to prove it. And I never saw anyone. But someone got Savannah and me from our dorm rooms. Or had access to our food and drinks. So they're looking into anyone who was at school with us then and anyone in my life now.

Not that they actually have to be in my life, but it's a starting point."

She rubbed a hand over her face.

"I explained a little bit to Harper about why you're staying here. No real details, I just let her know that the sheriff and FBI want to make sure we're safe and that's why you're going to be hanging out for a while. Which, you don't actually need to since the FBI—"

His expression darkened as he went into full-on protective mode. "Just stop. I'm not going anywhere."

She was silent for a long moment, watching him. She desperately wanted him to stay. Felt safe with him here. But not if there were strings or expectations attached. "Even if I never offer you anything other than friendship?"

He nodded. "Even then. I'm not here because I want something. I'm here because I want to be and because you need the support. You don't owe me shit for this, Serenity."

She liked that he didn't pretend not to understand what she meant. She'd never hinted that she wanted to offer more than friendship anyway, but she knew how he felt about her. Or at least a little bit. She had no idea if he wanted a future or just a hookup, though the way he was acting, she was fairly certain he didn't want the latter. He was acting as if she was precious to him, as if she mattered.

Even if she didn't owe Lucas an explanation, she was going to explain to him why she didn't want a relationship. He deserved it. "After what happened with Black, I met Olsen not too long after."

Lucas slightly straightened at the change in topic.

She continued, wanting to get all of this out at once. "He was a good man. Or at least not a terrible one. We had enough chemistry and... I didn't realize it at the time, but he liked being a knight in shining armor. He liked the thought of rescuing me. And to be honest, I didn't want to live anywhere near here back then. I wanted to run away from everything, to escape my past. And he was being sent on an international deployment. When he asked me to marry him, I said yes to escape. My mom had just died too and... I can see everything clearly now, but I was running away. And with his constant deployments, he was the perfect escape route."

Lucas nodded in understanding. Of course—of all people he would understand, considering he'd been deployed as well.

Since he didn't audibly respond, just listened attentively, she kept going. "Near the end of our marriage things weren't so great. They weren't awful or anything, just... I wasn't able to go with him on the last few deployments, and when he came back from them things between us were strained each time. While he'd been gone, I'd been spreading my wings a little, making friends, joining different clubs. Not to mention I'd been in charge of paying the bills and taking care of things around the house, and all the parenting duties. When he got back the last time, I wasn't ready to relinquish control of those things anymore. I did, eventually, to keep the peace.

"But it was a sign of issues we were already having. As time passed, and being on my own so much with Harper, I needed someone to look out for me less and less. I wasn't that damsel in distress he needed to save, and I now realize he almost resented me for it. Maybe that's too much of a jump, but our marriage had started to fracture. Then when he was killed in an ambush, I discovered he had a bunch of online gambling debts. It was like I didn't know him at all. He'd dipped into our savings, something I also hadn't realized. And that's definitely on me. I never checked our finances except to pay the bills, and he was gone so much. I let him handle all the big stuff like car insurance and homeowner's insurance..."

She paused, drew a deep breath.

"Our finances weren't a complete mess, but they weren't great. And when he died, I realized how little I knew about the state of our affairs. I didn't even have passwords to some things. I literally just let him take over my life and didn't question things like my retirement accounts or...anything. It was so, so foolish and I never want to do that again." Now she had a firm grasp on everything. Never again would she let anyone take over her finances and life.

Lucas was silent for a long moment, watching her. "I'm sorry about your marriage. I truly am. And for the record, I'm not looking to save you. I don't think you *need* saving. You are one of the strongest women I've ever met. I like you, Serenity. I like you a lot. I just want to be with you. And I want to help *keep* you safe."

His words warmed her from the inside out. "I don't know if I can ever be what you want." She deeply cared for Lucas too, but she wasn't sure she was willing to ever open her heart up to someone again. She'd gotten burned last time, and looking back, she'd never had that epic kind of love with her husband. She'd liked and respected him and she'd been grateful for the escape he'd afforded her. She'd truly been a mess back then. But becoming a mother had changed her inside, given her back her steel spine.

Lucas had started to respond when her phone rang. Glancing at it she immediately picked it up when she saw that it was Amy. "Have you found her?" she asked upon answering.

A long sigh. "No. I just wanted to let you know that we've reviewed the phone and videos texted to you. All the metadata has been stripped from it, which sucks, but we did find out where the burner phones were purchased—a gas station a couple towns over. Which lends credence to the idea of whoever doing this being a local here. Unfortunately they paid cash and there are no working security cameras at that place. Which was probably intentional on their part."

Her hope quickly crashed and burned as Amy laid out all the details. "So this person is somewhat intelligent," she muttered.

"Yes," Amy said. "But we have a lot of resources and we are using all of them to find whoever this is. We will find them."

Yeah, but how long would that take? "Thank you for calling. I appreciate it." Because Amy didn't have to.

"I'll keep you updated on anything that I'm able to. You already know that we've got someone stationed outside your house tonight, so get some sleep."

"I will. Thank you."

"No news?" Lucas asked after Serenity wrapped up her conversation with Amy.

"Nothing good." She quickly relayed everything to him before standing. The news that they weren't closer to finding Adeline sucked the rest of her energy out of her. "I'm going to head to bed." Not that she would be able to sleep. Again.

For a moment it appeared as if he might protest, but then he nodded. "I'll be up for a while if you want to talk or anything."

The "or anything" made her pause, but she simply nodded and headed to her room. She knew she needed sleep if she was going to be any use to anyone, but she wasn't sure she would manage to get any.

Not with her friend missing and a monster out there gunning for her.

## CHAPTER SEVENTEEN

Lucas was keyed up, unable to sleep for a multitude of reasons. He stared at the ceiling for another few seconds and finally got out of bed. Normally when he had trouble sleeping, he read for a while then usually crashed. Or if he'd had a nightmare, he tried writing therapy. Though as the years stretched out since leaving the military, he slept better and better. Time and distance were healing all unto themselves. For him at least. He knew that not everyone fared the same.

But being under Serenity's roof right now wasn't helping him sleep. Not to mention he missed Daisy. She sometimes slept at the foot of his bed, but usually she curled right up next to his leg, making sure at least her head or one paw made contact. When he'd gotten her, he'd sworn he would never have a dog sleep in his bed but she'd made the decision for him. Because once she'd finally figured out how to jump up on the bed he hadn't been able to kick her out. Saying no to those big brown eyes? Not possible.

He quietly made his way to the kitchen, careful not to disturb anyone, and to his surprise he found Serenity sitting at the table, mug in hand. Maybe he'd heard her in his subconscious and woken up.

"Hey," he murmured, stepping inside. It was normal and weird at the same time to be here with her. "How long have you been up?"

"Only about fifteen minutes. I'm about to head back to bed. I just couldn't sleep. I keep thinking about..." Sighing, she took a sip of what he guessed was hot tea.

Yeah, he could see the faint circles under her eyes. He poured some water for himself and leaned against the counter. "They're going to catch whoever is doing this."

She nodded, but he could tell she didn't believe him. Not that he blamed her. This had to be a nightmare for her—to move here after what she'd already been put through, settle in, start a business and then...this.

"I have a question, and if you say no it's okay. I was wondering if you would mind if I brought Daisy over here? She's fine at my mom's but I miss her and—"

Her eyes widened slightly. "Of course. I'm just sorry I didn't think of it earlier. I love that sweet girl."

"You've had a lot on your mind. Harper loves Daisy too, so this should be a good distraction for her," he added. He hoped she was for Serenity too. Daisy was like that; she seemed to know when you needed comforting.

Serenity's mouth pulled up in a ghost of a smile. "She'll be in heaven with Daisy here. In fact, you might lose her to Harper," she said, teasingly.

Daisy already adored Harper so he kinda figured she might bunk in Harper's room if Serenity allowed it. Which was fine with him.

"We lost our dog before we moved here," she continued.

His surprise must have shown on his face.

She nodded. "Yeah, I don't talk about her because it hurts. She was a rescue dog, a Maltese mix I got when I was pregnant with Harper. Her name was Dolly—after Dolly Parton. And I swear she knew I was pregnant before I did. She was tiny, but a fierce, protective little thing. Then when Harper was born, she was protective of her. She had heart issues, which is part of the reason she ended up at the kennel in the first place. She saved me as much as I saved her." There was a wealth of love and sadness in her voice.

Layers. This woman had so many of them. "Daisy saved me too," he said quietly, admitting to her what he'd never told anyone else. But it was true. Therapy had obviously helped, but Daisy? She'd been a huge help too. "Dogs are good for the soul." They were experts at unconditional love.

"I agree wholeheartedly. Bring her over as soon as you want." She stood then, finishing the rest of her tea. "I'm going to try and get some sleep. I don't even want to open tomorrow but the Feds think it's a good idea."

"Yeah, Lincoln said the same thing. It's better to have you there where the cameras are anyway."

"That's what Amy said."

Lucas knew the Feds hoped they might catch the killer on camera. Even if it would be monumentally stupid for whoever had killed Mrs. Rose to go in there, sometimes there was no logic to crazy. "They *are* going to catch whoever did this," he said again, wanting to emphasize what he truly believed. And until then, he was going to keep Serenity safe. She was his to protect, no matter what. He didn't care if they weren't together—if they might never be. He would do anything to keep her safe. He just hated that her friend Adeline had been taken. He might not know her well but she didn't deserve this. No one did.

She gave him one of those soft, sweet smiles and set her mug in the sink. "I know you don't want any more thanks from me, but I'm going to keep thanking you. Even with a Fed watching the house, I still feel better knowing you're here."

That was high praise indeed. He simply nodded and drank his water, however. He didn't want her thanks. He just wanted her, always. Forever. She'd been through so much, and knowing that she hadn't had a great marriage, damn. She deserved the world. She deserved a man who worshiped her, not someone with a savior complex.

After she left, he remained in the kitchen, trying to get his head on straight. All he wanted was to protect her and keep her safe. He hadn't been lying before—he truly did think she was the strongest woman he'd ever met. She'd survived hell and gone on to have a life, to become a mom and run her own business. She was independent, an occasional smartass, and fiercely protective of her daughter. He respected the hell out of all of that.

He downed his water and made his way back to the guest bedroom.

To his surprise, he found Serenity stepping out of Harper's room.

"I keep checking on her," Serenity whispered, shutting the door with a soft click. "It's like a compulsion. I think it's why I can't sleep."

"Do you have one of those baby monitor things?"

"Yeah. From when she was a baby. I guess I could put it in her room. I thought about just sleeping in her room, but I'm worried that'll make her realize how afraid I am." She ran her fingers through her dark hair. "Using the monitor would probably help me sleep a lot better." She stepped closer to him, clearly meaning to pass by as she made her way to her bedroom.

For just a moment, raw hunger flashed in her eyes as her gaze landed on his mouth. He felt that look all the way to his core as she practically scorched him. He told himself it didn't matter, to just let her go, but she took another step toward him. He wasn't sure who made the first move but suddenly his mouth was on hers.

Moaning softly, she dug her fingers into his shoulder as he backed her up against the wall.

They were too exposed in the hallway, his brain told him, even through the haze of lust fogging his mind. On the off chance that Harper woke up, he didn't want to have to explain any of this.

Holding Serenity tight, he guided them down the rest of the hallway and opened the guest bedroom door. Then he backed her up against it as it closed.

She arched her body into his, kissing him with a frenzy he hadn't expected. Hell, he hadn't expected any of this. He wasn't sure what this meant for them but he was going to take it. As far as she wanted it to go.

He wanted to banish all the pain and fear he often saw lurking in her eyes. He wanted to see her smile on a regular basis, wanted those circles under her eyes gone. She deserved happiness. She deserved to live her life without fear.

While he might not be able to take away the fear or find the monster after her, he was sure as hell going to give her as much pleasure as she could handle.

She kissed him with abandon, sliding her hands over his chest as she learned his body. He'd fantasized about this, about her touching him. And if he was dreaming, he didn't want to wake up.

It didn't take long until he got her little tank top and flannel pants stripped off.

For a moment she looked self-conscious as he stretched her out on the bed.

He paused, looking down at her, taking in every line of her curves and taut, lean body. No doubt about it—reality was far better than his imagination. "This goes as far as you want. I just want to taste between your legs." That was a lie because he wanted more, but for now he wanted to hear her come, wanted to hear her calling out his name as he brought her pleasure. What he wouldn't give to chase away all the shadows in her eyes.

Thanks to the lamp he'd left on, he could see the pink blush of her cheeks, the color matching her tight nipples. "Lucas," she whispered.

He knelt on the bed in front of her. "What? I've dreamed about tasting *all* of you."

The pink of her cheeks darkened to red, the color spreading down to her neck.

He kissed her again, deeper this time, cupping her cheeks with his hands. He loved the taste of her, the feel of her, everything about her. He had Serenity stretched out naked underneath him, her legs wrapped around his waist as he took his time teasing his tongue against hers. There was something to be said for simple kissing.

Well, kissing *and* Serenity's naked body underneath his. There was nothing in the world like this. She was fit and lean and appeared taller than she actually was because of all her muscle tone. He knew she worked out and took self-defense classes, and it sure as hell showed.

He reached between their bodies, trailing his fingers across her stomach and down between her legs. When he cupped her mound, she rolled her hips against his hand. God, she was so wet and soft. This almost felt like it was happening too fast, but they'd been building to this for months. All those weekly lunches and the low-grade flirting had been working toward something. He sure as hell hadn't expected this so soon—wherever this was headed tonight—but he wasn't stopping until she said to.

As he began slowly teasing her clit, she rolled her hips faster and faster, biting his bottom lip between her teeth. Oh yes, he would get her off. Hopefully more than once.

The energy humming through her was a palpable thing, practically buzzing in the air. All her earlier hints of self-consciousness were gone. Now it was just the two of them, here and now. No outside world.

He continued kissing her, blazing a path down her neck and chest, sucking each nipple until she threaded her fingers through his hair. Her body trembled as he continued.

By the time his mouth made it between her legs, she was clutching onto his head. And he loved the feel of her holding on to him. He flicked his tongue up the length of her slick folds, savoring the way she moaned out his name.

"Lucas."

Hearing his name on her lips like that was a fantasy. *Hell.* He was keyed up, his body desperate for release, but right now was about her. He continued teasing her, using his thumb to tweak her clit as he dipped a finger inside her. She was soaking wet, all for him.

And he was rock-hard between his legs because of her. There was no hiding his reaction, and he didn't want to. He wanted her to know exactly how she affected him.

She surged into climax faster than he'd expected. So much faster. The moans she made were the most erotic thing he'd ever heard, and when she collapsed against the bed he crawled up her body, capturing her mouth with his. He wanted to completely possess her, to make her his.

To his surprise, she pushed against his chest.

Disappointment filtered through him until she said, "My turn."

At her instructions, he flipped onto his back, watching as she shimmied down his body and knelt between his legs. Moving faster than the speed of light, he tugged off his shirt as she got rid of his pants and boxer briefs. For some reason he hadn't expected this boldness from Serenity, but he liked it. A lot.

Layers, he reminded himself. This woman had layers. And right now she was naked and all he could see, all he could think about.

Her jet-black hair fell around her shoulders in soft waves as she glanced up at him, looking every inch like a goddess. Keeping her bright blue gaze on him, she wrapped her fingers around his hard length and began stroking him, teasing him just as he teased her. The way she watched him as she touched him took his breath away. And when she leaned down and took him into her mouth, he forgot to breathe.

His hips jolted off the bed as he savored the sensation of her hot mouth on him. Sliding his fingers through the waterfall of her hair, he closed his eyes, moaning out her name. He wasn't sure how long she sucked him, but he was certain he came too soon.

He was pretty sure he'd died and gone to heaven. The fact that Serenity was in bed naked with him, had just come against his tongue and then gone down on him? It was too much. He tugged her up into his arms, cradling her against his side. She made a pleased sound as she pressed her body to his.

"I know it doesn't matter right this instant," he murmured. "But I've got condoms—in my truck." Fat lot of good they did him. He'd be more prepared next time. "And I'm clean."

"I've got an IUD…and I'm clean too. So if we ever…" She cleared her throat. "We won't need the condoms."

*All right, then.* Their breathing and the light rain pattering against the rooftop and windows were the only sounds in the room, making it feel as if only the two of them existed. At least for this moment. She trailed her fingers gently up his abs, then laid her hand over his chest.

"We're still friends, right?" Her voice was whisper quiet.

"We're definitely still friends. Naked friends."

She laughed lightly at that, cuddling closer to him. "I like being naked friends."

He wanted more than friendship and it was pretty damn clear she did too, even if she wasn't going to put a label on it.

That was okay with him for now. He'd been a Marine. He was very patient during an op.

And Serenity was worth fighting for.

## CHAPTER EIGHTEEN

Her heart rate kicked up as Paisley opened her town-home door. Stupid, stupid woman. Paisley should be afraid, but instead she was letting the monster walk right inside her door.

"Hey, come on in," Paisley said, her blonde hair pulled up into a messy bun that somehow still looked good. Because that was how Paisley was: perfect. Just like Serenity. They might be different in looks, but both women were beautiful with an air of fragility about them that men seemed to be drawn to.

Putting on a smile, she held up a bottle of wine. This was going to be so easy. And fun. "I brought sustenance."

Paisley laughed even as she sniffled. Given her red nose and slightly puffy eyes, it was clear she'd been crying. Her boyfriend Mitch had recently broken up with Paisley so of course she'd called. It was the only time Paisley wanted friends around—when she didn't have a man in her life. All she wanted to do was get married and have kids. Pathetic.

"I'm so glad you came over. It's been so tense around town," Paisley said.

"No kidding. I was worried even driving over here." She held back a laugh at the lie. She wasn't worried about anyone or anything.

"You can take off your jacket if you want," Paisley said, nodding at the row of hooks by the door.

She did even though she had no intention of staying long.

"Come on, I've got snacks in the kitchen. Do you want to go out or watch a movie?"

"Definitely stay in."

"Yeah, me too. It's crazy about Adeline…" She trailed off, clearly not wanting to talk about it.

"I know. It's awful. It seems mean to even think that if Serenity hadn't come back to town…" She trailed off, lifting a shoulder.

Paisley didn't respond as she pulled two wineglasses down from her open concept shelving. Then she said, "I feel bad for her. She lost her twin, survived hell, then lost her husband. She's barely thirty and she's already a widow and single mom. That's gotta be rough."

"Yeah. She seems to have bounced back pretty quickly though." Too quickly. And it sickened her how everyone felt sorry for *poor Serenity*.

"What do you mean?"

"Well, look at her and Lucas Jordan. She's not hurting for company." It was a struggle to keep the bitterness out of her voice. Lucas hadn't looked twice at anyone since he'd moved back to town. He was a sexy, wealthy bachelor and Serenity had just scooped him up.

"So what? She's a grown woman. I say good for both of them. He hasn't even dated anyone since he moved back to town anyway. Or I don't think he has. Not that I didn't try and make a move on him," Paisley added, a half-smile pulling at her lips. "You did too, if I remember correctly."

"Hardly," she snorted out. Even though she was annoyed that Paisley didn't agree with her about Serenity, she didn't let it show. Soon enough Paisley would know exactly how she felt about her.

After pouring their glasses of wine, she waited until Paisley was distracted by her phone and poured in a sedative. She'd stolen the ketamine from the local vet and she was pretty sure about the dosage. She just wanted to knock her out, not kill her. Well, not kill her right away. She was going to be joining Adeline soon.

"So tell me about Mitch. Has he called?" she asked, sliding the glass over to Paisley, wanting her talking.

Paisley's expression darkened as she looked up from her phone. She immediately picked up her wineglass and shook her head. "No. And I heard he took Cindy Morrison out last night. And stayed over. Bastard," she muttered.

She made appropriately sympathetic sounds as Paisley rambled on about her ex-boyfriend and drank her wine.

Considering her slight frame, after a half glass of wine it didn't take Paisley long until she started blinking as she tried to keep her eyes open. Then she gripped the countertop. "I don't feel so good."

"I'll help you sit," she said, gently easing Paisley onto one of the sofas. Just like that, her friend slowly drifted into unconsciousness, her head falling back against the cushion. Perfect.

Now it was time to get to work.

She grabbed her jacket and the wine bottle, and placed her things together on the counter while she busied herself wiping down everything she'd touched. Then she put on cleaning gloves, washed the wineglasses and put them back up so it wouldn't appear as if anyone had been there.

For good measure, she used Paisley's thumb to open her cell phone and sent a text to herself, canceling tonight. Immediately after, she sent one to Mitch from Paisley's phone, telling him that she missed him and asking if he wanted to come over and hook up.

She'd watched enough crime shows to know how to clean up after herself. She'd been over here on multiple occasions before so it didn't matter if her DNA was found here, but she wanted to wipe down what she could.

Careful, careful. That was what mattered now.

Getting out of here with Paisley was going to be tricky, but she planned to use Paisley's own vehicle to transport her to the waiting car. It was why she'd parked down the road and walked. So no one would remember seeing her car parked in front of Paisley's place.

She had all of this planned out perfectly. No one was going to catch her. She wasn't going to make the same mistakes her father had. No way.

She was having too much fun. And she was just getting started. Once she finished with Verona Bay, she was moving on to someplace bigger. With more people to choose from.

Somewhere she would have no problem blending in and disappearing.

## CHAPTER NINETEEN

Serenity ran a comb through Foxy's longer fur, smiling to herself as she purred like a cat instead of the Japanese Chin she was. She felt weird being in her shop, working like normal when Adeline was missing, but she was going to keep things as steady as possible. And she really hoped the Feds found something on the cameras they'd set up. Though it was horrifying to think about someone she knew doing this to her, she knew it was a real possibility that the killer might show up again.

After talking with Amy this morning, in her head she'd been going over names of who had been in college at the same time as her, when everything had happened. She'd blocked out almost everything when she'd moved away, cutting ties with almost everyone and trying her hardest to simply forget college.

Unfortunately a lot of people had gone to college with her and now lived in Verona Bay. Some of those people had been at school with her even though they were a few years older, so it didn't exactly narrow anything down. The people she saw on a weekly basis were Chloe, Paisley, Norah, Bianca, and Wilson, who worked at the local diner. And of course Lincoln, but she didn't count him.

There were a few more, but those were the people she remembered as being in close proximity to her and

Savannah during the insanity of the time Black was stalking their campus.

"How are things looking out there?" she asked Lucas when he stepped into the back room, Harper in tow. He'd taken her daughter out for a cupcake break while Serenity worked. As usual, when she saw him, her heart skipped a beat. Especially after last night. She hadn't expected that intimacy, hadn't expected any of it. But she'd embraced it and found herself warming up even as she thought of the way he'd brought her pleasure. She forced herself not to think of any of that as Harper bounced up and down.

Her daughter was so excited that Lucas had come with them today, and even though she was worried about Harper getting confused about his role in their lives, she loved seeing her so happy. Especially now with everything going on. She didn't want the ugliness of reality to touch Harper. Her daughter had her whole life to grow up and realize how awful the world could be. She was going to try to keep her oblivious of the bad things as long as she could.

"Great!" Harper answered for him. "All of the washing stalls are filled except one," her little girl said with pride. She loved the grooming shop and loved to tell her friends about all the dogs that came through.

There were stalls in the front where people could wash their own dogs. In the back was where Serenity did the actual grooming, which included haircuts, and then of course washing and nail trimming. But some people only needed a space to wash their pets. "How was the cupcake break?"

"Yummy. I had two and we brought you back some."

"Thank you," she murmured, looking over at Lucas.

In response, he gave Serenity a heated look.

She felt her cheeks flush and glanced away. After last night she felt almost nervous around him. This morning she'd told him that nothing would change between them, but she'd heard it for the lie that it was. No matter if she wanted things to stay the same—or to just be naked friends—everything had changed between them. She still didn't want a relationship, but she also didn't want a hookup buddy. Especially one who was already involved in Harper's life. Not that he'd implied he wanted that anyway, but still. Ugh, her head was a mess right now. She had no business getting involved with anyone.

Even so, thinking about last night... She felt her cheeks flush even warmer. Damn it, she needed to get her head on straight. It was hard to do that, however, when six-feet-plus of the sexiest, sweetest man she'd ever known was mere feet away from her. "So when are you going to bring Daisy in here again?" There, that was a safe enough topic.

"Soon. Though you're going to see her tonight."

"I'm so excited Daisy is gonna stay with us." Harper looked over at Lucas. "Can she sleep in my bed? Can I take her out for walks? Can I hold the leash?" She shot one question after another at him, not stopping to take a breath.

Serenity snickered to herself and turned back to the dog she was working on. Almost done. She'd let Lucas field all the questions for now. He'd proven that he had no problem holding his own.

Suddenly the door flung open and Paisley Long's mom stormed in.

Serenity stared in confusion at the slender older woman with hair a few shades darker than Paisley's. She didn't understand why the woman was here or where the Federal agent who was supposed to be manning the cash register was. "Ms. Long, you can't be back here," she said, frowning at the rage on the woman's face and her presence in general.

"What is the matter with you!" the woman screamed, her dark blonde hair wild around her face, eyes wide.

Lucas shifted in front of Serenity so quickly she barely saw him move. He pushed Harper gently behind him as he did, the action fluid.

Serenity grabbed her daughter even as she secured the now trembling dog. A few of the dogs in the kennels waiting to be groomed barked worriedly, clearly not liking the change in atmosphere. They'd tapped into whatever was going on fast.

"Ms. Long, what are you talking about?" she asked even as Lucas held up a hand, not letting her around him.

"You know exactly what I'm talking about!"

"No, I really don't. And I'm going to have to ask you to leave my shop if you keep screaming." The woman was lucky she wasn't hauling her ass out, but she knew from Paisley that her mother was an alcoholic. So maybe she'd fallen off the wagon.

"Paisley was taken last night and it's all your fault!"

She felt the blood drain from her face. "What?"

"And you're here working like it's no big deal when this is all your fault!" Her voice grew louder and louder.

The dogs started barking wildly and next to her Harper began crying, clutching onto Serenity's leg.

"You need to leave." Lucas's voice was firm as he took a step toward the woman.

"Don't you touch me! Don't you dare touch me!" She tried to dodge around him, lunging at Serenity, but he firmly gripped her shoulders. She started screaming even louder. "Get your filthy hands off me! I'm going to sue all of you! I'll shut down this shop!"

Lucas didn't seem to care what she said, because he steered her straight out of the back room. Serenity hurried after him, keeping Harper behind her, but stopped when she saw the FBI agent rushing out of the bathroom, adjusting her belt. Well, that explained where she'd been.

She took one look at Paisley's mom and took over for Lucas, ordering the woman to calm down as she hauled her out of the store, completely ignoring the woman's screams.

Swallowing hard, Serenity stepped into the back room with Harper and started calming her daughter down even though she was trembling inside.

Paisley had been taken too? It must have *just* happened. She needed to call Amy, to find out if this was true or if Ms. Long had just been freaking out because her daughter hadn't answered her phone. Maybe she'd just gone on a bender.

Although Serenity couldn't believe that Paisley's mom would have made such a spectacle if she wasn't a hundred percent sure her daughter was gone.

Serenity pulled a now sniffling Harper into her arms, holding on to her daughter tightly as she comforted her.

If this monster had struck again, that made *three* people who'd gotten caught in the crossfire. The only thing she could hope was that Paisley and Adeline weren't dead. Though she was terrified that whatever they were going through—

*No.* She swallowed hard, trying to banish all the thoughts and memories of her own time in captivity as they bubbled up to the surface.

It was hard, however, when they flashed in her mind like full-color photographs.

Waking up strapped down to that board. Seeing her sister strapped down next to her, fear etched into every line of her face. That monster cutting Savannah. Blood dripping.

She closed her eyes and only opened them when she felt Lucas's strong arms pulling both her and Harper into a big hug.

To Serenity's surprise, Harper latched onto him, wrapping her arms around his neck even as Serenity allowed herself to be comforted by him as well.

The whole nightmare from her past was starting again. It didn't matter if the details were different.

People were dying and there was nothing she could do about it.

* * *

Serenity tensed when she saw Chloe and Bianca standing outside the front door of her shop. She'd already closed up, having finished half an hour early with all of the day's pets. Thankfully Harper had bounced back after that shitshow with Paisley's mom. The federal agent had been in the bathroom for all of two minutes when the woman had stormed in, and felt terrible. It wasn't her fault. It wasn't anyone's fault.

"I can get rid of them," the agent said, glancing at the two women.

"Or I can," Lucas said, steel in his voice as he stood next to her.

"No, let me talk to them. Just keep Harper in the back?" She looked at Lucas.

He paused and then nodded, watching as the agent opened the door and then told the women to keep it short.

Wide eyed, both women nodded, Bianca glancing down at the gun visible on the woman's belt.

"Hey Lucas, Serenity," Chloe said as she stepped inside. Bianca nodded at both of them as the agent locked the door and strode toward the cash register, clearly not going anywhere.

"I'll be in the back if you need me," Lucas murmured, surprising the hell out of her by kissing the top of her head in front of everyone. All right then, so…that had happened. It wasn't a bold declaration but it wasn't subtle either.

"What's up, ladies?" she asked, dreading the answer. Maybe they were here to tell her that everything was her fault too. Yeah, she knew. And the guilt was clawing her up inside.

"We heard what Ms. Long did." Chloe's expression was annoyed.

"We just stopped by to tell you that she doesn't speak for everyone. She's worried about her daughter," Bianca added. "But she didn't have a right to come in here and start screaming at you like that."

"Nobody agrees with her," Chloe continued.

She looked back and forth between the two women, one sleek and lean, the other petite with a pixie haircut. Both appeared sincere. "Thank you. I didn't realize how much I needed to hear that, but I did." The Feds weren't even sure Paisley had been taken at this point, but she didn't like any of this situation.

"So have you heard anything about Adeline or Paisley?" Bianca asked.

Serenity shook her head. "They're following up on leads, but I don't know anything." Not exactly the truth, but she wasn't going to give them any information. She knew the only reason Amy had told her anything at all was because of her unique relationship to this whole case. And even if she'd thought of the other women as acquaintances-slash-friends, right now she wasn't sure who to trust. It was a shitty feeling, but the only people she could truly trust at this point were Lucas and his family. And Maris. That was it.

"Let us know if there's anything we can do," Bianca said.

"Yeah, we heard they might be setting up a grid search," Chloe continued when Serenity simply nodded.

"Tomorrow or the day after, depending on the weather." It was supposed to rain tomorrow and there was a chance of heavy fog, so it might be the day after. She planned to be there as well. There was a chance that Adeline wasn't even alive at this point. And now...potentially Paisley had been taken. The Feds and the sheriff's department were asking everyone who could help to do a search of rural areas surrounding Verona Bay. And if anyone objected to having people walk through their property, the Feds were going to look harder at them.

"I miss Adeline," she whispered, and to her horror a few tears leaked out. After losing her sister, she'd thought she'd cried all there was to cry. And to cry now in front of two women she wasn't even close to... *Ugh.*

To her surprise, Bianca stepped forward and pulled her into a hug, giving her an awkward pat on the back. "It's going to be okay."

"They'll find them. They have to," Chloe added, giving her an awkward pat as well.

Sniffling, she stepped back and swiped away the wetness. She wasn't doing anyone any good by standing out here crying. "Thank you guys for stopping by. I really do appreciate it." She just hoped that both Paisley and Adeline were alive and that they were found in time. She couldn't help but wonder if she'd get another text, another video, of Paisley this time.

A few minutes later Serenity stepped into the back room to find Lucas and Harper cleaning up. "The agent is waiting outside to follow me home," she murmured, her mouth curving up slightly as she watched Harper ineffectively sweep up dog hair into the EyeVac.

He lifted a shoulder at Serenity's look. "She wanted to help."

Despite the tension sitting in her belly, she let out a laugh. "You're doing a great job," she said to her daughter.

"I know," Harper tossed over her shoulder as she shoved a clump of fur in front of the machine. She giggled as it sucked it up. The only reason she wanted to help was because she liked the automatic function of the machine.

Lucas spoke. "So I was thinking, my parents' estate is large and—"

"We're going to stay at Lucas's parents' house. They have horses!" Harper shouted over the sound of the running machine.

Serenity looked at Lucas, eyebrow raised. "Uh, what's going on now?"

"My mom called and offered to let all of us stay at their place. It's huge, has incredible security. And there are horses and other things to keep everyone busy." He nodded at Harper.

"It sounds like an adventure," Serenity said, keeping her voice light for her daughter's sake. She'd been to the

Jordan estate once. It was incredible, and she couldn't imagine anyone breaching that fortress. It probably was the safest place for her daughter, and right now she would welcome safety. Even if it was an illusion, to an extent. She'd briefly toyed with the idea of leaving town but it made more sense to stay put where the Feds and sheriff's department were here, hunting this killer.

"You're really okay with this?" he asked.

She gave Lucas a wry look. "You didn't really give me a chance to say no."

He actually winced. "When my mom called, I started talking about it in front of Harper...I didn't think," he murmured.

"It's okay." He'd been so incredible, staying over at her place when he absolutely didn't have to. Not pushing her for more than she was willing to give. She wasn't going to get mad at him for something like this. "That's very generous of your parents. I just need to go by our place and pack up some things. And I'll need to let Amy know where we're going."

"Of course." There was a simmering heat in his green eyes and she wondered how she'd never noticed how he looked at her.

Now that she'd acknowledged to herself how attracted to him she was, it was impossible to turn that part of herself off. She wasn't sure what that meant for tonight. This morning she'd woken up early and slipped out of the guest room, not wanting Harper to find them together.

Tonight they'd be at a new place and...she didn't think she had the mental energy to consider their sleeping arrangements. She wasn't sure what she wanted, and it felt wrong to try to decide before this mess was over.

And it had to be over, eventually. One way or another.

## CHAPTER TWENTY

"Thank you again for letting us stay here," Serenity said to Louise Jordan, Lucas's wonderful mom. It was just the two of them in the massive kitchen. Harper had run off to explore and Lucas had offered to give her a quick tour. Louise had asked Serenity to stay back so they could talk in private, so she'd obliged.

The woman's sandy blonde hair fell a couple inches past her shoulders, always perfectly styled, and now was no different. "There's no need to thank me. Everyone feels awful about what's happening and I feel better knowing the two of you are under our roof. Plus I love having my boy over as well. He'll stay here as long as you two do, so you can stay forever as far as I'm concerned."

Serenity smiled at the word *boy*. Lucas was all man, but she understood the sentiment. Harper was always going to be her little girl no matter what.

"How do you feel about Harper going on a horse trail with me and Jack? It's perfectly safe and she can ride Rocket—who is not fast, despite his name."

"I'm fine with that. I'm sure Lucas wants to go as well." Serenity wasn't very skilled at horseback riding but Harper had done lessons and had taken to it quickly. Serenity, however, liked to give the big beasts a wide berth.

Louise just clucked her tongue once. "I'm not inviting the two of you."

Serenity lifted an eyebrow. "Ah...okay."

"I have a feeling you and Lucas need some alone time, so I'm giving it to you. It looks like rain the next few days so now's a good time to let Harper get some riding in."

Serenity's entire face warmed up at the woman's words, even though she'd brushed right past the "alone time" comment. She also did *not* know how to respond to the implication that they needed "alone time."

"Oh, we're not— That is—" she spluttered, trying to find the right words. She wasn't sure what she and Lucas were. They'd gotten naked together but...that didn't mean they were together, *together*. Still, something settled inside her knowing that Mrs. Jordan was basically accepting her. She'd allowed her into her home despite the danger and she wasn't making her feel guilty or indebted to her. She was simply opening her home to Serenity and her daughter, offering them safe haven.

"Yeah, that's exactly what I thought. We'll take her out for the next hour or so. There are some short trails around here and our entire property is secure with cameras. Not to mention you know Jack doesn't go anywhere without his pistol in case of rattlesnakes. She'll be fine with us. But only if you really are okay with letting her come," she added. "There's plenty to do closer to the house."

Harper had spent time with Louise Jordan in the past, so Serenity trusted the other woman with her daughter's safety. And Harper loved riding horses so much it felt wrong to say no. Harper had been uprooted from her home and Serenity was terrified of all this scaring her daughter.

"Yeah, it's okay." And not because she needed alone time with Lucas. She actually wanted to set something up in one of the spare rooms and she didn't want Harper around to see what she was doing. Now would be the perfect time. "But will you keep your cell phones on you?"

"Of course."

Almost as if Harper knew that she was being talked about, she strutted into the room, wearing little cowboy boots with sheriff stars on the side.

"Check these out! These used to be Mr. Lucas's."

Serenity grinned at the sight of her daughter stomping around in the boots, her pink skirt flaring wildly around her thick leggings.

Lucas looked at his mom. "I can't believe you kept these."

Mrs. Jordan just shrugged and smiled. "I'm saving them for my grandkids." When she gave Lucas a pointed look, Serenity noticed that he studiously avoided responding.

And Serenity looked anywhere but the other woman as well. Whatever Louise Jordan thought was happening between her and Lucas, grandkids was not it. She turned to her daughter instead. "How do you feel about going horseback riding?"

Harper squealed in delight. Well that answered that.

It didn't take long for Louise to get Harper bundled up in an extra jacket and out of there.

Serenity settled against the countertop as soon as Lucas's mom and Harper were gone. "I feel a little guilty for letting your mom take over. But I'm so exhausted and it's nice to have someone to help out." She was terrified of leaning on other people, but at the same time she knew she needed it right now. Her brain was completely taxed with fear and worry. And this place was safe. Sure, they couldn't stay forever, but for now? She wanted Harper to be able to relax. And no one knew they were over here. The Jordans weren't telling anyone and there was a Fed watching this place now too.

"My mom is more than happy to do this. She told me it will give her practice for when she gets grandkids." He rolled his eyes. "She's been on me and my brothers for ages about it."

Serenity half-smiled at that, but didn't want to touch on the subject. "Look, I have a weird request. Do you have an extra guest room I could use? I brought a bunch of old photos and scrapbooks from when I was in college. I know the FBI has way more resources than I do but I kind of want to set something up and cross-reference who was in school with me and who I'm in contact with now. I don't know that it will do any good, but I don't like feeling useless. After Savannah died, I tried to block out all of college basically. But with Adeline and Paisley missing, I can't do that anymore. If I can help them figure out who is doing this, I'm going to."

"There's an extra office you can use."

Good. She couldn't just sit around and do nothing when her friends were being targeted.

# CHAPTER TWENTY-ONE

She glanced over from her seat at the dimly lit bar top to see a familiar face walking through the door.

Surprise flickered through her to see Wilson Hart this far out of Verona Bay—but she was here too, so who was she to judge? She came to this shithole dive in Bishop's Creek because she needed to get away from all the locals of Verona Bay when she wanted to find someone to fuck. Tonight was no different. After killing Carol Rose and taking the two other bitches, she needed to find a release. Sex was the easiest way to do it. She'd sneaked away only once to see Adeline, to watch her suffering, but she hadn't wanted to stay too long. She needed to find a place and a town with no link to her so she could take her time.

Right now she desperately needed to take the edge off, especially because of what had happened with Paisley. She'd made a mistake. Something she wasn't going to think about now. She was here to forget, to regroup.

For a little while she'd thought about going after another target tonight, but it was too risky. The Feds were everywhere, and though she couldn't be certain, she thought they might be watching her. She'd heard from multiple friends that they had tails and everyone she knew in town was locked down tight. For all the Feds knew, she was too. Sneaking out had been a risk, but she'd needed it. And she was certain no one had followed her either. She wasn't stupid enough to take her own vehicle or come here directly.

Seeing Wilson provided an interesting dilemma. He might not even recognize her tonight. She was dressed completely out of character, wearing a short leather skirt, a leather bustier and a jet-black wig as well as non-prescription, trendy-looking glasses. Not a stellar disguise, but if he had on beer goggles, it would be enough.

He sat down next to her at the bar, his baby blue eyes doing a once-over of her before he motioned at the bartender.

*Take him*, the voice whispered.

Yeah, he didn't even seem to recognize her, though his interest was clear. Wasn't like they'd ever dated or hung out in the same social circle, but damn.

His not realizing it was her pissed her off. It was like she was invisible until people wanted something.

Before the night was out she'd make sure he paid for that. *Yes, yes, take him. Make him suffer.* The voice was louder tonight.

She waited until the bartender took his order and placed a beer in front of him. "How are you doing tonight?" she purred to Wilson.

Seeming surprised, he turned to look at her, a charming grin spreading across his face. "Better now, darlin'."

Oh, barf. She knew he'd dated dozens of women in Verona Bay, and "date" was a loose term for what he did. He was a pig. After tonight she'd be doing the women of Verona Bay a favor.

"Why don't you finish your beer, then you and I get out of here?" She grinned at him, knowing he'd take the bait. A guy like this was so damn predictable.

He seemed positively stunned, but grabbed the green bottle and slapped a bill on the table. She'd only been drinking Sprite with lime and she'd already paid. So she slid off her seat and linked her arm with his as he chugged down his beer. Real classy.

As they stepped out into the cool air, her mind started working overtime. She could take what she wanted from him tonight. She could do whatever she wanted to him and no one would ever know.

"You look kinda familiar." His words were slightly slurred, telling her he must have been drinking long before he got there.

"I just have one of those faces."

"You've got a gorgeous face."

She resisted the urge to roll her eyes. "Which car is yours?"

"That big ol' Ford is my truck, darlin'."

She inwardly winced at the faux cowboy accent. Did he think this shit was charming? He must. And so must a bunch of other women, because as far as she knew this fool never wanted for female company. Gross.

He went around to the passenger side and lifted her up because it was so jacked up. Clearly he must be over-compensating for something with a truck this big.

As he made his way around to the other side, she glanced around the parking lot. She'd been here enough times that she knew they didn't have working video cameras. It was one of the reasons she came here. She wore different disguises, didn't bring her cell phone or pay with a credit card either. She liked to be anonymous, to have no way for anyone to track her.

It was easy to pick up guys when she wanted to leave no trace behind. She liked dressing up as different people. It gave her a rush. When she was herself, she was simple and boring, but disguises and makeup turned her into someone else. Someone other people wanted to know, wanted to be friends with.

Tonight she could be whoever she wanted to be—a seductress.

As Wilson got into the driver's side, she quickly slid over and straddled him, shoving her leather skirt up to her hips. A rush of heat flooded between her legs as she thought about watching the life drain out of him.

"Hell yeah, you're a feisty little thing."

Oh, he had no idea. "Let's see if you can handle me." She reached between their bodies and rubbed her hand over his growing erection. It didn't feel too impressive through his pants but that didn't matter for what she had planned.

As he started pawing at her, tugging her panties to the side, she reached over with one hand and grabbed her purse. It wasn't large, but was big enough to pack a compact Taser.

He cupped her mound, just jamming his finger in her, not even taking his time to get to know her. She gritted her teeth at his lack of finesse. What the hell did women see in this fool?

"Damn, girl, you're already wet. Is this all for me?" He made a gross groaning sound as he gyrated his hips.

She was wet, but not because of him. She was turned on because of what she was going to do to him.

"Oh yeah, all for you cowboy," she purred as her fingers clenched around her weapon.

He wasn't paying attention to anything but her pussy as he kissed at her neck, the scent of beer and his cologne filling the air.

She flipped on the Taser and jammed it against his neck. He jolted against her, his entire body trembling in shock as his hand fell away from her.

Now she got even wetter—getting rid of him would be fun. Especially since he didn't even seem to recognize who she was. He deserved this, and she'd be doing the town of Verona Bay a favor for getting rid of him. She'd make sure he suffered too.

As she slid off him, she started to drag his body over to the passenger side when she saw a couple stepping out of the woods at the edge of the parking lot. Adjusting their clothing. *Oh, shit.*

She hadn't even thought people would be getting busy in the woods when it was so cold out. Hopefully they wouldn't even notice her and Wilson.

"Wilson, that you?" someone shouted.

*Double shit.* She vaguely recognized the couple as two redneck assholes, Beau and Clarice.

She slid off him and adjusted her skirt. As they stumbled over to the driver's side window, she grabbed her stuff and jumped out of the passenger side, her boots thudding against the gravel of the parking lot.

"I think he's had too much to drink. He couldn't even get it up for me," she shouted in her best Southern accent as she made her way to her car.

She heard the man guffaw loudly even as they opened the door to check on their friend.

Heart racing, she picked up her pace and slid into the front seat of her car. As she tore out of the parking lot, she glanced in the rearview mirror. Wilson probably had no idea what had happened. Which was just as well.

Going after him without proper recon had been poorly thought out. It had just seemed so easy running into him tonight. And that voice had urged her on, telling her to do whatever she wanted.

But she needed to take people without the threat of being caught. She needed to have some control. She wasn't going to be stupid like her father. She was going to prove to him that she was a hundred times better than him.

She didn't need anyone to help her. Unlike him. He'd never have taken all those girls without her help. He'd never been there for her growing up. Had never even acknowledged her. But she'd helped him anyway. And look how stupid he'd been. She wasn't going to be like him.

She wouldn't end up in jail, stripped of her power.

## CHAPTER TWENTY-TWO

Serenity looked around the table, humbled that Lucas's family had invited her into their home. Louise had also invited Maris over because the two of them were lifelong friends and she'd known how close Maris and Serenity were.

His parents were at one end of the long dining room table, joking around with Easton, who'd shown up late then devoured a plate of food, wearing a Verona Bay FD T-shirt that stretched across his muscular chest. She could understand why so many women of the town all fell for him.

But not all, because while she could see that he was attractive, he didn't even compare to Lucas. No one did.

Lucas and Harper were intently discussing something a few seats down, and it sounded as if they were "arguing" over what kind of cupcakes were better. Which just made her smile.

"It's good to see you smile," Lincoln said quietly across the table from her.

She glanced at him. "It feels weird to. But I'm grateful Harper hasn't been touched by the ugliness of everything." She kept her voice low, for Lincoln's ears only. "With the exception of Paisley's mom coming in to my place earlier." That had been a shock.

"She was drunk and upset. I've talked to her since then and she feels terrible." He wasn't excusing her, just stating a fact.

Serenity wasn't even angry. Not anymore. She had a daughter and she could understand blind panic and fear. She couldn't imagine herself ever reacting in such an unhinged way, but the woman was terrified. "Have the Feds told you anything? Anything they might not tell me?" He might not be able to say one way or the other, but it didn't hurt to ask.

"No. But I have been interviewing different people from their list of potential suspects."

"From what I've heard, the list is long."

He nodded, his expression grim. "Yeah, that's the problem. There are too many possibilities."

"Do you have any maybes on your list?"

"Kinda. And there are a lot of them. And the only tying factor is that they were in college with us."

"Oh, wow." That didn't narrow anything down at all, which just made that hard knot in her stomach tighten even more.

"Exactly." He looked just as frustrated as she felt.

"Are you keeping an eye on Autumn?"

He jolted at the mention of his neighbor, Autumn Perez.

"What did I say?" she asked.

"Nothing." His expression went carefully neutral. And wasn't that interesting. "I didn't even realize you two were friends until recently."

"Yeah, I like her. She's not from here, and even though I am, sometimes I feel like an outsider since I was gone for so long. She keeps to herself, but she is very sweet." And smart, with a sarcastic edge that Serenity found refreshing. Autumn never acted like Serenity was broken or needed to be "handled." She said what was on her mind but was incredibly mindful of people's feelings. The woman seemed very authentic, which was refreshing.

Lincoln nodded. "She's a good neighbor. I talked to her about staying safe."

"Good." Serenity wanted to push him further but decided against it since it was clear he did not want to talk about her.

When Lucas motioned to Lincoln that he wanted to talk to him, Harper jumped up and started dancing around in her "new" cowboy boots. Her little girl was a lot of energy, but Lucas's family, especially his parents, seemed to not mind at all. They seemed to adore Harper, which made her feel less guilty about staying here.

As Lincoln stood, Maris sat down next to her, an exhausted smile on her pretty face. "So how are you doing?"

"As decent as can be expected." As she took a sip of her red wine, her gaze was drawn to where Harper was happily stomping around, attempting what she assumed was line dancing. Lucas's parents seemed to think it was hilarious as they encouraged her.

"I'm glad you're staying here. At least you'll be safe."

She snorted as she absently ran her finger up the stem of her wineglass.

"You know what I mean." Maris touched her arm gently. "I'm just so sorry this is happening."

"Thank you. Look, can you be honest with me? Is everyone in town gossiping about me?" Serenity was fairly certain Maris would be straight with her. There wasn't a dishonest bone in the woman's body.

"There is a *little* gossip, but mostly it's just people scared and worried. Especially now that Paisley has gone missing. People just want to pitch in and help, and most everyone is feeling helpless."

"Really? Bianca and Chloe came by the shop as we we're closing up today and they were pretty decent. But...I don't know, I just feel like everybody is judging me."

"Why would anybody be judging you? This isn't your fault." Maris's tone was blunt and to the point as she pushed up the sleeves of her sweater to her elbows. Today her sweater had dancing llamas wearing top hats. The silliness was incongruent with her no-nonsense attitude.

"Whoever is doing this is doing it to taunt me, so it is kinda my fault." She knew it wasn't true, but logic didn't have a strong foothold right now when guilt was eating away at her.

"Whoever is doing this is doing it because they're an asshole," Maris murmured, glancing over to make sure Harper couldn't hear her. "This isn't on you."

She lifted a shoulder. "I still feel guilty."

"Nah, you're just worried for your friends." She reached out and squeezed Serenity's forearm, her expression sincere.

"Whoever is behind this sent me a video." She kept her voice low. She knew she wasn't supposed to tell anyone but this was Maris, and of all people the woman could keep a secret. She ran a private shelter for women escaping their abusers. If anyone was a vault, it was Maris. "It was of Adeline chained to some kind of radiator thing. She was asleep or unconscious, I'm not sure. But breathing, thankfully. She was wearing the same clothes she was last seen in. And they've been leaving me little mementos. Jewelry taken from Black's original victims."

Maris sucked in a sharp breath. "Jesus. So was that bracelet on your windshield the real deal?"

"According to the Feds, yes."

She cursed again. "I'm really sorry." Maris paused, eyeing her for a long moment.

"What is it?"

"I have no idea if this will help or even if it's important, and I don't know what the Feds are looking for, but Norah has been talking a little bit of garbage about you. It's benign stuff, but she's one of the few people who thinks that everything has been brought on by you. Or your presence in town."

Hurt lanced through Serenity, sharp and fierce. "Norah has?" She owned the local quilting shop and had always been friendly to Serenity. More than, even. She bought pet toys from her and she'd opened up her place to local business owners on Thursday nights. She rarely ever showed up to the meetings, but she let them use her facility.

"It's just the fear talking, but yeah, she's had a few ugly things to say," Maris said. "No one is agreeing with her, but I've been keeping an ear to the ground."

Serenity shoved out a jagged breath, surprised at how much hurt she felt over this. "Thank you for telling me."

Maris had started to say something else when a chime rang through the air. Serenity knew that the Jordans had a security system and cameras here—and someone had to drive down almost three-quarters of a mile of driveway just to get to the front door. And they'd be caught on camera doing so. Not to mention there should be a Federal agent parked in the driveway keeping an eye on the place.

She frowned, looking down the table at Louise and Jack.

"We're not expecting anyone," Jack said. Tall and handsome, he was an older version of Lucas.

Lincoln stepped forward. "I've got this."

Lucas was right with him, and to her surprise he pulled out a small pistol. Good lord, she hadn't even realized that he'd been carrying a weapon. Though she shouldn't be surprised. Of course he was. Both he and Lincoln—followed quickly by Easton—hurried out of the dining room and disappeared from sight.

Moments later they returned, with Amy Lin in tow.

She looked around the room before focusing on Serenity. "I'm really sorry to bother you."

Serenity shoved up from her chair, fear curdling in her gut, the wine she'd just sipped roiling around. "It's fine. What's happened?"

"Nothing. I just wanted to know if you had some free time to go over some things." She kept her words vague, something Serenity understood.

Some of her fear eased. If something had happened, she was pretty sure Amy would tell them all.

"We've got Harper," Louise said. "Go do what you need to do."

"I'll come with you," Lucas said.

"It's okay. Just stay here with your family." She would love to have him with her for this, but she couldn't justify leaning on him even more, on becoming more of a burden.

He looked surprised, then hurt, but she knew this was for the best.

"I'll drive and bring you back." Amy said.

After kissing her daughter goodbye—and thinking about kissing Lucas but deciding against it in the end because she didn't want to confuse Harper—she headed out.

"You want to tell me what all this is about?" Serenity asked once they were on the road.

"We've narrowed down our suspect pool."

She glanced over at her in surprise. "Seriously? How?"

"A lot of cross-referencing. Unfortunately we haven't been able to find any incriminating emails, texts, random property owned where they might be hiding Adeline or

Paisley...nothing. I don't think whoever did this is necessarily brilliant, but they are covering their tracks. And this is personal. The biggest mistake they made was sending you the mementos. It gives us something to go on."

She rubbed a hand over her face. "Anything else from Black?"

"No, but we are working an angle on that end. I believe he's getting messages out of the prison, and sooner or later I'm going to figure out how. Or more specifically, through who."

"What...like through a prison guard?" she asked.

"Don't sound so surprised. It happens far more than anyone wants to think about."

"Where are we headed?"

"A safe house."

She nodded, not asking any more questions. By the time they'd made it, she found that it was a two-story house in a normal-looking subdivision. But inside, the living room had been turned into a conference room basically. It was clear the Feds had been working overtime. She looked at a whiteboard they'd set up.

"Normally we're more high-tech, but it's easier to set things up this way here. And these are our suspects." Amy went to stand next to it, hands on hips.

Serenity's stomach twisted as she looked at the board, at the twelve familiar faces. "Why these people? Other than they attended college with me at the same time as Black's murder spree?"

"None of them have truly confirmable alibis for when the bracelet was left on your vehicle, when Mrs. Rose was murdered, and the other women taken. And all of their cell phones pinged off the tower closest to Mrs. Rose's house during the time of her murder. Which doesn't mean much because this town is so small, but it's another thing linking them to the area. We're working with what we've got here."

She frowned at the board. "Even Bianca? She was hurt when Adeline was taken."

"She could have done it herself. I've seen it before. So she stays on the board until I can prove she's not involved. Now tell me what you know about each of these people. I want impressions, any weird personal arguments. Or non-personal issues, something to do with business—anything at all. Something that we haven't found through our digging. We're going to catch whoever this is, and my money is on it being a woman, but... At this point I'm not ruling out these guys." She pointed to three men who had gone to college with Serenity, each of them owners of or working at various businesses in Verona Bay.

"Well, I'm pretty sure Bianca had a thing for Lucas, which seems like a crazy reason to come after me. But if you want details, I'll give you everything. She hit on him more than once but he's always rejected her. Same with Paisley. Not that she's a suspect, but...I also heard that Norah has been displeased about my presence in town." She quickly relayed what Maris had told her, and Amy nodded as if this wasn't news. "You knew?"

"It's my job to know."

Serenity wondered what that even meant. Oh...they were probably wiretapping or something along those lines. That's what Feds did, right? Something she had no idea about, but she was pretty sure the FBI had a pretty big purview right now. And she knew better than to push for more details because she certainly would not get them.

For the next hour she gave them as many details as possible about every person on the board while one of Amy's people recorded everything.

When she was finished, Amy raised her eyebrows. "This is a hell of a lot more information than we got eight years ago."

"Yeah. Because you got the guy last time." And the truth was Serenity had tried to block out everything once Michael Black had been imprisoned. "Do you think it would help if I talked to him?" she blurted.

"Him who? Wait—Black?" Amy's dark eyes widened and Serenity noticed that a few others in the room went completely still at their laptops, staring at her.

Serenity looked around at them, then focused back on Amy. "What?"

"I think it *could* be beneficial, but...I would never put you in that position. I know what he took from you, what he did. You're a civilian—I don't expect you to talk to that monster. You faced him down in court. That's enough."

She was silent for a long moment but mulled it over in her mind. Serenity was terrified to face him again but she would do anything to make this stop. To make sure her daughter was safe again. Sitting across from Black, talking to him... A cold flush punched through her and she had to focus on anything but him or she wasn't sure her knees would hold her up. "Do you need anything else from me?"

Amy shook her head. "I think we're good for now. I'm really glad you're staying at the Jordan estate. That place is locked down pretty tight. Are you going to be at the grid search tomorrow?"

"I am. Why...do you think I shouldn't?"

"No, I'm glad you're coming. It's almost a hundred percent chance that whoever's doing this will be there. They're going to want to revel in the havoc they've caused. I'm going to have an agent on you and I know Lucas won't be far from you either. If anyone acts suspicious, we'll take them down."

"Good to know. I'm ready to go if we're done here."

"I'm going to have an agent drive you back if that's okay?"

She nodded, not caring who took her back. She simply wanted to see her daughter and Lucas. She'd hurt him when she'd told him not to come with her.

He was already going above and beyond what a friend—or whatever they were—should ever do. He had to be getting tired of all her shit and she wanted to spare him if she could.

By the time she made it back to the Jordan house, the gate was closed for the night. Luckily Louise answered the intercom and opened it. Lucas was nowhere in sight when she met his mother in the foyer, and Serenity was too chicken to ask where he was. Instead she headed for Harper's room and found her in bed, reading to Daisy.

"What's all this?" she asked, her heart warming as Daisy yipped to see her.

"Mommy!" Harper set her book down and sat up, jumping into Serenity's arms.

She hugged her daughter tight as she got into the bed, pulling her close. Daisy licked Serenity's face before cuddling right up next to Harper, her sweet little shadow.

"Are you reading to Daisy?"

"Yes. She has a lot to learn."

Serenity laughed when she saw that the book was one of her many "Biscuit" books, featuring a cute puppy who got into mischief.

"Is everything okay with your friend?" Harper left the book open in her lap as Daisy nudged her with her nose, not so subtly begging to be petted.

Harper rubbed her head as Serenity answered. "Of course. I just needed to help Ms. Amy with a couple things." She'd decided to go with Ms. Amy instead of Agent Lin. It sounded less intimidating.

"Okay." Harper turned back to her book, seemingly unworried. In fact, she seemed to think all of this was an adventure.

Which was just fine with Serenity.

As Harper started reading, she flipped on the little dome light on the table, that she'd brought from home. Little blue and green stars danced on the ceiling.

Considering how much her daughter was slowing down, it was clear she would be going to sleep soon. Half an hour before bedtime, even, but Serenity had a feeling she was just as exhausted as everyone else. Minutes later, and before she'd finished the book, Harper had drifted off, Daisy's head still on her lap.

Serenity eased the book out of the way, tucked her in and turned the lamp off, but left the twinkle lights on.

Their rooms were connected by a bathroom so she headed into the other guest room, but left Harper's door open so she could hear her if needed. Then she simply sat for a long moment, gathering all her thoughts. Going over all that information with the Feds had mentally taxed her. So she was going to allow herself a few minutes of quiet, even if she was finding it almost impossible to turn her brain off.

After checking her cell phone to make sure Amy hadn't called with news—not that she'd really expected it—she went in search of Lucas.

She found him and Easton in the kitchen, Lucas with his muscular arms crossed over his chest as he and his brother talked about something quietly.

They both stopped talking and turned to look at her. His expression was unreadable, making her stop in her tracks. "Should I come back later?"

"No, it's all good," Easton said. "I've got to head back to the station house anyway. I'm on call starting in two hours."

She nodded, half-smiling when he basically patted the top of her head as he passed. Easton was like this giant, affable puppy you couldn't help but love.

Lucas was his polar opposite, much more serious. "Hey, is everything okay?" she asked, stepping farther into the room. It was the first time they'd been alone in... Since last night, she realized, her cheeks warming up.

"Yeah, just talking about family stuff."

Despite the tension in the air, she moved closer to him, leaning against the granite countertop. She wanted to erase the awkwardness between them. "I know you're coming to the grid search tomorrow, but what's going on with your work?" He'd been fairly quiet about that and she didn't like the thought of his work suffering because of her.

"Tobias is taking over for the next week. Unless there's an emergency, he's got things handled." His expression wasn't cold, but he seemed distant, his hands shoved into his pockets as he stood in front of her.

She didn't like the wall between them, but knew it was her fault. "Okay." Good, she'd been worried about that. "I think Daisy is going to sleep with Harper, if that's okay?"

He finally smiled, though it was only a half-smile. "That's more than okay. Daisy has been following her around like a little shadow."

She wanted to say more, then Lincoln walked in to the kitchen. He looked just as tense as Lucas. What was going on with these two?

"Got a second?" Lincoln asked his brother. From his body language it was pretty clear this was a private conversation.

"I'll let you guys get to it. I'll see you in the morning," she said.

Lucas simply nodded, not correcting her or attempting to stop her. *All right, then.*

She headed back to the guest room and collapsed into bed after changing into her pajamas. She'd stay awake a little longer and talk to Lucas before she crashed. At least that was what she told herself as sleep completely pulled her under.

## CHAPTER TWENTY-THREE

*Serenity's feet were cold, wet as she walked through the dewy grass. Where was she? And why was she outside in her pajamas?*

*"Help me," whispered a voice through the fog and mist.*

*She recognized that voice. She hurried forward, her feet sluggish as fear clawed at her spine. What was going on?*

*The moon was high in the sky and it looked wrong. It was completely red, casting a macabre glow over everything. Shadows loomed from the forest.*

*She jolted to a halt when she saw Paisley Long stretched out in the grass in pajamas.*

*Her skin was far too pale. Even as she approached to check her pulse, she knew Paisley was dead. Serenity had seen death before.*

*Suddenly Paisley's eyes snapped open, her irises ringed in red. "She's coming for you," she whispered.*

*Serenity's skin flushed hot, then ice cold. She tried to take a step back when she saw the gleaming points of Paisley's teeth. She looked inhuman.*

*"She's going to take everything that matters to you. You are going to die slowly, painfully." Her words were still a whisper.*

*"Who?" she rasped out.*

*Paisley shook her head from side to side, the jerky action unnatural. "No, no, no. Tick-tock, tick-tock." Her voice was singsong now, sending more chills down Serenity's spine. She took a small step back, the effort taking unimaginable effort.*

*Paisley shifted slightly, crawling forward, her fingernails pointed just like her teeth as they dug into the grass. She reached forward, pulled herself toward Serenity.*

*"Tick-tock, tick-tock," she taunted.*

*Serenity opened her mouth to scream, to do something, but she was frozen as roots sprouted from beneath her and wrapped around her ankles. Oh, God! They started pulling her down.*

Her eyes snapped open and she jolted up in bed, her heart a staccato beat in her ears.

It was just a nightmare. An awful, terrifying nightmare. Shoving the covers off her, she swung her legs over the bed and leaned forward. She put her head between her knees and dragged in lungfuls of air, taking deep breaths to steady herself.

As soon as she could stand, she stumbled through the attached bathroom and checked on Harper.

Familiar little twinkle lights glittered across the ceiling. Harper was sleeping peacefully, as she should be.

Daisy raised her head once to glance at Serenity, but went back to dozing within seconds, Harper's protector.

She sagged against the doorframe, watching her daughter for a long moment.

It was only a nightmare, she reminded herself. One that would *not* come true. That nightmare had been ghoulish, scary.

She was tempted to write down the nightmare and try some writing therapy, but even the thought of doing so scared her. She did not want to relive that. Not now. It was too soon. In a few hours she knew the images would fade, but for now they were etched into her mind.

She thought about going to Lucas but things had been weird between them earlier. She knew he'd be okay with her coming to him but she didn't want awkwardness. No, that wasn't true. She couldn't run to him with this, couldn't depend on him for everything. Because she could easily get used to him and everything he offered.

Stepping back, she eased the door shut and stripped off her sweat-soaked clothing. A shower would help.

Or at least banish some of the nightmare.

Until the next one.

## CHAPTER TWENTY-FOUR

Serenity shoved her hands in the pockets of her windbreaker as she listened to Lincoln bark out instructions to everyone from Verona Bay who'd come to help with this grid search for Paisley. Behind him, quiet and at attention, his deputies were all wearing uniform shirts, cargo pants and windbreakers with the sheriff department emblem on them. Despite the overcast morning and the fog lingering on the ground, a few hundred people had gathered here for the search.

Almost all shop owners downtown had closed up and posted signs letting others know where they were if they wanted to help.

Serenity felt vulnerable out here, knowing that the killer was likely here, that they could strike out at her at any time. She also felt as if everyone was watching her, silently judging. Even with Lucas by her side, being so exposed right now was beyond unnerving. Like one of her nightmares come to life. His presence was the only thing helping her keep it together.

Amy's FBI profiler didn't think the killer would attack her out in the open. No, this person didn't want to get caught. The poison suggested a hands-off type of killing, and the way Adeline and Paisley had disappeared with no witnesses further added to the profile that whoever this was didn't want to get caught.

Still, it was hard to shake that icy ball of fear congealed in her gut.

Lucas took her hand in his and squeezed once, offering silent support. He'd been quiet, almost distant all morning, but he also hadn't left her side.

She wondered if he was regretting getting involved in all this, and getting closer to her. She certainly wouldn't blame him if he did. She was a magnet for danger, apparently. And she was pretty sure she was too broken to ever have a real relationship. She'd run away with the first man who'd offered an escape and she hadn't had a relationship since him. And she woke up on the regular sweating buckets because of a nightmare. *Ugh.*

Lincoln motioned to her and Lucas when he was done speaking. Then his deputies started breaking people into groups and going over various grids on the maps set up.

She was surprised when Lincoln moved Norah and Bianca into her group, but there was a subtle look that passed between him and the agent shadowing her.

Okay, so maybe this was intentional. Yeah, it had to be. She knew from Amy that the Feds were keeping a close eye on all their top suspects. It creeped Serenity out that they were in the same group as her but she forced herself not to show her fear.

"I'm surprised to see you out," Norah said once Lincoln had finished going over everything.

"Why?" she asked bluntly, facing the other woman, looking her directly in her blue eyes. After what Maris had told her, and after everything she'd been through, Serenity was over caring what people thought of her.

"I just mean… You know…"

"No, I don't know. Enlighten me." Serenity watched Norah intently for a long moment, a perverse pleasure sliding through her when Norah's cheeks got pink. Sure she could talk trash behind Serenity's back, but it was a whole new ballgame when she was right in front of her. Norah was older than her by about two years, and she'd once been interested in a boy who Serenity had dated in college, but that seemed like a strange reason to hold a grudge. Or the kind of grudge someone was willing to kill over. Even though fear still simmered under the surface, she gained back some of her power as she faced Norah down.

Ignoring the other woman, she turned toward Lucas, who almost looked as if he was fighting a grin.

"I'm ready if you are," she said.

He nodded, even as his brother drew a square around the map on one of the boards the deputies had set up. "Don't forget, this is your perimeter. Stay in this area. We don't want any crossover and we need this group to stay staggered like this." He motioned to various points already drawn on the map.

She nodded even as Lucas said, "We've got it."

The reason for the search was twofold. The Feds weren't technically sure Paisley had been taken by the same person who'd taken Adeline and killed Mrs. Rose. It was very likely considering the circumstances, but at this point they were covering all of their bases.

Paisley had a standing weekly breakfast date with her mom and had missed it. Her cell phone and all of her other belongings were at her house, but her vehicle wasn't. And her car had been found abandoned near a local park, which backed up into a national forest. They were searching a good portion of it right now.

The fog swirled around their feet, a few birds chirping as they headed off into the woods. She'd worn knee-high rain boots because it was still damp out, and even if it was cold out, snakes could be hiding anywhere.

"Can we talk about last night?" she murmured as she and Lucas broke off onto their directed path. In the distance she heard people calling Paisley's name sporadically.

Instead of responding outright, he made a sort of grunting sound. Then he glanced over his shoulder and she did the same. Amy's agent was about twenty feet behind them, wearing a plain jacket and outdoorsy hiking clothing. The dark-haired man nodded once and continued walking behind them.

"Come on, Lucas," she said, then called out Paisley's name, her voice echoing against other calls. "Please talk to me." She couldn't stand this coolness from him. Not on top of everything else.

"Last night you could have brought me with you. Instead you brushed me off as if..." He shoved a hand through his hair. "It doesn't matter."

"Obviously it does matter. I didn't want you to come because I didn't want to be a burden. Your whole family has been incredible. I figured you didn't want to be dragged off—"

"That's the problem. You figured and didn't ask me what I wanted. I've been about as blunt as I can about my feelings. I'm in this thing, Serenity. I don't want casual with you. If an FBI agent shows up and wants to take you somewhere, I want to go with you like a partner."

She was surprised by the intensity of his words and felt the blood drain from her face. "I thought we were just going to stay friends." Okay, that was lame, but it was all she could get out.

"You can tell yourself that, but it's garbage and you know it. We crossed a line the other night." His jaw clenched once, his emerald eyes shooting fire. "Yeah, I know what you told me, but I also know it's bullshit. You're keeping a wall between us that doesn't have to be there. I'm not running away—you're pushing me away." As two of the volunteers drew closer, moving into their space, Lucas snapped his jaw shut.

And she wasn't sure how to respond, regardless. What he'd said was...true. She *was* keeping him at a distance. She zipped up her jacket when a few little droplets of rain tickled her face. She called out Paisley's name again even as she ran over what Lucas had said. He was right about her keeping up walls, but she wasn't sure she was capable of letting them down.

She didn't know if she was ready to let someone else into the life she'd created for her and Harper. She'd gotten burned before, and while she could never regret her daughter, she regretted a lot of her past choices. She didn't want to make another one based out of fear or neediness.

After two hours of walking in their grid area—and ignoring the awkwardness between them—there had been no good news from anyone else. And the stark reality started to sink in even more. She couldn't help but think about Paisley's mom, desperate for information. Just like her own mom had gone through when she and Savannah had been taken. Only her mom had never gotten good news. Not truly. Because Savannah had died and Serenity hadn't come back whole. The scent of the forest, the rain lingering in the air— She had to shove back old memories as they assaulted her senses.

"Serenity," Lucas said firmly, and she was suddenly under the impression that he'd said her name more than once.

She blinked, wiping away some of the mist that had settled on her cheeks. "What?"

"We need to head back. We're at the end of the perimeter." He frowned down at her.

She glanced around, and realized how deep into the woods they'd gone. It was impossible to go any farther through the thicket of the forest.

She nodded and turned back around with him, calling out Paisley's name again, though in her gut she didn't think the woman was out here.

The fog had gotten thicker instead of waning, and though she couldn't see his face clearly, the federal agent was visible through the mist.

She kept imagining the fog turning into fingers, snaking up around her ankles and pulling her under, like in the dream. *Hell.* She rolled her shoulders, banishing the images.

Suddenly, the agent was next to them, his footsteps wraith quiet as he put a gentle hand on her forearm. "They've found her body."

She stopped, turning to stare at him while her pulse thudded in her ears. "Who?" she rasped out.

"Paisley Long. Not here...in your back yard."

## CHAPTER TWENTY-FIVE

S erenity didn't remember the walk back to the parking lot and she didn't remember the drive to her house. She was only vaguely aware of Lucas's strong, steadying presence. Thank God he was here to drive even though he told her he didn't want her to go to her house.

He'd made his opinion known, but he hadn't argued with her. Which was good—she didn't have enough steam left in her right now. Paisley Long was dead and had been left in her yard. She had no more details than that but she was going to get them.

She saw the reflection of the flashing blue lights bouncing off her neighbors' houses even before they reached her house.

Crime scene tape sectioned off part of her yard and the half-opened gate of her privacy fence.

She saw Amy before she saw anyone else, the petite woman talking to one of her older neighbors, Demarcus Hall. His hands were shoved into his jeans pockets, his standard Braves cap on his head.

Amy glanced over when she and Lucas pulled up. Her entire body language changed and she said something to Serenity's neighbor before hurrying over to the curb.

Lucas rolled down the window as she approached.

"You don't need to be here," Amy said, her jaw tight.

"What happened?" Serenity asked.

Sighing, Amy opened the back door of the extended cab truck and slid in. "Someone dumped her body over the back fence. I've had someone watching the front. One of the neighbor's dogs was going crazy barking, so my guy checked out your backyard and found her." Amy's tone was sharp, but Serenity heard the underlying anger.

Whoever was behind this was getting bolder.

"What happened to her?" Serenity managed to rasp out.

She only paused for a moment. "I can't know for sure, but it looks very similar to what happened to your neighbor. Ketamine overdose if I had to guess."

Serenity closed her eyes as she held back a curse. "I'm going to see Black," she blurted, the words pouring out of her. He hadn't talked to Amy but maybe he would talk to her. She at least had to try, to appeal to whatever sense of...a conscience he might have.

The interior of Lucas's truck went deathly quiet.

"Serenity—"

"Nope." She cut Amy off. "I'm going, but I need you to pave the way for me. I know you can get me in. Especially now."

"Okay. As soon as I'm done here—"

"I don't need you to go with me. They record those meetings, which I know you can get. I'm going right now. As in, this instant. It's only a couple hours' drive from here. I can be back before dinner." The maximum-security prison was in north Florida, only a couple hours from Verona Bay, a fact that Serenity was very aware of.

She'd have to miss Carol's funeral but she would let her daughter know why. "Maybe he'll talk to me. And we'll never know if I don't try. He wanted desperately to talk to me years ago after the trial, something you know."

Lucas let out a savage curse, then grew silent and she could practically see the steam coming out of his ears.

"Okay," Amy finally said. "I'll have one of my people follow you." Then she looked sharply at Lucas. "Obviously you're going too." Not a question.

"No shit." His expression was dark and he didn't take his eyes off Serenity.

"I'm going to put another agent on the Jordan estate as well," Amy continued.

"Thank you," she said. She needed Harper to be safe.

"Keep your phone on you at all times."

She nodded and Amy got out of the truck, already on her phone. Hopefully calling the prison warden or whoever she needed to set this up.

She turned to Lucas. "You don't have to drive me if—"

"Just stop right there," Lucas said as he pulled away from the curb. "First, we're going to go to my parents' place, get changed and you can say goodbye to Harper. I'm going to pack a small cooler for us because even if you're not hungry, you need to eat. And I know you're not going to feel like stopping somewhere. You also probably want to call Carol's daughter and let her know we won't be making it this afternoon. Then we're heading out. That will take an extra fifteen or twenty minutes max, so don't argue."

"That's…very organized and well thought out."

He simply grunted.

"I kind of can't believe you're not arguing with me," she said a moment later.

"Because I already know how the argument will go. I think it's bullshit, but you'll tell me that you want to help—"

"I do want to help!"

"Exactly."

"It's a long shot, but maybe he'll tell me something. I feel so useless sitting here while people are dying. If I can do something to stop this, I have to." Her words were impassioned and she felt every single one of them.

"And that's why I'm not going to argue. I want to go on record as saying I don't like this, but you know your mind. And it might help talking to him, and give you, I don't know, closure, if that's even possible. Maybe it will be beneficial. Or maybe it will help find whoever is tormenting our town." His jaw tightened now, and another rush of anger from him popped to the surface. It wasn't directed at her, however. He was just as pissed as she was about what was happening.

She certainly hoped this visit with Black would do some good. "I had a dream last night," she blurted, needing to tell someone. To get the words out there. "Nightmare, actually. Paisley was in it. She was already dead and she told me that 'she' was coming for me. And the she wasn't a reference to herself, but to someone else. The nightmare was…terrifying." She shuddered as the vivid details of the foggy forest came back. It was easier to talk about it now, however, that she'd gotten some distance from it. She was used to nightmares but this one had stuck with her, digging its talons in tight.

"She? She who?" Lucas's voice was sharp.

"I have no idea. And it could mean nothing." But her gut said otherwise.

"You could have come to me." His words were quiet now, laced with some emotion she couldn't define.

"I know. I..." She couldn't think of anything that didn't sound lame.

"Dreams or nightmares, sometimes they tell us things that our subconscious already knows."

"Yeah, maybe."

"Years ago, during my first tour, I had a dream about a mission we had planned for the next day. In it...one of my guys told me not to storm a certain house. I brushed it off. There was no reason to listen, not when literally everywhere we went we could be ambushed." He was silent for a long moment and Serenity figured he wasn't going to continue.

She reached out and squeezed his leg. Of all people, she understood that it was hard to talk about things from her past. She would never pressure him to do the same.

"I should have listened to that dream," he finally said. "We lost two men. Two of my friends. I'd seen something in our recon that didn't register until I was asleep and my brain was relaxed. At least that's what I assume happened. I've never ignored another dream or nightmare again. Sometimes a nightmare is just a nightmare. Sometimes it's more."

She nodded slowly, laying her head back against the headrest as they turned down the driveway to his parents' estate. "The nightmare was like something out of a horror movie. I don't even know what to make of it." Serenity shuddered again and turned the heat on high to fight the shakes she knew were coming.

"The 'she' is interesting."

"Amy thinks it's a good possibility that the killer is a woman. Their profiler does, anyway."

Lucas nodded and reached out to squeeze her hand in his before he put the truck in park. "They're narrowing it down."

Yeah, she just hoped they narrowed it down to one person, and soon.

## CHAPTER TWENTY-SIX

Even though the back of her neck was sweaty and her palms were damp, the rest of Serenity's body was ice cold as she stood outside the guarded room. The industrial hallway had a weird echo to it, the sound of a heavy metal door clanging shut in the distance sending a chill up her spine. And the smell was oddly sterile, like a hospital—and absolutely no one she'd come in contact with since arriving at the prison smiled. But the main thing that surprised her was how quiet everything was. Maybe it was just this area though.

Amy must have a lot of clout to get this meeting for her, and so quickly. Some of the guards had been surprised about this, but the warden had made it clear that Serenity was to have this meeting with no interruptions from them or anyone else.

Serenity hated being here, hated being anywhere close to such a monster, but she was going to do this. The fact that Lucas was with her was pretty much the only reason she wasn't having a full-fledged panic attack.

"I'm right here when you're done," Lucas said. "You escaped him. You got away from him. And then you faced him down in court. He has no power over you. And when you're done, you're walking away and he's going back to a shitty cell."

She nodded even though it didn't feel true. Because she still had nightmares, and she lived her life a certain way because of what Black had done. No longer was she the free-spirited young woman she'd been before him. Her life had been bisected into before and after. Before the kidnapping, torture, and murder of her sister. And then after.

Even though she was afraid of splintering in two, she reached for Lucas and held him tight, taking all his strength. "Thank you," she rasped out, her throat scratchy.

He pulled her close, his grip around her fierce and protective as he kissed the top of her head. His spicy scent was barely perceptible in this place, but it gave her comfort. Hell, him simply being here gave her comfort on the most primal level. Lucas would never let anything hurt her. Not if he could help it. That knowledge punched right through her and rearranged everything inside her right then and there.

Taking a step back, she dragged in a steadying breath. She could do this. She would do this. If she said it enough maybe it would be easier.

"We're going to be standing outside the entire time," one of the prison guards said, his tone surprisingly gentle. Her gaze flicked down to his name tag. Jake Carter.

As she moved into the small, square room with gray walls, gray floors and an industrial steel table, she reminded herself why she was doing this. Maybe it would do no good, but just maybe he would tell her something.

A freaking pipe dream, she knew, but screw it. She was going in.

Even as the door shut behind her, the lock clicking into place, she told herself that she wasn't stuck. She could leave when she wanted. This wasn't a nightmare. The guard remained in the corner as she sat at the table, forcing her breaths to remain steady.

Less than ten seconds later, the opposite door of the sterile room opened and in shuffled Michael Black.

The monster from her nightmares.

Shock stole through her as she looked at this man who'd always seemed to loom larger than life in her nightmares and in her memories. He was about six feet tall but he seemed smaller, his shoulders stooped as he made his way to the chair, the chains dragging with him.

His blue eyes were bright as he looked at her. But they looked paler than she remembered and he'd lost a lot of weight. The prison orange hung off him, his arms almost skinny, with no muscle tone. And his dark hair had started graying—and thinning in the way that came from not having the proper nutrition. He didn't look anything like the man she remembered.

Though her heart still beat out of control, something inside her shifted. She straightened in her seat as she regained more of a sense of self. The guard who'd escorted him inside locked his handcuffs to the table and his feet to the chair so he had limited range of movement.

She was surprised he'd even agreed to see her. Even though Amy had made it possible for her to see him, he could have said no.

"Why did you agree to meet with me?" She was the one that got away. He was in prison because of his crimes but she'd testified against him, had helped put the nails in his coffin. And now he was shackled, imprisoned for the rest of his life before he got the needle.

He lifted a shoulder, much of the pride and arrogance she remembered from before gone. Now a sad, middle-aged man sat before her.

*Okay, then.* She wasn't sure where to go now. She'd needed to see him, to see if she could get something from him, but she didn't have a psychology degree. God, what the hell had she been thinking? When panic started to set in, telling her what a fool she was, she shoved it back down and found her voice. "Someone is stalking me and I believe you are helping them. I don't know how you are, but the Feds will figure it out." Or at least she had to believe they would.

He was silent, watching her with a sort of subdued mania. She could see it right beneath the surface.

Staring at him now, she didn't feel afraid. And she didn't feel pity for him because he deserved what he got, but…he wasn't intimidating anymore. Facing him in the courtroom had been hard. He'd been in an expensive suit, polished and charming-looking, and she'd been a mess, still in therapy, still dealing with Savannah's death. Now…he was pathetic. A shell of what he'd once been.

"Your partner has gone off the rails," she said, searching for a button to push. "Killing my neighbor—a great mom and grandma—and they don't care who they hurt. And if I die, my little girl won't have a mom anymore."

She stomped on the only button she knew might get a reaction. He was such a psychotic narcissist that she wasn't sure he would even care, but he'd been so damn adamant as he'd told the entire world about why he'd gone on his killing spree. He'd wanted to kill women before they had a chance to procreate and potentially abandon their kids, just as he'd been abandoned. Though he'd referred to it as a "cleansing." But once they became mothers—they were off-limits, even with his mommy issues. It was all bullshit though. He simply hated women and wanted to hurt them.

His jaw twitched once. "I don't have a partner. And I'm not ordering anyone to do anything." He might be telling the truth, but it was impossible to read him.

"Pardon me if I don't believe you," she said, her words coated in ice. When he didn't say anything more, she continued. "Well if you're not directing them to leave presents for me, then they're doing it on their own. They aren't going to stop."

He cleared his throat. "The jewelry... It's real?" he asked carefully.

She knew Amy had already told him about the jewelry when she'd questioned him. "If you mean does it belong to your victims, yes. Now, who is stalking me?" she demanded, rage rising inside her in a tidal wave. She was ninety-nine percent sure he wasn't going to tell her. She had to try, however. Had to face him down. It was taking all her self-control not to lunge across the table and start choking the life out of him, to hurt him for taking away her twin sister. That kind of violence would accomplish nothing right now—even if it would feel good.

He leaned forward, his chains clanking against the table. "I'm not directing anyone to do anything." His pale eyes were intense. "I swear it."

He seemed almost desperate for her to believe him. Fat chance. Not when his word meant exactly shit, but she kept that thought to herself. Instead she leaned forward, putting on her most imploring expression. "I'm a mother now. I have a daughter who means everything to me. My husband died, which you probably know. If something happens to me, my little girl will have no one to look out for her. She will be all alone in the world. She'll have nothing and no one. Do you want her to grow up without her mother?" she asked softly. Maybe the demanding approach was the wrong way. Maybe this softness would work instead.

His expression changed ever so slightly, but she couldn't get a read on whatever emotion he betrayed. Because just as quickly a neutral mask fell into place. "I can't help you."

Yeah, but he'd agreed to see her for a reason. Maybe the reason was simply because he wanted to see her, sick freak that he was.

"Then I have nothing left to say to you," she said, standing. She'd come to face him, to get answers. But she couldn't force him to give them to her—no matter how much she wanted to bash his face in and make him talk.

"Wait..." He clenched and unclenched his fingers.

"What?"

"What is this person doing exactly? This person you think is my partner?"

Shouldn't he already know? Maybe he didn't have the details, but he would have to know the basics. "They're hunting me. Killing people." She wasn't going to give him more than that, however. He'd probably jack off to them. "And let me tell you something. If she comes for me, I'm going to kill her." She used the pronoun "she" intentionally, watching his reaction.

He jerked slightly in his seat, his hands tightening into balls before he relaxed them, letting his fingers go limp.

But she'd struck a nerve, she had no doubt. Even if he was trying to cover it. Amy and the Feds might be able to see something more when they watched the recording of this meeting later. "I'm going to kill your daughter," she whispered, leaning forward on the table. She was on a fishing expedition right now but it was worth a shot to see if she could get under his skin, get him to break.

He jerked back as if she'd hit him. Jaw tight, he turned away from her. "Get me out of here!" he shouted.

Heart pounding, she turned away from him and nodded at the guard in the corner, who immediately opened the door for her. Maybe it wasn't the jackpot, but it sure felt like it. Did he have a daughter? She could hear the other door opening and Black's chains clanking against the table and floor. But she didn't turn around.

It took all her self-control not to look at him. She wouldn't give him the satisfaction. She was never coming back here.

And he was going to die here. It was the only thing that gave her a modicum of comfort. That and the fact that she was going to stop whoever was working with him.

"I won't insult you by asking how you are," Lucas said a few minutes later, turning to face her in the cab of his truck.

She sat there, turned toward him in the seat, not bothering with her seat belt yet. It was bright outside, with little white clouds dotting the sky in every direction. The setting was incongruent with the darkness of the prison, the barbed wire surrounding them, even where they sat in the parking lot.

"Thank you for coming with me," she said quietly, reaching across the center console, her fingers cold and numb. "It was harder than I thought, but at the same time I'm glad I did it." Even though she hated that she'd missed Carol's funeral, she actually was glad she'd come—and she was pretty sure her friend would have understood. "Seeing him like that..." She shook her head, her jaw tightening. He might have looked sad and weak, but she was still dealing with the emotions of seeing him and knew she'd have more nightmares later. They would probably be worse this time. But she'd faced that monster down and she was never going to see him again.

He held her hand tight. "You are the bravest woman I've ever known."

She snorted softly. "Says the man who fought in war zones. I'm not brave. I was afraid I was going to throw up on the table."

"And you went anyway."

"He looked...not good. In my nightmares, he's so much bigger. Intimidating and scary." She snorted derisively. "For obvious reasons. But seeing him in person, seeing how he's aged. He looks like a sad, aging man. Pathetic."

"He *is* pathetic," Lucas said, heat in his voice.

"So...this might sound crazy, but I think he really might have a daughter." He'd reacted to her threat so clearly.

Lucas went still. "What did he say?"

Lucas listened as she went over the conversation she'd had with Black. She hadn't been in there long with him and he hadn't thought she'd gotten anything useful, but he was glad to be wrong. A daughter? Holy hell.

"Trust your instinct," he said when she was finished. "At the very least we've got to tell Agent Lin."

"I plan to. I just needed a moment," she said, her voice cracking. When tears started spilling down her cheeks, her strong façade breaking, he pulled her to him, wrapping his arms around her as she clutched onto his shoulders, sobbing into his neck.

For some reason the tears surprised him, though they shouldn't. So often she kept herself so rigid, so controlled for everyone. He understood why, but it was a sharp reminder of how much she kept bottled up inside. He rubbed a hand up and down her spine, making soothing sounds as he simply held her. He wished he could take away all her pain—hell, if he was getting wishes granted he wanted Michael Black dead and gone.

Eventually Serenity's grip on his shoulders loosened but she remained where she was. Then she shifted slightly and laid her cheek against one of his shoulders. "I'm sorry," she murmured.

He tightened his own grip. "You don't ever have to be sorry." He would be her shoulder to cry on anytime.

"I'm sorry for not just this." She pulled back, her eyes red-rimmed as she dashed the remnants of her tears away. "I swear I'm not trying to mess with your head, Lucas. I just don't think I'm ready for a relationship. I feel like I'm broken half the time, like I'm barely keeping my life together. Some days I feel like a champ, then others...it's all I can do to get out of bed. And if I'm being really honest, Harper is the reason for that. I don't know if I have room in my heart right now for anyone else. I'm so sorry," she whispered.

His throat clenched as he clasped her hands in his. "Okay." He wasn't a saint but he would accept that for now. Because he cared for her. More than simply cared for her. He didn't have a savior complex, but he wanted to help her, to love her. To be hers.

"Okay?"

He nodded. "Serenity, I'm your friend. No matter what, I'm here for you." It carved him up to say it, but it was the truth. He wasn't going anywhere, even if she never let him fully in.

# CHAPTER TWENTY-SEVEN

"What did Serenity say?" Frank asked Amy as he parked in the driveway of the quiet residential neighborhood.

They were paying someone a surprise visit and she hoped it paid off. "She pushed him on his partner, used the pronoun 'she' with Black. And she thinks she got a reaction from him when she mentioned him having a daughter. My gut is telling me that whoever is behind this is a woman and that it's his daughter. Somehow he had a kid and no one knew about it."

Which definitely wasn't out of the realm of possibility. If her DNA wasn't in the system, they would have no idea. And if the mother never put his name as the father on her birth certificate, there was no way to track who she was. If she even existed. But Amy's instinct was telling her that this woman was real—that she was their unsub.

"I'll watch the recordings as soon as we're done here," she continued. The warden would have already sent them to her email as she'd requested.

"You ready?" Frank asked. As usual, he was just a little rumpled. Somehow it made him seem more approachable and they always used it to their advantage.

She nodded and stepped out of the car with him. She was used to cracking cases sooner. And she did *not* want anyone else to die or be taken in Verona Bay. Right now they had all the suspects under surveillance, and after this, she was going to go pull every single one of them in for interviews. They either talked to her team or they didn't. She would give them the option, and if they rejected her, she would keep someone on them until they made a mistake.

And whoever was behind this *would* make a mistake. This whole case was personal, and when emotions were involved people screwed up. Which made her job a lot easier because humans were often emotional creatures.

She and Frank strode to the door of the house, not caring that it was suppertime. She knocked sharply three times.

A few moments later a slightly older woman with a cap of brown and gray hair smiled at them. "Hello?" There was more than a hint of question in her tone and expression. She glanced down at their badges hanging around their necks, her eyes widening. "Can I help you?"

Amy nodded. "We're here to speak to Steve Crow."

"Oh, my husband, yes. Ah, may I ask who is here?" she asked even as they'd started pulling out their IDs.

"I'm Special Agent Amy Lin and this is Special Agent Frank Quittner. We're with the FBI and working on a case in town right now alongside Sheriff Jordan." She paused, waiting—and saw the moment that the connection clicked into place for the woman whose name she already knew. Betty Crow, wife of local veterinarian Steve Crow.

"Oh my goodness, those poor women. Yes, yes, please come inside."

Frank eyed the menagerie of statues on the shelves of the foyer curio cabinet. Little elephants of glass, stone and crystal and in every shape and size covered the shelves. Some were kinda cute. At least it wasn't creepy little girl dolls. Because Amy had seen those before in a suspect's house. She shuddered at the memory of that freak.

"Would you guys like some cookies or coffee? If it's too late for coffee I've got—"

"We appreciate the offer," Frank said, his tone a lot softer than Amy's would have been. "Nothing is necessary, though we do appreciate the hospitality." Damn, she could hear his faint South Carolina accent, though he hadn't lived there in decades. He was laying on the charm thick.

"We really need to speak to your husband," Amy added, trying to hide her impatience.

"Of course." She motioned for them to follow her into a country kitchen decorated in roosters. This woman certainly like themes. "Just take a seat," she said and opened a door that led to the backyard, leaving it open as she shouted. "Steve, the FBI is here!"

Less than a minute later, a man with graying hair and garden gloves stepped into the doorframe, his face smudged with dirt, his expression concerned as he pulled his gloves off.

His wife shut the door behind them and immediately went to pour him a glass of what Amy assumed was sweet tea as he leaned against a nearby countertop. "How can I help you guys? Also, I'd like to see your badges."

In his early fifties, he looked exactly like his driver's license. Gray hair, a sharp face, pale blue eyes. His credentials were excellent as well. There was nothing in his history to suggest that he would be helping someone overdose, kidnap, or kill women, but they were covering all the bases at this point. They had to. Detective work wasn't like on TV. It involved a hell of a lot of interviews and running down leads that usually turned into nothing. And people were very often *not* accommodating.

"I'm here about the case you've probably seen on the local news. I don't have a warrant to search your veterinary practice, but I can get one. I came here to see if you have any missing ketamine."

The man sighed, his expression morphing into one of frustration as he pulled out one of the empty chairs and sat with them at the table. The scent of freshly cut grass and soil wafted on the air. It was pretty cold out to be gardening, she belatedly realized.

"I just contacted Sheriff Jordan this morning about it," he said. "I left a message with the sheriff department because he wasn't in—he was at the grid search, I discovered later."

She straightened in her chair. "You did?"

"Yeah, they told me he'd call me back and I didn't want to talk to anybody else but him."

"Explain exactly why you called."

"Over the last month I've noticed things moved around in my business. Little things. I thought maybe I moved things and didn't remember." He rubbed a hand over his head, agitated. "Then I noticed a couple vials of ketamine missing this morning. Things had been shifted around in one of my refrigerators so I don't know how long they've been gone. I don't want to accuse anyone I work with but...I don't know how else to explain what the hell is going on. I'm not sure how that relates to your case though," he said frowning. "I called Lincoln...ah, Sheriff Jordan so I could talk to him, one on one. Away from the clinic."

Amy shared a pointed look with Frank. Then she turned back to the vet. "Mr. Crow, would you mind going down to your office with us tonight? I'd like to take some fingerprints off the fridge where the vials were kept. And if you've saved them, I'd like to see your security recordings. If you want to wait for the warrant—"

He shook his head. "No, no. That's not necessary. Is this about the missing girls...girl, I guess? And the murdered women?"

Amy simply nodded.

His jaw clenched as he stood from his seat. "I'll help in any way I can. I didn't know Carol Rose that well, but..." His eyes widened slightly as he trailed off. "Is that how she died? Did someone give her ketamine?"

Amy didn't respond, simply stood. She couldn't give a potential suspect any information on an ongoing investigation. The only reason she told Serenity things was because she had a unique perspective on the case and Amy knew she'd keep her mouth shut. She'd refused to talk to reporters years ago and now was no different.

The man cleared his throat nervously and followed suit, standing. "If you don't mind, let me just put on a fresh shirt and wash my hands and face. Then we can head out."

"We'll wait in the driveway for you." Amy paused, then asked, "You're gardening this time of year?"

He blinked in confusion, then half-smiled. "I've got a greenhouse I work on when I'm not with my animals."

Amy nodded, making a note to check if he actually did have a greenhouse in his backyard even as Frank smiled politely at the man's wife.

"Thank you for your hospitality," Frank murmured. "We'll be in the car waiting."

"How are we doing on the warrants?" she asked once they were alone in the car. She hadn't gotten any weird vibes from the vet and she'd be checking with Sheriff Jordan about the supposed call the man had made about the ketamine.

Frank checked his phone as he let the car idle. "We'll have them in the morning. Porter found the right judge."

Amy allowed herself a modicum of relief as she leaned back in the passenger seat. She might be a superstar within the Bureau, but she still had to follow all the rules, and for good reason. It didn't matter what her instincts told her—she needed evidence. And unfortunately, she didn't have enough right now to search all the places she wanted to. But after Serenity's visit with Black today, she had enough to get warrants for the houses of the women she suspected.

At least her team was watching every house, and her people weren't being subtle about it. All of those women knew they were under surveillance, which was a good thing. She hoped to God the killer stayed put. Or if they made a move, that her team would take them down.

## CHAPTER TWENTY-EIGHT

She stared down at her captive, soaking up the raw fear in her gaze. Watching the life drain from her was exhilarating and she hated that she'd waited so long to do this.

"You're a monster," Adeline whispered through dry lips, her eyes barely open. Her wrists were bloodied and bruised, her brown skin was paler than normal and her eyes had deep shadows underneath them. Her hair fell limp around her face as she found the energy to open her eyes and glare. "A pathetic monster."

Rage popped inside her. *You're in charge*, the voice whispered. *Make her respect you, notice you.*

She kicked her in the stomach. That's right, she was in charge. No one else.

"Monster," Adeline rasped out again as she coughed, her frail body spasming in pain. "You'll pay for this. Eventually they'll catch you."

She kicked her again.

She'd given her prisoner very little food, no blanket, and enough water because she hadn't wanted her to die too quickly. And she hadn't been able to check in on her as much as she'd wanted because of the damn Feds. It had been two days since she'd been back here and she'd needed a fix. The sheriff had called the FBI in too quickly and she hadn't expected it.

Unfortunately, this morning time had slipped away from her, as it did sometimes. She'd lost three hours just watching Adeline, taunting her.

Now it was time to go.

"You're going to die soon," she whispered. "And you're going to wish it was sooner. Enjoy." She hurried out of the small cabin, scanning the forest as she stepped onto the dilapidated porch. No one was out here. No one even knew about this old FEMA trailer. And it was almost impossible to find unless you knew where you were going.

When she checked her watch, her heart rate jumped. She had to get back to her house. The sun would be coming up soon. The Feds couldn't know she'd been out. She raced through the woods, her boots and pants getting soaked from the morning dew. She'd just wanted to check on Adeline, to watch her suffering—to watch the life drain from her. She shouldn't have stayed so long.

As she ran, the memory of the last couple hours replayed over in her mind on a loop, soothing the voice in her head, the one that wouldn't let up, telling her to hurt more people. To take more victims.

She'd been invisible, lonely, her entire life. No one ever noticed her unless she dressed up, changed her appearance. Now everyone was taking notice even if they didn't know she was behind everything.

Everyone was scared, terrified. They were all talking about Serenity and what was going on when they came into her shop. A thrill shot through her every time someone brought up the case.

Even in college she'd been invisible, passed over for extra assignments by her teachers for other students. Usually stupid males or whores who flirted mercilessly to get what they wanted. She'd graduated at the top of her class, but she'd been asked to leave her internship early because she'd pushed back on ideas that had been stupid.

And she'd had no problem saying so. People just didn't want to hear the truth.

Now everyone was hearing her truth.

Her heart raced as she sprinted through the forest, only slowing when she reached the edge of the clearing. She'd parked her car down a ways on the side of the highway, in a hidden little turnoff impossible to see from the road.

The overgrown underbrush covered the little car for the most part, especially this early in the morning. It wasn't hunting season so no one would be out anyway.

She hadn't had any hits on her security system or the cameras at home, so no one had approached the house. And she knew the Feds were watching the front of the house.

Not just hers, or she might have packed up and left town. No, the Feds were watching a lot of people they considered suspects, waiting for one of them to make a mistake. Well, that wasn't going to happen. She'd already made one mistake by killing Paisley by accident. She'd thought she'd had the dosage perfect but she must've given her too much. Maybe Paisley's metabolism had been too slow, who knew. Next time she would just stick with bashing her victims in the head or tasing them. It was easy enough.

When she reached her car, she popped the trunk, stripped off her boots and pants, and slid on her dry jeans and sneakers. Then she headed home, though she wouldn't be parking in her driveway.

Since she was keeping an eye on the house of a neighbor who was out of town for the month, she'd been using their vehicle. It had provided the perfect place to stash all her things and then use her neighbors' backyards to move in and out of her house by entering through her back door. The Feds were so stupid—and understaffed. If they'd had someone watching the back of her house, she couldn't have moved around so freely.

She'd even set a few of her interior lights to go off using a timer. That way it looked as if she'd been home, and got up to go to the bathroom a couple times over the last few hours. It was child's play for her. She wasn't sure how that agent had ever caught her father. Maybe her father really was inept. A stupid, stupid fool. She wanted to write him a letter, to tell him what she thought of him, but she was done with him.

He'd gotten a message to her, telling her to stop. Begging her to. Telling her to just live her life and stop killing. That the Feds would eventually catch her. He'd used code, of course, so the message had been benign, but it didn't matter. She hadn't responded. She didn't care what he thought. She might as well have been invisible to him too. He'd used her for what he wanted, but he'd never truly seen her. Never appreciated how smart she was.

Power had flooded through her as she'd read then burned his letter. He didn't get to tell her what to do. He was nothing but a rotting bag of bones.

The drive home was quick and it didn't take long to hide the neighbor's car in their garage then make her way through backyards, knowing exactly where to avoid floodlights. She had half an hour until sunrise. Still, she couldn't stop the racing of her heart. She should have been home hours ago, not pushing it so close to dawn.

She didn't like how much time had gotten away from her. As she slipped in the back door of her house, she quickly disarmed her security system. She was back. Safe.

Now she had to figure out how to kill Serenity. No more taunting. It was time to take her prize.

As she ran over scenarios in her mind, she headed to the bathroom. She needed a shower, to wash off everything from the last few hours. It didn't matter that she'd changed clothes. When she heard her doorbell ring, followed quickly by the alert on her phone that someone had set off the motion sensor of the security camera out front, she froze.

She pulled up the live view and saw that two federal agents were on her doorstep. *Oh shit.*

Did they know? Sweat rolled down her spine. She could try to run but she didn't have anything ready to go. No, they couldn't know what she'd done or they'd have rammed the door down.

The doorbell sounded again, followed by someone's fist pounding on her door.

Despite the fear lancing through her, she quickly looked herself over. She stripped off her jeans, tossed them into the hamper and grabbed a robe from her bathroom door and put it on. Hoping she looked as if she'd been about to get in the shower, she cracked open the door. "Yes?" she rasped out, staring at them in what she hoped looked like confusion.

"We have a warrant to search your house," the woman she recognized as Agent Amy Lin said. "Here it is. You have the right to read it over and understand its contents. You are not under arrest. We are simply doing a search of your property and we'll also be searching your place of business. We would ask that you get changed and come down with us to the sheriff's station so we can ask you some questions."

"Do I have to answer your questions?" She stepped back, letting the small team of agents in her house. They wouldn't find anything here.

"You don't have to say anything. But you are entitled to a lawyer."

She shook her head. "I don't understand why you're here but I don't need a lawyer. I haven't done anything wrong."

The woman eyed her for a long moment and simply nodded. "That is your prerogative. Please get changed and come with me."

"Fine," she muttered. "I assume I'll have a few minutes of privacy to change?"

The agent nodded but still followed her into the house, shutting the door behind her. She could hear the other agents moving around and felt her ire rise. They were touching her things, putting their dirty hands on all her stuff. And she couldn't stop them. That rage bubbled up again but she pushed it down, ordering herself to remain calm on the outside. If she let her temper show, they would zoom in on her. *Stay calm.*

Grabbing a change of clothes and her phone, she shut and locked her bathroom door behind her. As she did, her phone buzzed once, twice.

*OMG, the FBI is searching my house!*

Another similar text quickly followed. Relief surged through her. At least two of her friends were having their houses searched as well. So this was a blanket type of thing, the FBI hadn't singled her out.

She could get through a stupid interview with them. Because they sure as hell weren't going to find anything incriminating at her house. She was too smart for them.

And as soon as she was done with the interview, she was going to prepare to run. But only after she'd taken care of her final loose end. She would kill Adeline, then Serenity.

Whatever it took, she was killing that bitch before she left town.

Even if she was done with her father, it was still Serenity's fault that he'd been caught, taken from her. She had to pay for that.

## CHAPTER TWENTY-NINE

Lucas glanced over from the coffee pot as his brothers Easton and Lincoln strode into the kitchen. He hadn't even realized Lincoln was here. He was still feeling sluggish after the drive back from the prison yesterday and Serenity was still sleeping.

"When did you get here?" he asked Lincoln—he knew Easton had gotten in a few hours ago.

Easton had said he wanted to be here until all the bullshit was taken care of—aka until Serenity and Harper were completely safe. Something Lucas appreciated. His brothers obviously had their own places but they all cared about Serenity and her daughter. And his mother was happy to have all her boys home, even if the circumstances were shitty.

"Just now. The Fed waved me through then Easton let me in."

Good. Even with the vastness of the estate, no one should be getting past the watchdog out front. "You want coffee?"

At their nods, he poured two more mugs. "Any news?" he asked, knowing his brother would tell him even if he wasn't supposed to. This entire situation was personal.

"Between us, yeah, looks like the Feds are getting search warrants for some of their suspects. Probably already have them."

Lucas's eyebrows rose at the news. Until now it was his understanding that they'd had far too many suspects to narrow things down seriously. Grabbing his coffee cup, he said, "Come on," motioning for his brothers to follow him. Serenity and Harper were still asleep and he wasn't going to bother them. Harper had school today but Serenity had decided to keep her home, something he understood. In the long run, it didn't matter if she missed a day or two of first grade.

"What's all this?" Easton asked as Lucas flipped on the lights of the office where Serenity had set up all her stuff.

"Damn," Lincoln said, eyeing the whiteboard. "This is thorough. It looks similar to what the Feds have."

"Yeah, that's what Serenity said."

"Pretty sure she can take the men off the board now." Lincoln motioned to the pictures of the three males. "All the search warrants are for women."

Easton snorted as he looked at the board.

Lucas frowned. "What the hell could be funny right now?"

Easton rubbed a hand over his tired-looking face. He'd been out late last night on call. "I was just thinking about a story I heard about Wilson Hart recently, that's all."

"What?" Lucas's gaze strayed to the bottom of the board where the three lone males were posted.

"He thought he was getting lucky at some bar over in Bishop's Creek and some chick tased him." Easton snorted. "Dumbass."

Lincoln straightened slightly. "Tased him?"

"Yeah. He had his dick out and everything. They were in his truck when she shocked him." Easton kept laughing as he shook his head. "He was so sure he was going to get lucky when some woman he'd never even seen before convinced him to head outside and hook up. Seriously. Dumb. Ass."

"I'm sure she didn't have to convince him very hard," Lucas muttered.

"No doubt. From what I heard, they were getting it on and the next thing he knows, electricity is shooting through his body." His brother's grin was huge now. "I kinda wish I'd been there to see it even if I don't want to see that asshole's dick."

Lucas snorted but stopped when he saw Lincoln's intense expression as he eyed the board. "What?"

His brother lifted a shoulder. "Everyone who has been targeted has had a connection to Serenity. She's not friends with Wilson but they went to college together. It's still a connection. Maybe it's nothing but...I don't like these odds."

Lucas straightened and looked at the board again. "Hell."

"I'm going to talk to him now," Lincoln said, glancing at his watch. "He should be at work."

"I'm going with you." And Lucas wasn't asking.

Lincoln's jaw tightened. "It would be pointless to tell you to stop, right?"

"Well, it's a free country and I know where Wilson works. I'm either going with you or meeting you there. Are you questioning him in an official capacity or just talking to him?"

His younger brother sighed. "Get dressed. I'll wait." That was answer enough. This wouldn't be official, but a social visit—more or less.

"You guys aren't asking me to go?" Easton asked.

Lucas shook his head at his older brother. "You just got off a long shift. Go get some sleep."

Easton shrugged and took a sip of his coffee. "Nah. I'll wait until Harper and Serenity wake up and keep them company. I hate that they're dealing with this. Maybe I'll get them out riding horses."

Lucas clapped his older brother once on the shoulder. "Thank you." He felt better leaving knowing that Easton was here. Military trained and now a firefighter—no one was getting through him. Even if there was a federal agent outside keeping guard, he trusted his brother more.

Lucas wanted to stay home today with Serenity but he was pretty sure she needed space. And if he was being honest with himself, he needed to be doing something. To be active with this case, even if he had no right to be. He would do anything to find who was hunting Serenity.

* * *

*"Help me," the voice whispered.*

*Serenity didn't want to open her eyes. No, she kept them squeezed shut even as icy fingers danced up her spine. She didn't want to be in the woods again, did not want to see Paisley lying there looking like a zombie. Nope.*

*"Help me, she's coming," the familiar voice whispered.*

*She opened her eyes and found herself looking at Adeline.*

*Her friend's wrists were shackled to the radiator, just like in the video Serenity had been sent. Adeline's eyes were barely open, her breathing shallow. "I'm so hungry," she murmured.*

*Oh God, no. No, no, no. "Where are you?" She tried to take a step forward but her feet were rooted to the spot, her legs leaden.*

*"Help me," Adeline said again instead of responding.*

*"I want to help you! Tell me how. Where are you?" she demanded, even though she knew the request was ridiculous. Adeline couldn't tell her where she was.*

*"Help me!" Adeline screamed. Her eyes opened wide, and just like Paisley's had been, they were rimmed in red as she screamed over and over to Serenity. "Help me!"*

"Mommy." Harper's soft voice cut through the haze.

Serenity's eyes flew open and once again she was damp with sweat. She blinked, saw faint light streaming in through the blinds.

"Hey sweetie," she murmured, willing her heart back into her chest.

Harper frowned at her, still in her princess pajamas. "You said help me. Are you okay?"

Nodding, she lifted Harper up from the ground and pulled her into bed with her. She kissed the top of her head as her daughter settled against her. "Yeah...I was just dreaming about ice cream. I needed help getting it off the top shelf of the freezer." Okay, as far as lies went, it was pretty lame, but it was all she could come up with on such short notice. "I hope I didn't wake you."

"No, Daisy woke me up by licking my face. She ran off, to go use the doggy door, I think."

Serenity laughed lightly, some of that tension coiled in her belly easing. "That seems like a fun way to get woken up."

"Since we can't keep Daisy, I want to get another dog. I'm ready."

Nightmare pushed to the side for now, Serenity tried to find the right words. "We'll see. Maybe after summer."

Harper's expression turned sullen. "I know what maybe means."

"We're still getting settled in. Let's just give it some time."

"Is this because someone wants to hurt you?" Harper asked, her little voice trembling.

In that moment Serenity wanted to bash in the face of whoever was doing this. For making her daughter scared. "No, baby. I just want to do some research first, to make sure we get the right kind of dog for us. We got lucky with Dolly. I want to look at some rescue dogs and see if one of them might be a good fit for us."

"Okay. I'm hungry." Like usual, Harper changed subjects at warp speed.

She gently tickled her tummy. "You're always hungry."

Harper giggled and jumped out of bed. "Feed me," she said in her best Cookie Monster impression.

She laughed even more. "Give me a second to change." She needed to get out of her damp pajamas. "Then we'll go hunt down some food."

Even as she stripped, the remnants of the nightmare clung to her like kudzu, holding on, spreading everywhere. She had to help Adeline. Had to save her.

She just didn't know how.

## CHAPTER THIRTY

Lucas glanced around the diner, glad that it was clearing out as he sat down with his brother. They were here to question Wilson Hart who worked as a short-order cook.

"Sheriff, Lucas, it's good to see you boys in here. Any news on the case?" Janice asked as she stopped at the table, already pouring both of them coffee since she knew what they liked.

"We're working on some leads. Is Wilson busy right now?" he asked.

Lucas put some sugar in his coffee as she said, "Yeah, he's in the back. You need to talk to him?" Her accent was pure Georgia, which fit since she'd moved down here from Athens a decade ago.

"Whenever he gets a chance, if you wouldn't mind sending him out here I'd appreciate it." His brother smiled politely but even that smile made Janice blush slightly.

She nodded and then gave a little wink to Lucas before heading into the back.

"So...now that it's just the two of us, what's going on with you and Serenity?" Lincoln asked bluntly.

Lucas had been wondering when his brother would ask. The tension between him and Serenity was palpable. If he'd ridden here in the same vehicle with Lincoln, he had no doubt he'd have already been questioned about this. "I have no idea." And he didn't. He might have to live with the fact that she could never give him what he wanted. The thought created a hole in his chest but he ignored the pain. He could live with it as long as she was still in his life.

Lincoln simply grunted, not looking convinced. "Have you eaten?"

"I'll get something since we're taking up a table."

At that, Lincoln turned around and let Janice know that they both wanted the day's special—two eggs over easy, grits, a blueberry muffin and a side of sausage. No substitutions allowed.

"So what's up with you and your neighbor?" Lucas asked, turning the tables on him. Serenity had mentioned something to him about Lincoln acting weird when he'd talked about Autumn.

Lincoln narrowed his gaze at him. "Why?"

"Just curious." He started to say more but Wilson appeared in the doorway to the kitchen, wiping his hands on his long white apron. He took off his hairnet and tossed it down as he strode over to meet them.

The guy was good-looking in a sort of Florida surfer boy type of way, Lucas realized. He didn't have much drive, and Lucas was pretty sure the only reason he showed up to this job was because he was afraid of Janice—who was also his distant cousin. Plus he needed to pay the bills. But he was fairly shiftless. Certain women seemed to love him though, and Lucas couldn't understand it.

"I heard you wanted to talk to me?" Wilson looked between the two of them, shoving back a chunk of his dark blond hair.

Lincoln smiled politely and motioned for him to sit down. "I heard you got tased the other night and was just wondering why you didn't make a report or anything. I was concerned about you, wanted to make sure you're doing all right."

Lucas smothered a grin. His brother's words immediately put Wilson at ease. It wasn't the real reason they wanted to talk to him—not exactly—but now that Wilson knew he wasn't in trouble, all his guards would lower.

The man snorted and sat down next to Lucas, who slid over toward the window. "It was the craziest thing. But if I'm being honest, I'd had a few drinks. And what the hell am I going to do, make a report about some woman I didn't know? Seemed pointless. Besides, I was on the border of Bishop's Creek. Wasn't sure if I should call you or their department." He lifted an arm, slung it along the back of the booth.

Yeah, right. He'd probably been drinking and driving, so of course he hadn't wanted to call the sheriff.

"You remember what she looked like?" Lucas asked.

Wilson glanced over at him, frowning. "What do you mean?"

Lucas didn't think the question was that hard, but kept his tone neutral. "What color hair did she have? How tall was she?"

Wilson shrugged, his mouth curving up. "She was hot. Not tall, really, more compact and sexy. Ah...she had black hair and was wearing a leather skirt even though it was cold out. And she had on some kind of strapless leather top pushing up her tits. And man, she was ready to go." He lowered his voice when Trixie Davis walked in, a woman Wilson had a former relationship with.

Or maybe not so former, considering the way she smiled and waved at Wilson—who grinned right back at her.

Lincoln cleared his throat, drawing Wilson's gaze back to the table. "Yeah, so anyway, she was kind of tiny, like petite I guess is the right word," he continued. "And her hair was long. Extensions or a wig probably."

Lucas raised an eyebrow. "Seriously?"

Wilson shrugged. "I've been with enough chicks to know when a woman's hair isn't real."

*All right, then.*

"So what exactly happened?" Lincoln asked.

Another shrug. "We were going at it and then all of a sudden I can barely move. Now, I've been tased before. It's the only reason I knew what had happened when I finally woke up. A couple of my friends found me in the front seat of my truck, twitchin'." His jaw tightened, his annoyance clear. "I've never forced a woman in my life and I sure as shit don't need to. She's the one who dragged *me* out to my truck. She's the one who straddled me and started grinding up on me. So why the hell she decided to tase me, I don't know. It's not like she robbed me either. Though that could've been because my friends showed up."

"Sounds like she didn't have time to rob you," Lincoln said.

"Yeah, maybe. I mean, my friends did find me, and they said they saw the cute little thing rushing out of my truck. Bitch told them I couldn't keep it up." The first sign of real anger lit his tone. "That's some bullshit right there."

Lucas shot his brother a dry look.

"Would you recognize her if you saw her again?" Lincoln asked.

"Ah...maybe. It was dark, and like I said, I'd had a few drinks by that point."

"A few?"

"I'd polished off a six-pack—in the parking lot. I wasn't drinking and driving," he tacked on.

*Yeah, right.*

Lincoln's expression remained stoic, however. "You remember around what time it happened?"

He quickly answered, and once Lincoln got all the information and Wilson had left their table—and stopped by Trixie's to flirt—Lucas said, "So what do you think? Are you heading out to Bishop's Creek?"

"We've helped the Bishop's Creek PD before at that bar. It's a dive. Bikers like to hang out there sometimes. The woman could've been a biker looking to rob him blind."

Lucas nodded. "Maybe."

His brother pulled out his phone. "Give me a sec. I want to text Agent Lin everything he just told me." After he was done, he tucked his phone back into his pocket. "I know there aren't any cameras at the bar, but I'm still going to check the place out, see if the bartender remembers anything. You want to come?"

"Yeah." As if that was even a question. Maybe this was nothing, but maybe this woman was the same one who'd killed Ms. Rose and was stalking Serenity.

If she was, they were going to stop her. He just hoped it was in time.

\* \* \*

Amy looked at Norah Miller across the rectangular metal table in one of Sheriff Jordan's interview rooms. During her team's search of the woman's house, they hadn't found anything useful. They were currently going through her laptop but Amy wasn't sure what the hell they would find. If Norah was communicating with Black, she wasn't doing it by email. But maybe they'd find something. The woman was fairly small, with darker hair similar to Black's, but she didn't look like him. Not that Amy could see.

"Tell me about your parents," Amy said.

The woman blinked at her, clearly taken off guard. "What? How about you tell me what the hell your people are searching my house and shop for?" she snapped. Her dark hair was pulled back into a ponytail and she had her arms crossed over her chest.

Amy watched her body language. Norah wasn't under arrest and she didn't have to be here. So Amy would play this carefully because the woman was very hostile. "We're searching many houses today and you are simply part of that group." Her words were soft-spoken and she kept her arms loose at her sides, not wanting to appear confrontational. "I just want to eliminate you from our suspect list. Help me do that."

Norah shoved out a breath. "I don't even know why I'm here! Is it because I talked a little trash about Serenity? So what."

"So you don't like her?"

"I don't *not* like her," Norah said. "We both run businesses downtown. But we're not friends. Friendly enough, yes. I mean, she's all right, don't get me wrong. Not liking someone isn't a crime."

Amy flipped open a file that had absolutely nothing to do with this case and pretended to read something. Then she flipped the file shut. "I see that you guys were friends during college?"

"No. Not really. I'm not much older than her, and she and her sister were too friendly and bubbly for me." She rolled her eyes.

That was interesting. "Friendly and bubbly?"

"Perfect types, you know? Lots of friends, didn't seem to see anything wrong with anyone."

Amy kept her expression neutral. "So you're originally from here?"

"Yeah. I am." She folded her arms across her chest, all but glaring at Amy.

"Tell me about your mom."

Another blink of surprise. "What's there to tell? She's dead. You're with the FBI so obviously you know that. What the hell does she have to do with anything going on right now?"

Amy ignored the questions. "She was an alcoholic, yes?"

Her expression shuttered slightly. "Yeah. She was. And before you ask, I have no idea who my father was. Some asshole who up and disappeared. No idea if he even knew she was pregnant with me."

"Would you consent to a DNA test?" Amy asked bluntly because there was no other way around it at this point.

Norah blinked. "Huh? Are you kidding me? No I won't consent to a DNA test. I don't know what you guys are up to but this is bullshit. I don't have to stay here, do I?"

Any was quiet for a long moment, tapping her fingernail on the table. It was difficult to get a read on Miller when all the woman was putting off was anger. Maybe that was intentional. Or maybe Amy was giving the woman too much credit. Still, she had an impressive business degree, and by all accounts ran a profitable business—online sales, mostly. Amy didn't want to underestimate her. "You don't have to stay. But—"

Norah shoved the chair back. "I'm out of here. If you want to talk to me again, I'm getting a lawyer. And you better not have trashed my house!"

Sighing, Amy sat back in her chair and winced as the door slammed in the wake of Norah's exit. They were using the sheriff's department offices to question everyone. Right about now, most of her team was currently going through their suspects' downtown shops as well. So if Norah was headed that way, she would only be allowed inside in a very limited capacity.

"That could have gone better," Frank said, stepping inside.

*Yeah, no kidding.* "How'd you do?"

"Neither Bianca Copeland or Chloe Thompson would give up their DNA either."

Amy cursed. Of course they wouldn't. People didn't like to give up personal information, and definitely not DNA if they didn't have to. And Amy's team hadn't made any allies by searching these women's homes and their shops.

Her team was making these women look like potential criminals in a small town, in front of their neighbors and friends. There would be absolutely no love from any of them, not even the innocent ones, after this. *Dammit.* She shoved to her feet, stretched. "I need a coffee."

"Yeah, you and me both. I would say we could head downtown but I don't think Copeland will be serving us anytime soon."

She snorted. There was a coffee maker in the break room, and whatever shitty coffee the sheriff's department had would do for now.

Amy wasn't stopping until they had their killer. And her gut told her they were damn close. "We focus on the three women who refused their DNA, hit their online presence and cell phone history hard. Rip their lives apart."

Frank nodded in agreement. "We'll get her."

Amy hadn't failed a case yet. They'd catch whoever was behind this—her fear was that more people would die before that happened.

## CHAPTER THIRTY-ONE

Serenity knocked on Lucas's bedroom door, though it was already half open.

He glanced up from where he lounged in the bed, looking at something on his laptop. Of course he was shirtless, and she hadn't been prepared for the sight of him. Especially since it had been a couple days since they'd been intimate with each other.

She knew he'd been giving up work for her and she couldn't fight the guilt that welled up because of it. If he was getting stuff done, she wouldn't take him away from it again. Even if she wanted to spend time with him. "If you're busy, I can come back?"

He stretched his arms above his head, his arm muscles flexing. "Nah. I was just going over some reports. Real exciting stuff." He gave her a half-grin she felt all the way to her core. "Even Daisy left me, she was so bored."

Her mouth kicked up even as she resisted the urge to stare at all that bare expanse of skin she wanted to run her fingers—and mouth—all over. "Harper's asleep and Daisy is keeping watch."

He gave her a full-on sexy, mouthwatering smile now. "I'm pretty sure I lost my dog to her."

"Maybe so," she said laughingly as she stepped farther into the room, some of the tension inside her easing. Not all, because she wasn't sure where they stood with each other—and that was definitely her fault.

He moved his laptop to the nightstand and stood. "Is everything okay?"

"Yes. No. I don't know. I talked to Lincoln and he told me the Feds pulled in a bunch of their suspects today." If he hadn't told her, she'd have heard through the small-town gossip grapevine anyway because Maris had also let her know. "I don't know, it's terrifying that any of those three women could have done this. I'm not exactly friends with them, but I'm not enemies either. And none of them stick out for me during that time at school either." She and Savannah had been twins, best friends, confidants, and they'd spent most of their time together. Yes, she'd had outside friends, but at the end of the day, it had been her and Savannah. It had always been the two of them. Until it hadn't.

Lucas gently shut the door behind her and motioned for her to sit by the chaise at the window. "They're closer to finding the killer." He sat on the end of it as she pulled her legs up to her chest. "Soon your life will go back to normal. Ish."

Yeah, that was what she kept telling herself. She wouldn't believe it until Adeline was found. "I think I'm going to send Harper to school tomorrow." And she was curious about his opinion.

"I think it's a good idea. And she'll be safe. The Feds are watching those women closely and she'll have someone on her at school."

That had been Serenity's reasoning too. "Could you have ever suspected any of them?" she asked, desperately trying to wrap her mind around all of this. Bianca, Chloe and Norah. The top three women the Feds suspected right now seemed so unlikely.

"No. But people wear masks every day. You can't truly know everyone. Even if you think you do."

She knew that more than most but for some reason all of this still surprised her, made her question everything. "It's just hard to deal with, I guess. I heard that Paisley's funeral is going to be in a few days. I...don't know if I should go. I want to. But I don't want to upset her mom."

Reaching out, he took her hand in his. "I can have my mom reach out to Ms. Long, see if you're welcome."

"Thank you." She squeezed his hand back.

"Of course. Listen, Wilson Hart was tased by a woman we think might be one of the three suspects."

"What are you talking about?"

She was silent as Lucas quickly went over his morning and afternoon with Lincoln.

"It could just be a random woman," she said when he was done.

"True. But the Feds are showing him pictures of all three women, seeing if any of them look familiar."

"Hopefully." Or maybe not. She wanted this person found, but she didn't want it to be anyone she knew. Except...it *had* to be someone she knew. "I'm scared for Adeline," she whispered, finally getting the words out. It was weighing on her, day and night.

"I know. I am too." He squeezed her hands gently in his again.

She savored his strength, the comfort of his mere presence. She stared into his green eyes, trying to hold back the words, but they just tumbled out. "I keep wondering if I've done something to bring all of this on." Saying it out loud lifted something off her chest.

He frowned, his eyes flashing. "What? None of this is your fault."

"I know that in my head. I *do*. But I just keep thinking 'what if.' Over and over. Like, what if I hadn't come home? What if—"

"Stop. You can do that until you're blue in the face. Anyone can. It's like berating yourself for taking a left on a certain street and getting into a car accident. Or stopping for milk at a gas station and being there for a robbery. You can't control other people. And 'what if-ing' won't change anything. You moved home and started a business. You've given your daughter roots." He looked as if he wanted to say more but instead just tightened his jaw.

His words wrapped around her, comforting her. "If I hadn't come back, I never would have met you," she whispered, unable to keep from lifting her hand to cup his cheek. She needed to touch him.

His eyes heated when her fingers grazed his cheek, going white-hot as he pulled her into his arms. The action took her off guard even as she settled in his lap— over his growing erection. God, she'd missed him the last few days, missed having privacy.

"Stay with me tonight," he growled out. The rumble of his voice rolled through her, making her nipples tighten in anticipation.

She still wasn't sure where her head was at, but she knew she wanted him. That had never been an issue. She wanted this man more than she wanted her next breath. And she trusted him in a way she'd never trusted another man. "Lucas—"

"I don't expect more than tonight." The possessive gleam in his eyes said otherwise.

But she found herself leaning into his hold, searching out his kisses. She wanted more than one night too, even if she couldn't vocalize it. She would though, soon. For now, she simply wanted him. All of him. To be possessed by him.

He took over immediately, his mouth crushing hers in a heated expectancy for one hot second. But he slowed a fraction, his tongue tangling with her own as he explored her mouth with surprising gentleness. Every tease, every flick of his tongue felt possessive, hungry, mirroring exactly how she felt.

She might not know exactly what she wanted, but she wouldn't share him, wouldn't do casual. The thought was unthinkable. She found herself plastered against the chaise as he pinned her in place. Groaning, she wrapped her arms and legs around him, savoring every second of his mouth and body against hers.

No matter what tomorrow brought, she desperately needed this and she knew that he did too. She needed to feel good again, wanted to be completely free with Lucas.

The longer she was around him, the more she realized she could be herself. She'd admitted more to him about herself than anyone. He knew the truth about her marriage, about her past, her nightmares, everything.

She moaned into his mouth as he slid his hands up under her top, quickly getting rid of it and her bra. The man moved with incredible efficiency, something she appreciated right now because she felt as if she might come apart at the seams.

When he cupped her breasts with his callused palms, she moaned again. They were actually doing this.

She felt as if she was a ball of nerves right now; everywhere he touched set off her nerve endings. She was already wet and they'd barely started. Even though she hadn't been with anyone in years—other than the brief intimacy they'd shared days ago—this felt right. So right it scared her.

Reaching between their bodies, she shoved at his pants, needing him bare so she could feel him everywhere. She'd already seen how impressive he was, stroked him, tasted him, and now she would feel him inside her.

Thankfully he had more control than she did because he stripped off his pants without her help. Then he was wonderfully naked as he carried her to the bed. She barely got a chance to see his hard body—which she'd been fantasizing about even before the other night—then he stretched out on top of her.

She promised herself that she'd get her fill later, even as she reached between their bodies and wrapped her fingers around his hard length.

He hissed, his abdominal muscles pulling tight as he stilled on top of her.

"Not yet," he rasped out, clearly on the edge of control.

Shifting down her body, he finished undressing her, his movements jerky now. So he wasn't in control like she'd thought. Good, because she was barely hanging on.

The way he looked at her—with a mix of protectiveness and possessiveness—as he moved up her body took her breath away. He looked at her as if she was everything he wanted on Christmas morning, and then some.

She didn't deserve it, wasn't sure why he wanted her so badly. Part of her was terrified that once he got to know all of her, he'd realize that he'd just built her up in his head. And deep down she knew exactly what she wanted.

Lucas Jordan in her bed, in her life, in her daughter's life. Forever.

But she was still afraid to say it aloud. Fear and doubt bubbled up inside her, but she ruthlessly shoved them down as she reached for him, needing to touch him, hold him. For this one night she would enjoy herself, block out everything else.

He cupped her cheek as he lowered his mouth to hers, his kisses gentler this time, though his body still trembled above hers.

She could feel the energy pulsing through him but he kept his kisses shockingly soft and teasing. Arching against him, she shivered at the feel of her nipples brushing against his chest.

She wanted all of Lucas and she wanted him right now. She'd always enjoyed sex before but this was different. More. All her muscles were pulled taut in anticipation and she walked a tightrope of control. This was too much and not enough.

She wrapped her legs around him, rolling her hips against his as she clasped his hard length in her fingers. The man was utter perfection.

A groan tore from him, his big body shaking at her touch. As she enjoyed stroking him, he reached between her legs, shuddering as he slid a finger inside her.

"So wet," he growled.

She was beyond words at this point. She needed him inside her, needed release—needed to take the edge off, and she knew one time with him wouldn't be enough.

She was afraid that nothing would ever be enough, that she would want more and more of him. That she would come to depend on him.

With trembling fingers, she tightened her grip on him and guided him between her spread thighs. Not that he needed the help.

He let out another one of those sexy groans as he slid inside her, his thick length filling her up.

She sucked in a sharp breath as she adjusted to him. It had been a long damn time and she hadn't been prepared for his size. It didn't matter that she'd brought him to climax before, feeling him inside her was too much. And not enough. He kissed her again, not as gentle as before, his kisses needy and hungry, mirroring her own emotions.

He remained still inside her, clearly waiting for her to set the pace.

She didn't need slow or gentle. Biting down on his bottom lip, she rolled her hips and it was like a starter pistol at a race went off. Something set off inside him and he started thrusting in long, sensual strokes.

She met him stroke for stroke, savoring every second of him, of this. She wasn't sure how long they lost themselves in each other but when he reached between their bodies and tweaked her clit, she rushed over the edge. As her orgasm punched through her, she fell into pure bliss.

Her climax had barely started as he let go of his own control, his thrusts becoming harsher, wilder as he came inside her.

When they finally collapsed against the sheets, she knew that was just the beginning for tonight. Normally sex made her sleepy but she was revved up, hungry for more.

And by the heated look in Lucas's eyes, he felt the same.

## CHAPTER THIRTY-TWO

*S*erenity *opened her eyes and found herself back* there *again. The cabin. Everything was so vivid, so clear, but she* knew *it was a dream.*

*A nightmare.*

*Savannah sat on the board, her legs dangling off the side, her skin a grayish color as she watched Serenity. "You've got to get out of here," her sister whispered.*

*"I did get out of here," she said. "But you didn't."* Wake up, wake up, wake up.

*Savannah looked right at her with achingly familiar blue eyes and for a moment she swore her sister was real, that this was real. Maybe it was. Maybe she'd never left at all and was trapped in this nightmare forever.*

*"Don't trust her," her sister whispered.*

*"Who?"*

*"Run!"*

*Behind her, she heard the door opening up, the rain slapping the porch. Lightning flashed, illuminating the dimly lit cabin like a horror show. He was back.*

*She refused to turn around. She'd left him back in that prison cell. She had, she reminded herself.*

*She squeezed her eyes shut. "Wake up, wake up, wake up."*

Sucking in a breath, she opened her eyes. She was in bed with Lucas.

Sweet, wonderful Lucas, who was flat on his back, his hand lying on his bare stomach, looking sexy as anything. He was so peaceful, and watching him helped calm her.

Her breathing was jagged and her heart was a staccato beat in her chest, but she wasn't a sweaty mess this time. So her nightmare must've been shorter. And she clearly hadn't been loud because she hadn't woken him up.

Still, it messed with her head, seeing her sister like that. Talking to her.

She wanted nothing more than to snuggle closer to him, to lose herself in his embrace—to go another round—but when she saw that it was five in the morning, her heart rate kicked up again.

It was time to get back to her bedroom. She didn't want Harper to come looking for her and find her room empty. And she *really* didn't want Harper to find her in bed with Lucas.

She wasn't ready for that kind of conversation. Though she knew it would be coming sooner than later because things had definitely changed now. She wasn't walking away from Lucas. And unless he'd changed his mind, she knew he was as serious as she was.

Without making a sound, she shifted out from under his arm, pausing when he mumbled something in his sleep and pulled the pillow close to him.

He looked so peaceful she didn't have the heart to wake him.

Grabbing her clothes, she quickly dressed and hurried back to her own room. And she was glad she did because the second she slipped under the covers, Harper came stumbling in, her stuffed unicorn tucked under one arm.

"Mommy," she murmured, jumping into bed next to her and curling up on her side.

Serenity wrapped her arms around Harper and closed her eyes. She wouldn't be able to go back to sleep again, but she could enjoy the quiet with her daughter for now.

She just hoped this new day brought news about her missing friend. Good news.

## CHAPTER THIRTY-THREE

She hadn't slept all night, hadn't been able to. Nothing was going according to plan. She shouldn't have been called in to be interviewed. And the Feds wanted a DNA sample. Which meant... They must suspect or know that Michael Black was her father. It was the only thing that made sense. Why else would they want her DNA? She hadn't left any at her crime scenes—she'd been careful. And if they had DNA and truly suspected her, they could force her to give it. No, this was for something else.

But how? Had he told them? Would he have betrayed her? She'd started killing on her own but he shouldn't have a problem with it. Maybe he was angry at her, but he wouldn't betray his own daughter, would he?

She snorted, stopping her pacing to look at herself in the mirror. Of course he would. Everyone betrayed everyone in the end.

She hadn't been arrested, which meant they didn't have enough evidence. But could they get it? By denying them a DNA sample, she was certain she was higher up on their suspect list now.

And she had left a loose end...one she didn't want to think about. She'd been fucking Paul Covington, one of the techs who worked at the local vet's, to get access to the ketamine. He had no clue she'd been stealing, and even though she was just using him...he liked her for her. He'd never ignored her. If anything, he was smitten with her. She didn't want to kill him.

*Do it,* the voice whispered. *You can make it quick.*

"Shut up," she muttered, shelving thoughts of Paul for now. He was out of town anyway, fishing with his dad.

Maybe she just needed to split town now. She wouldn't crack if the FBI brought her in for more questioning, but she didn't want to risk being arrested. Because once she got put into the system, there was no way she would get bail. They'd lock her up and throw away the key.

"Time for a new plan," she muttered to herself. She needed to leave town. She could easily start over somewhere. She knew how to blend in. And she had enough money saved that she would be okay for a while. She'd simply change her identity and start over. But she wasn't leaving without making sure Serenity was dead.

Hurrying to her closet, she pulled down a duffel bag and started packing. She wouldn't bring enough for anyone to notice. Just a small bag of clothes and her laptop. She'd have to stop and pick up the money she'd stashed away as well.

Then she'd put her other plan into motion. The one that would bring Serenity to her. It was a risk, but she was going to take it. She had to.

She couldn't leave if Serenity was still alive. But she needed to give the Feds something before she left.

Something to distract them while she made her getaway. And she had the perfect idea.

## CHAPTER THIRTY-FOUR

Amy stepped out of the local diner, a to-go cup of coffee in hand and Frank by her side. He was on some weird health kick now and was only drinking green tea or water. *Blech. No thanks.*

They'd narrowed down which guard they thought might be passing messages from Black to someone on the outside and planned to pull them in for questioning today. And they were going to pull in the three women at the top of their suspect list again. Not to arrest them, but to put more pressure on them. Currently her team was tearing apart their personal assets, cell phone histories, anything that might be helpful.

"Just got a tip that someone saw Bianca Copeland tossing something in the dumpster of the local thrift store," Frank said, looking at his phone.

"That's on the opposite side of town from her shop." She had her own dumpster; she had no business using another place's trash disposal.

Frank handed her the keys. "You drive."

It didn't take them long to reach the thrift store. As they pulled into the back of the place, she automatically looked for security cameras. "I see one there." She nodded toward one positioned over the drop-off area.

"It's a fake."

"Dammit, I think you're right." She was so used to dealing with CCTVs and having access to a hell of a lot more security footage than was available in a small town. If it was up to her, everyone would have security cameras at work and at home. But that wasn't how small-town life worked. "Want to rock-paper-scissors who goes in the dumpster?"

Frank cast her a sideways look. "I'll do it this time. But you owe me breakfast for a week."

"Considering you're now eating like a bird, deal."

He snorted as she pulled to a stop by the unloading area. Giant metal bins were either half full or completely empty, with the actual dumpster about twenty feet from the bins.

Amy headed inside to talk to a manager or whoever was in charge, and Frank headed straight for the set of dumpsters. By the time she came back out after letting the manager know what they were doing, he'd already finished and was holding up a plastic garbage bag in his hands. Frank triumphantly pulled out a Tracfone with a gloved hand.

"It looks like you hit the jackpot." She eyed the bag, which appeared to have some heft to it.

"Five phones. And thankfully there was no food in the dumpster. Just broken kids' toys—junk mostly. This is the only thing that looks like it could be anything she would have dumped."

"Verified the camera is a fake. They don't have a problem with stealing, but sometimes teenagers like to cause trouble back here on the weekends so they installed the camera. Kids don't know it's a fake because they haven't had any trouble since the install." She pulled her cell phone out of her pocket as she spoke. "Let me see that one." After he handed it to her, she took a picture of the IMEI number and sent the image to Walker.

A second later she got a text that made her smile. "This phone is from the same batch our unsub bought." Whoever had bought the bundle of cell phones, including the one used to send a video of Adeline to Serenity, had bought them all at the same time, making it easier for them to track. And this matched one from their file. Looked like the unsub wasn't unknown anymore. "Let's bring Copeland in."

"I'm driving this time." Frank grabbed the keys from her, already heading toward the car.

"Fair enough." He'd spared her from having to go dumpster diving, something she immensely appreciated.

Her adrenaline spiked as they headed out of the parking lot. They were so close to wrapping up this case. If they got Copeland to talk, Amy just hoped she could convince her to tell them where Adeline was in time.

If she was even still alive.

\* \* \*

"Hey," Serenity said as she stepped into the huge kitchen at the Jordan estate.

"Hey yourself." Lucas's tone was friendly but his expression was unreadable.

She'd just returned from dropping Harper off at school, and while she hated having her daughter out of her sight, she knew this was for the best. Harper had a federal agent watching out for her at school, and this way she wouldn't get behind in her work.

She glanced over her shoulder to make sure Lucas's mom or one of his brothers wasn't lurking around. "I left this morning because I didn't want Harper to find us in bed together," she murmured as she stepped closer to him. If she'd had time, she'd have woken him up and taken advantage of him.

He set his coffee cup down, the tension in his shoulders easing slightly. "Do you have any regrets?"

"No." She didn't regret sleeping with him. How could she, when it had been incredible? He was as giving and wonderful as she'd imagined. She was just terrified of the feelings he evoked inside her and was afraid she wouldn't live up to what he thought of her. She knew that was her own baggage but it didn't matter—she was still scared. "How about you?"

He made a soft scoffing sound and reached for her, resting his hand possessively on one of her hips. "Not possible."

"Really?" she murmured, stepping closer, warmth spreading throughout her body. A weight she hadn't even realized had been pressing on her lifted off her shoulders. She wanted to wrap around him again, to completely lose herself with him.

She'd started to place her hand on his chest when his mom and Lincoln stepped into the room. Feeling as if she'd been caught doing something naughty—which was utterly ridiculous—she dropped her hand and turned to face them.

"You get Harper off to school?" Lincoln asked, his tone carefully neutral.

"Yep. What's up?"

"I shouldn't be telling you this, but I'm going to anyway. The Feds are looking for Bianca Copeland. They're going to arrest her."

Her breath caught in her throat. "Is she behind all this?"

"It looks that way. It also looks as if she's tried to skip town. Some of her clothes are missing and she never showed up to open her shop."

Serenity blindly reached behind herself, needing something to steady her, but Lucas was there, pulling out one of the bar stools. She collapsed onto it. "Bianca? It's so hard to believe that she could be behind this. I mean, I know we aren't close friends or anything, but..."

Mrs. Jordan hurried over to her and wrapped an arm around her shoulders, nudging Lucas away. Serenity wished he was holding her right now, that they were alone, but she couldn't very well say that. And she appreciated Louise's kindness.

"The important thing is that she will get caught," Lincoln continued. "There are a whole team of federal agents hunting her down. Soon this nightmare will be over."

Serenity tried to wrap her mind around all this, to focus. "I hope they find Adeline." She was hoping against all hope that her friend was still alive. Considering the way they'd found Paisley she thought that might be a stupid hope, but something deep inside her refused to admit that Adeline was gone. Her friend had been through enough; she didn't deserve to die so young. And if she was dead, Bianca would have dumped her too, right?

"Will you guys give us some privacy?" Lucas asked, his blunt words surprising her.

But Lincoln and their mother hurried out of the kitchen.

He pulled up a stool right next to her, his knees touching hers. "They'll get her." Pure confidence was in his tone.

She was grateful for it even as her mind rebelled at his words. He couldn't know that. "Right now I'm terrified for Adeline, wanting her found and this to be all over. I feel like I've dealt with enough crazies to last a lifetime. I just...I want Adeline home," she rasped out. She'd been keeping her rage and fear on lockdown but she wanted to lash out, to scream at the injustice of it all.

He took her hands in his. "Linc and the Feds are doing everything to find her. Listen—"

She heard his phone buzz in his pocket, and not for the first time since she'd stepped into the kitchen. But he was studiously ignoring it.

"You can answer your cell. It's work, right?" she asked, wanting to talk about anything but Bianca right now. She was a shaky mess, though she was trying to keep it locked down.

"It's fine. It's nothing." Not a denial.

She nudged him with her knee. "Come on, I know you've been putting work off to stay with me. And I know you guys are working on a big project. The Feds are going to find her. I will be absolutely fine here at your parents' house." Maybe if she said it enough, she'd believe it.

He started to shake his head.

"So if we're in a relationship, are you going to argue with me about stuff like this?"

"Well, I sure hope stuff like this doesn't come up often enough to— Wait, are you saying you want to be in a relationship? Not just friends who get naked together?" His entire body language changed as he straightened, his gaze guarded.

"I'm pretty sure you're going to regret this, but yes. I'm putting it all out there that I'm not completely sure about anything, but I know I want to be with you. Exclusively. And fair warning, I clearly have baggage. I have nightmares, I'm a single mom, and my daughter is always going to come first." Maybe she should have waited to tell him, but she knew how he felt about her— and she felt the same. Waiting would only hurt him and she couldn't do that. "I know Bianca will be caught but...if something happens, I want you to know where I stand. I want you to know where my heart is.

Eyes filled with that familiar possessiveness, he leaned forward and brushed his lips over hers. "How do you feel about more kids in the future?"

She stared at him for a long moment, surprised by the bold question. But maybe she shouldn't be. "I'm not opposed to it. But like, not next year."

"Okay, then."

"Okay, then?"

He lifted a shoulder. "I'm a pretty simple guy. It's something I wanted to know. Everything else... You're human, just like me. You have as much baggage as I do. And I have nightmares too... And if you don't want more kids I'll be disappointed, but that's okay too. I want you, Serenity. And I want to be a father figure for Harper. I know you two are a package deal and I love that kid."

Despite everything, even the pressing fear for her missing friend, something loosened inside her, solidifying that she'd made the right decision. Lucas was it for her, and she knew it on a primal level. This man had stolen her heart long ago, no matter how much she'd wanted to fight it. And with the way he was talking, he was serious about everything. Which was good, because she couldn't half-ass something with Lucas. "So we're together? Full in, you and me exclusive?"

His grin took her breath away. "Definitely exclusive, because I don't share." He leaned forward, this time kissing her harder, deeper.

She leaned into it, tightening her fingers on his shoulders, but she paused when she heard the buzzing again. She pulled back slightly, letting out a little laugh. "Just answer it. You know it's Tobias. And please go and take care of whatever it is you need to. I will be completely fine. I'm only going to be picking Harper up from school

today and the Feds will be here until they catch Bianca."
Ugh, she didn't even like saying her name now.

She could see he wanted to argue, but his phone
started buzzing again so he pulled it out of his pocket.
She went to the coffee pot and poured herself a mug as
he took the call, talking in quiet, urgent tones. Somehow
she managed not to spill any, even though she was still
shaken by the news about Bianca.

Though she only heard snippets of the conversation,
it was clear that Lucas needed to be there for this. Otherwise his cousin wouldn't have been calling him so con-
sistently. He ran a huge construction company—of
course he was needed. He had to make a lot of decisions
that affected people's jobs.

When he was done, he tucked his cell phone in his
back pocket and looked at her apologetically.

"Please don't apologize," she said before he actually
could. "You've been perfect. More than, even. Thank
you for all you've done."

He kissed her again, this time more chastely on the
forehead. "When this is all over, I'm taking you away for
a long weekend. You, me and lots of sex."

She felt her face flush at his words but she nodded.
She shouldn't even be thinking of the future, of anything
other than her missing friend, but for the first time in a
long time she could see a good future. A real one filled
with the man she…was pretty sure she loved.

She was afraid to say the L-word out loud, however.
If she did, she was terrified he'd be taken from her.

## CHAPTER THIRTY-FIVE

Serenity pushed her laptop slightly away from her and shut her eyes for a long moment. Since Lucas had left a couple hours ago she'd been catching up on various administrative things that inevitably had piled up in the last week. She was keeping her shop closed the next few days, so now was the perfect time to catch up—and keep her mind occupied instead of obsessing over how little control she had over anything. She could easily spiral if she focused on Bianca and whether or not Adeline was still alive. And she was dangerously close to it.

Years ago, after Savannah's death, she'd gone into a dark, downward spiral of depression. Having Harper, having someone be so completely dependent on her had changed everything.

Now, thinking of what Bianca had done, what she was capable of… It shook her to her core. They'd been in school together at the same time, but they hadn't been close. Still, Bianca had always been friendly enough, not outwardly hostile. Nothing to make Serenity imagine that she could be behind any of this.

Swallowing hard, she mentally shook herself. The Feds would catch her. They had to.

Her cell phone rang, breaking into her thoughts. Her heart rate kicked up to see Harper's school number on the caller ID. "Hello?"

285

"Is this Serenity Washington? Harper's mom?" The woman's voice was slightly nasal and vaguely familiar. The school had hired some new admin staff this year and she hadn't met everyone.

"Yes," she said, dread building inside her.

"There's been a little accident at school. Nothing for you to get too worried about, but Harper has broken her arm—"

"What!"

"Listen, she's all right. She's in the nurse's office and we've called an ambulance. I'm calling to let you know that you can meet us here or down at the hospital."

Everything around her funneled out as she quickly got off the phone, grabbed her purse and keys and headed for the front door.

When she reached the front door she remembered that her vehicle was blocked in by Louise's truck. *Damn it.* She called Louise's cell phone but got no answer. *Double damn it.*

She raced through the downstairs, looking for Louise, but couldn't find her or Jack anywhere. The property was too damn vast for her to go on a manhunt when she needed to get to her daughter's side. When she saw Louise's keys on the hook in the kitchen, she snagged them and tried calling her again. No answer.

She palmed the key fob and hurried to the huge driveway. She paused when she didn't see the FBI vehicle normally sitting there. Maybe Amy had taken the agent off her?

Shaking her head, she raced toward the truck, her heart beating erratically. If they'd taken the agent off the Jordan estate, then they definitely must have Bianca in custody.

Heart pounding, palms sweating, she raced down the long driveway, telling herself that everything was fine. A broken arm wasn't the end of the world, but Harper was so little. God, this never should have happened. That fierce protective instinct welled up inside her, demanding she take away her daughter's pain.

She inwardly berated herself for not asking more questions—like how the hell it had happened—but she'd been in such a panic, wanting to get to Harper as fast as possible. Instead of going to the school and potentially missing her, she was heading straight to the hospital.

As she sped down the highway, she saw a familiar car on the side of the road, hood popped up, smoke billowing out from under it.

"Shit," she muttered when she saw Chloe Thompson leaning over the hood.

Serenity almost kept going—was severely tempted to—but she pressed her foot on the brake. She couldn't help Chloe with her engine issues, but she could at least give her a ride to the hospital. And Chloe could figure things out from there. But she couldn't just leave her stranded on the side of the road with no help. Cell phones didn't always work out here.

She stopped, leaving the truck idling as she rolled down the window. "Everything okay?"

Chloe shoved up from the engine and cursed, wiping her hands on her jeans. "I have no idea what's going on. It just started smoking and then shuddered to a stop. And I can't get any damn service out here. Can I get a ride into town?"

"Sure. Hurry though, I'm on the way to the hospital. I can't take you anywhere else." The hospital was central to everything so she would be able to get to a mechanic.

"Is everything okay?" Chloe asked as she grabbed her purse from the interior of the vehicle. Petite and pretty, she had short blonde hair and reminded Serenity of Tinker Bell.

"I'm sure it will be," she said as Chloe jumped up into the passenger seat. "Just got a call from my daughter's school."

Before she could kick the truck into gear, Chloe shifted closer and suddenly a shock of energy jolted through Serenity.

Her fingers gripped the wheel as she fought the waves of pain. Her mind screamed at her to fight, but her body wouldn't listen. Suddenly Chloe shoved a cloth over her mouth and darkness swept her away.

## CHAPTER THIRTY-SIX

A my glanced over at the soft knock on the door of the interview room of the sheriff's office. Right now they were teamed up with the Sheriff's Department and using their building to work together. She'd pulled in Copeland's ex-boyfriend and some of the woman's neighbors to talk to.

She was going to find this woman no matter what. Copeland had packed a small bag with clothing and her laptop. And her car was missing. "Excuse me," Amy murmured to the man across the table as she stood. Her people wouldn't interrupt her without good cause.

Pushing down her annoyance, she stepped out into the hallway of the sheriff's station. "What is it?" she asked Shelley Reburn, one of her best tech people. As Reburn spoke, Amy glanced down the hallway where Alec Wafford was talking to Lincoln. She frowned to see Wafford here. He was supposed to be watching the Jordan estate. "Wafford, in there," she said pointing to the room she was using before she turned back to Reburn.

"Warden Brumley is on the line," Reburn said, holding out a cell phone in her perfectly manicured hand. "He's got intel."

"What have you got?" she demanded into the phone. There was no time for niceties.

"I found out which of my guards has been sending messages from Black. He saw the news about the missing woman and others who have died. Guilt has been eating away at him. I'm going to preface this by saying that he kept all the messages he passed along for Black. I've looked at them and none of them were about committing crimes or anything like that. They were all very benign, like a father talking to a daughter."

Amy didn't give a shit. "I want his name."

"I'll give you his name. But I have something better. You don't need to interview him. He told me how he used to leave messages for Black—who had the settlor from his trust pay my guard in cash. The withdrawals can't be linked to Black or my guy."

That explained why her people hadn't been able to find a payoff trail. *Come on, come on.* Amy didn't care about any of that. She wanted something tangible, something she could work with.

Before she could interrupt Brumley again, he said, "After my guy left the messages at their designated spot, a couple times he stuck around to see who picked them up. It's a woman. And one time he got a picture. I'm texting you the image but also emailing you, so you can blow it up or do whatever it is you need to enhance it. It's in your inbox right now. It's pretty clear as it is, but now you've got it."

"Thanks. I'll be in touch once I've wrapped up this case. Your guy isn't walking away without repercussions." And she was going to have a talk with the settlor of Black's estate. Without waiting for him to respond, she hung up. She'd find out who the guard was later and there would be consequences. But for now, the only thing that mattered was clarifying that Bianca was the one in the picture. Amy wanted an airtight case to bring this woman down—and she desperately wanted to find Adeline.

She stepped into the small meeting room where her laptop was set up. Wafford was on his cell phone but he started wrapping up his call as she pulled up her email.

"What's up?" he asked, tucking his cell away.

"Why aren't you watching the Jordan estate? You're supposed to be monitoring Serenity, so she'd better be with you." Her people were good so she expected nothing less, but she needed to confirm regardless. They were so damn close to wrapping this case up and there was no room for error.

"Wait…what are you talking about? I got a text from Frank, calling me in. Said you needed me here."

Lead congealed in her gut. "No, he didn't. Get everyone in here now," she snapped as she pulled up her email account. She clicked on the link from the warden and pulled up the attachment.

As everyone piled into the room, she turned her computer around to reveal a picture of Chloe Thompson, a petite, vulnerable-looking woman. "We're not looking for Bianca. Or if we are, she might be a victim. We need eyes on Serenity ASAP and we're going to bring in Chloe Thompson."

Ben Walker hurried in, his phone up to his ear, catching the tail end of everything. Before she could ask him what the holdup was, he shoved his phone into his pocket. "Just got off the phone with Paul Covington." One of the vet techs they'd been trying to hunt down. "He's been off fishing with his dad and didn't have phone service on the lake—anyway," Walker nodded at the image on screen, "he said he's been sleeping with Chloe Thompson on the sly, lets her come down to the office after hours. He seems to think this is a big mistake, that she couldn't possibly be behind any of it."

Yeah, this was no mistake. "Good work."

Amy had started barking out orders, sending everyone to their duties, when one of Sheriff Jordan's guys hurried in and signaled for Lincoln's attention.

Lincoln held his phone away from his ear as his deputy said, "Your mother's truck was found abandoned on the side of the road. I recognized it because of the sticker on the back. I got a hold of her and she's fine. But Serenity isn't at the house. She's gone, and it appears to be her cell phone and purse that are in the truck. I checked the ID from her wallet."

Amy held back a curse. She refused to let Serenity die. That woman had been through too much.

"Everyone listen up!" she shouted to her assembled team. "Sheriff, I want you to send out a media alert to the local news with Thompson's picture. I want her image plastered everywhere in a hundred-mile radius. She's not getting away."

It was a gamble, blasting her picture out for everyone to see—it could preempt her plan, leading her to kill any potential victims and run—but it was also the only way the public could potentially help them. Chloe was wilier than she'd thought, but given her degree in computer information systems, some of the things she'd done made sense. She must have cloned the FBI's phones to be able to text Agent Wafford. And that wasn't easy to do. *Fuuuuck.* She must have done it when she'd been called in for an interview. Either that or she'd spoofed their phone numbers—which was a lot easier than cloning if you knew what you were doing. Fuck, fuck, fuck. That was likely what she'd done.

Amy would berate herself later for not seeing through Thompson—who hadn't raised any red flags during her interview. Maybe she was a sociopath like her father. They had to find her immediately—and find Serenity and Adeline. Though Amy didn't have much hope for Adeline at this point.

She just prayed Serenity was still alive.

## CHAPTER THIRTY-SEVEN

Serenity opened her eyes and dragged in a painful breath. An ache spread through her ribs as a chill skittered over her bare arms. Where was her coat— Wait, where was she? She frowned at the wooden slats of the ceiling above her. None of this looked right.

"She kicked you in the ribs," a familiar voice rasped out.

Serenity blinked, banishing the cobwebs from her mind as it all came rushing back. Chloe had tased her and then shoved something over her mouth. She rolled over slightly, and realized her wrists were shackled and the chain was attached to a wall. *Oh no. No, no, no!* She rolled over to face Bianca—who was also chained up on the wall a few feet away. Bile welled up but she swallowed it down.

Sweat trickled down her spine despite the freezing room. "How'd Chloe get you?" Her throat was scratchy as she spoke, her heartbeat rushing in her ears as she tried to come to grips with this reality.

"I was taking the trash out this morning at work. I hadn't even opened the shop yet. I was prepping for the day and she jumped me. Never saw her coming."

Serenity's eyes widened as she spotted a still figure across the room. *Adeline!*

"Adeline." She slightly raised her voice but not too loud in case Chloe was nearby outside.

There was slight movement but her friend didn't raise her head, didn't say anything. Serenity recognized her dark hair and clothing, even in the dim room. She fought the fear swelling through her as she took in their surroundings. They were in a small, one-room cabin shaped like a shotgun-style house. It looked like one of the FEMA trailers she'd seen pop up after the last hurricane. Two windows were covered over with dark blue sheets, but a little light filtered in through the tears in the material.

"Where is she?" Serenity asked, looking at Bianca again. No need to clarify who.

"I don't know. She dumped you here, kicked you, then stomped off, muttering to herself. She's batshit crazy."

*Yeah, no kidding.* "We have to get out of here." Obviously. Serenity yanked on her chains, seeing if there was any give. She had a little slack but the shackles on her wrist held firm.

"They're solid." Tears streamed down Bianca's cheeks as she tugged on her own chains. They rattled against the floor, clanking together.

"Not that it matters, but did she say anything else? Is anyone helping her?" Serenity tested her chains again, tugging to see if she could squeeze her wrists out of the shackles. Tears sprung to her eyes as she yanked hard.

"A little. She's really proud of herself." Bitterness laced Bianca's voice as she did the same, yanking again. "She

apparently called in a tip to the Feds to tell them someone saw me dumping a bunch of burner cell phones she'd
been using."

Wow. So Chloe had really thought all this through.
Which was terrifying. Serenity thought of her daughter,
of Lucas. She did not want to die. She didn't want her
daughter to grow up without both parents—and she really wanted a future with Lucas. *Think, think, think.* They
had to get out of here. Could Chloe really be Michael
Black's daughter? Had he instructed her to do this?

Serenity shook her head. Right now that didn't matter. They had to get free—she would see her daughter
again. She had to. Tears rolled down her cheeks now as
she yanked down harder this time. The shackles were
too tight, nearly cutting off her circulation. There had to
be another way to get free— If she could break the chain
off the wall maybe—

They both jumped at the sound of a car door shutting.
A moment later the door flew open, slamming against
the interior wall.

Chloe stood in the doorway, a small red canister in
her hand. The wind picked up behind her, making a
howling sound. Her eyes were wide and manic as she
looked right at Serenity. "You're finally awake," she practically sang. Stepping inside, she slammed the door shut
with her foot. "I should have done this a long time ago.
You took everything from me when you took my father!"

Serenity stared at her in horror. It was true, then.
"Black is your father?"

Chloe sneered, taking a step forward, her sneakers squeaking against the old, rotting wood. "That's right. And I helped him all those years ago, you stupid bitch. You were supposed to die, just like your sister. We were going to keep going but you ruined everything!" She picked up the canister and started dumping the contents on the floor. "Stupid, stupid bitch. You'll pay," she muttered, more to herself now than them. "You should have stayed away from here."

Holy hell, was this really the woman she'd gone to quilting classes with? The woman whose technology repair shop she'd used on multiple occasions. A woman she'd been alone with in her own grooming store. Serenity was frozen as she looked at the splotchy red face of this...stranger. She'd actually helped her father take other women? It was unfathomable.

She stared as Chloe splashed the liquid on the walls, confused for all of a second until the scent of kerosene blasted her senses.

*Oh, God.* She was going to set the place on fire with them in it.

"That's right," Chloe said, stepping farther into the room. "You should be afraid," she snapped, clearly reading the fear on Serenity's face.

Her heart rate tripled as Chloe stomped around the room, splashing accelerant everywhere. When she got closer to Serenity and Bianca, Serenity lashed out with her foot, trying to knock her down. If she could just get close enough, she'd attack with her damn feet. If she could knock her down she would. But she barely grazed Chloe's ankle.

Startled, Chloe jumped back, her eyes narrowing as she moved around them, giving them a wide berth. "I wanted more time with you, but my time here has come to an end. And so has yours. Your pretty face is going to melt right off." Venom dripped from every single word as she gave Serenity a Cheshire cat smile.

Fear slid down her spine, ice cold. "It's not too late to let us go. At least let Bianca and Adeline free. They're not part of this." Serenity knew her pleading was pointless, but she had to try. She didn't want to die, especially not like this. She wanted to see Harper grow up, get married, have kids of her own. She wanted to see her little girl happy. Safe. She wanted a future with Lucas.

Oh God, she wanted forever with Lucas. She wanted to marry that man. And she'd been a fool to push him away. She should have embraced him with everything she had. Not been keeping him at arm's length, keeping up stupid walls that hadn't saved her from anything. Because here she was, about to be burned alive by a crazy woman.

"Everything came so easy to you and your stupid sister. You pretended to be my friend in college, but I know how you really feel about me," Chloe snarled.

Serenity had no idea what she was talking about. They'd been friendly, and had occasionally hung out in the same circles, but she'd never thought anything mean about the woman in front of her. Not until now.

"Then you came home and you stole Lucas, had the whole town fooled by your sad martyr act." Her face was mottled with rage. "You should have stayed away!"

"Did your father tell you to come after me?" As long as she kept Chloe talking, she wasn't setting them on fire. It was the only way she could stall. Serenity was desperate and fairly sure that no one was coming for them, but she couldn't give up hope. She would keep Chloe talking as long as she could. Maybe, just maybe the Feds had figured things out.

Chloe made a scoffing sound as she stepped back toward the door, canister in hand. "Of course not. He wanted me to live a normal life. What he didn't tell me was that it was boring. He let me help him before, but he wouldn't let me take part in his kills. If I'd known how good it felt, I would've been doing this a long time ago. I would've killed *you* years ago."

Serenity couldn't tear her gaze away from this woman—this monster. "Why Mrs. Rose? Why Paisley?"

"Because I can!" she screamed. She wrenched open the door behind her, leaving a trail of fuel out the door and down the steps. "I really, really wish I'd had longer with you." Smiling widely, she dropped the can and lifted a Bic lighter.

Serenity stared in horror as the kerosene can exploded and flames shot up the steps and into the cabin. The fire spread in a circle, following the line of fuel, dancing up the walls in a sweep of motion.

*No, no, no.* Heat blasted them in the face. She cringed away from the ravenous flames.

"We've got to get free!" Bianca screamed, tugging on the chains, the rattling sounding in time with Chloe's maniacal laughter as she ran toward her waiting vehicle.

*Think, think.* Sweat poured down Serenity's face and neck as she tried to stand. The chains were short, giving her limited movement. She knew they couldn't break the chains or shackles but maybe they could smash through the old wood. These old FEMA trailers weren't made to last forever and they were never put on concrete slabs. They were raised off the ground.

"Kick at the wall," she said to Bianca who was wildly pulling on her chains. "Try to dislodge the metal base."

Adeline hadn't moved, too weak to do anything. She hadn't even turned over, opened her eyes. Her body was so still. Oh God, was she already dead?

As Bianca started kicking and punching at the plaster, Serenity slid the chain under her sneaker and started slamming her feet against the flooring. When she heard a crack, she worked harder, combating the smoke and fire filling the cabin. Even as she coughed, she kept slamming down.

All around them, flames licked up the walls, the heat and smoke nearly unbearable.

*God, Lucas!* She prayed against all hope that he would find her. Even in her state of fear she knew it wasn't likely but she still called out for him even as she slammed her feet against the floor again.

When the wood made a cracking, crumbling sound, hope launched inside her chest.

## CHAPTER THIRTY-EIGHT

*Twenty minutes earlier*

Lincoln stood with his men and women along with Special Agent Lin and her people as she barked out orders to all of them. Her people had two possible locations they thought Serenity and Adeline—and probably Bianca—were being held, and they were all ready to roll out.

Tension hummed through him as he checked his weapons and gear. He was trying to keep his head in this, to stay focused. It was a hell of a lot harder to be detached when you knew the people who were involved. And he could admit that he was scared for Serenity, for all of them. The thought of Harper growing up without her mom... Hell. His head snapped up when the door to the meeting room flew open and his brother stormed in.

The room grew quiet as Agent Lin stopped talking and turned to Lucas, her expression softening only a fraction when she saw him. "You need to leave," she told him quietly.

"Serenity is missing?" Ignoring her, he stared at Lincoln.

Swearing under his breath, Lincoln stepped forward. "I've got this."

She nodded and turned back to her people and his.

303

"You're not going to handle me," Lucas snapped as Lincoln steered him out of the room, gripping his upper arm tightly.

His administrative assistant stood there, wringing her hands. "I told him he couldn't go back there."

"It's fine," he said, marching his brother down to his own office.

"Mom told me that her truck was left abandoned on the side of the road and that Serenity is gone. What the fuck is going on?" Lucas was vibrating with anger as Lincoln shut the door behind them.

"We know who took her." Before his brother could say another word, he held up a hand. "Chloe Thompson is behind everything. We know beyond a shadow of a doubt. We're also concerned that Bianca Copeland might've been taken by her too. Unless they're working together, but we don't think so. Agent Lin's team found a lead on two properties connected to Chloe that they missed before. The information was buried deep. And over the last year Chloe's cell phone movements show it pinging off an area in the grid where the Feds have picked up a satellite image of an old FEMA trailer. We're heading out now to search it, so I don't have any time to sit here and discuss this."

"Where?" Lucas demanded.

"Lucas—"

His brother shoved him against the wall, grasping his shoulder as he got in his face. Lincoln didn't react only because of the raw fear on his older brother's face. "I'm going with you. I'll follow you if you don't take me, so either arrest me or I'm in."

Lincoln shoved Lucas's hands off him, then pushed his keys at his brother. "Go wait in my truck. There's an extra tactical vest in there—put it on."

"If you leave me behind, I will never forgive you."

Yeah, he knew that. There might be consequences for bringing Lucas, but Lincoln would deal with them. He couldn't leave his brother behind. He adored Serenity and was afraid for her right now too. No way he'd keep his brother back from helping. "Go."

Without waiting, he jogged down the hallway to the conference room to find everyone spilling out. It was time to get out of here.

Agent Lin stepped out last wearing a tactical vest over her long-sleeved thermal shirt. "You ready?"

He knocked his own vest once. "Yep. And Lucas is coming with me." She started to argue but he shook his head. "He's got a closet full of medals from all of his military experience and he's got more training than most of my guys. There's no way in hell I can keep him from following me. So either arrest him, or he's coming with me."

"He stays in the truck," she snapped out.

There was nothing more to say at this point so he turned and started jogging down the hallway. The sheriff's department might not have the resources the Feds did, but he had a hell of a lot of training and experience with taking down terrorists. So did Lucas.

He just prayed that they were in time. If anything happened to Serenity, he wasn't sure his brother would survive it.

* * *

Lucas gripped the side handle of his brother's truck, biting back the urge to bark at him to drive faster. Lincoln was already going thirty miles over the speed limit, tearing down the two-lane highway. His blue lights were flashing but he'd kept his siren off. It didn't matter because the few cars on the road moved out of the way when they saw him coming.

He couldn't believe Chloe Thompson was behind this. That she was Black's daughter. That she'd been hiding in plain sight this entire time. He would've believed Bianca or Norah had been behind this before the petite, soft-spoken tech shop owner. She seemed so nonthreatening and quiet.

As they drove, he was grateful that his brother didn't offer him platitudes by telling him things would be okay. Shit went sideways every single day and Serenity was in true danger. The woman he loved was being held by a monster.

He bit down hard, forcing himself to stay under control. He was trained, and losing focus wouldn't do anyone any good. "Smoke," he said as they neared the turnoff, stating the obvious because Linc could see it too, wafting up past the trees.

On the outskirts of town, the area hadn't been in the grid search. It was too thick with trees and swamp, and they'd thought it had been owned by a group who leased it out during hunting season.

Lucas's adrenaline spiked as Lincoln took a sharp turn at the dirt road turnoff. Dust flew up behind them as Lincoln stepped on the gas. Without looking, he knew the SUV of Feds was right behind them.

As they flew into a small clearing, Lucas already had his fingers wrapped around the door handle. Smoke and flames billowed out from a pale pink FEMA trailer. His whole chest was tight, fear blasting through him. Screw staying in the truck. If Serenity was in there, he was getting her out. Or he'd die trying.

He grabbed Lincoln's half-empty bottled water and poured it over the front of his sweater, then over his head and face. He would need help breathing.

"Lucas—"

"I'm going inside." And there was no point in arguing with him about it, something his brother must have realized because Lincoln didn't say anything more.

It registered that recent tire tracks had left a deep impression in the dried mud, but all of Lucas's focus was on that house. On getting to Serenity.

As Lincoln jerked to a halt in front of the burning trailer, Lucas jumped out and raced up the rotting stairs. The door was open, smoke billowing out in waves.

"Serenity!" he shouted before he tugged his sweater up over his face. His eyes burned as he moved through the entrance, though he couldn't see much. Heat blasted him but his brother was right next to him, small fire extinguisher in hand.

As Lincoln started spraying around them, Lucas called out again. "Serenity!"

He heard a muffled sound from...somewhere. Crouching down, he started crawling, feeling around as smoke and the white foam from the extinguisher filled the air. His throat was too raw from the smoke and heat, even breathing through his wet sweater, to call out again.

His heart rate kicked up as he wrapped his fingers around a chain secured to the wall. With his hands, he followed it to a big hole in the smashed flooring. *What the hell?*

Coughing, he pulled his phone out and used the flashlight. Holding it down in the hole, his heart nearly stopped.

Two bodies were connected to chains. *Oh, God.* Serenity and Bianca.

"I found them!" He ended up coughing it out as he jumped down into the hole and crawled toward Serenity. *Please be alive, please be alive...*

*Yes!* Her eyes were closed but her chest was rising and falling. Bruises covered her knuckles and hands and her wrists were still shackled. Bile rose in his throat. He had to get her out of here. Had to get both of them free.

He turned to Bianca. Bits of her pants had been burned off and her wrists were both shackled but the chain was free from the wall, dragging behind her. And she was breathing too.

The sound of the wood cracking above them and his brother spraying the fire extinguisher filled the air as he popped his head back up through the hole. "Serenity and Bianca are down here!" he shouted, testing Serenity's pulse. Too thready. *No.* "We're in the crawl space! Need help!"

"On it!" Agent Lin's voice carried through the smoke.

"Ambulance is on the way," his brother followed, coughing as he jumped into the hole with him, getting on all fours. "And they've got Adeline out."

*Oh shit.* He hadn't even seen her. "Serenity's chain is bolted to the wall." He lifted it to show Lincoln, who had a handkerchief tied around his face.

"I've got it." Lincoln grabbed the chain and followed it back through the hole.

Parts of the floor had started to fall through, the heat creating a hot box around them, so he covered Serenity's body with his own. Even though she was unconscious, he cupped her face in his hands. "I'm going to get you out of here. I won't let you die. I love you, Serenity!" Damn it, he just wanted her to wake up. To look at him with those beautiful blue eyes and tell him that she was fine.

As he kept his body over Serenity's, he reached out and checked Bianca's pulse again. Strong enough.

*Come on, come on.* What was taking so long?

*Pop.* He felt the chain slacken as it broke free. They would get the shackles off them later but for now he would drag them to safety.

Lincoln dove back into the hole just as someone started punching through the wooden lattice base a few feet away.

Lucas crawled toward the edge of the crawl space and kicked at the lattice as well. It splintered, opening up a hole. "We're over here," he called out to whoever the hell was out there.

Lucas hooked his hand under Serenity's armpit and dragged her with him as quickly as possible in the small space, trying to get her toward the Federal agent ripping the lattice free.

"Take her," he ordered, pushing her out in front of him. He allowed himself a fraction of relief as her feet disappeared through the hole, then turned back and took Bianca from Lincoln. Another Fed was there, pulling her out.

Cool air blasted him as he and Lincoln finally crawled out.

"They're both breathing, some burn wounds, nothing serious. But they need oxygen," one of the agents said as he crouched down next to Serenity.

Lucas knew the women also might have internal injuries. For now, getting them away from the fire and smoke was the most important thing. At a creaking sound, he heard a whoosh and glanced back just as one of the walls caved in.

Lifting up Serenity as gently as possible, he stood with her, his heart racing. "Gotta move them." One of the agents had lifted up Bianca before Lincoln could.

"Lucas," Serenity rasped out as they raced around to the front of the house. He knew his brother had a first aid kit in his truck and he wanted to start tending to her wounds.

He looked down at her pale face, rage simmering under the surface as he thought about how close he'd come to losing her. "You're okay, you're okay." He bit down, because he was saying it for himself.

"Chloe," she rasped out. "She did this."

"We know. Save your energy. There's an ambulance on the way." He wanted that monster caught and punished.

He moved to Lincoln's truck and eased open the passenger side as she started crying. Ignoring the frantic movement of the federal agents and deputy sheriffs around them, she buried her face against his chest as he settled her into the seat. As he wrapped his arms around her, holding her close, he heard the sirens in the distance and allowed another fraction of relief to slide through him.

Rubbing a hand up and down her spine, he made soothing sounds. "You're okay and so are Adeline and Bianca. We'll get these chains off you soon."

She'd be dealing with this for a while, but she was going to be okay.

She was strong.

Even though he needed to tend to her wounds, he gently wrapped his arms around her and held her close for a long moment. He shuddered as she tightened her grip and he closed his eyes.

"You came for me," she whispered.

His throat was so tight he could barely answer as he held her to his heart. "Always."

## CHAPTER THIRTY-NINE

Serenity opened the hospital door and peeked inside to see Adeline sitting up in bed, flowers and other gifts surrounding her, and a green Jell-O cup in her hand.

Her friend's eyes widened even as she smiled, putting the cup down on the table. "Hey! The doc said you'd been hounding him to come see me. Glad you finally got the okay."

Wearing hospital scrubs herself instead of one of those awful gowns, she stepped farther inside, holding the door propped open.

"I'll wait out here," Lucas murmured, leaning against the outside wall. "Spend time with your friend. I'll say hey once you guys are done."

"Thank you." He hadn't left her side in the twelve-plus hours since she'd been admitted to the hospital with Bianca and Adeline. And the Feds had put someone on all of their doors so they weren't left unguarded.

"He can come in," Adeline said, even as the door shut behind her.

"I'm going to be selfish and spend some time alone with you first." She hurried across the room and pulled her friend into a gentle hug. Tears sprang up as she held Adeline tight.

"I'm so glad to be alive," Adeline rasped out, her own cheeks wet with tears as Serenity pulled back.

"Me too. You look good," Serenity said. Adeline's left arm had a light bandage where she'd been slightly burned. She'd also suffered some smoke inhalation, they were monitoring her for kidney damage, and they had her on an IV of fluids because she'd been so dehydrated.

"I feel good, considering," Adeline said as Serenity grabbed a chair and pulled it close to the bed. The blinds were up, letting the morning light in. "I'm just pissed they haven't found that bitch yet."

"Yeah, me too." She wanted Chloe behind bars forever. Just like her father.

"How are you doing?" Adeline asked, motioning to Serenity's hands.

Her knuckles had little steri-strips on them and her right calf was bandaged up where she'd suffered shallow burns. They'd also put her on antibiotics to stave off any infection, but otherwise she was good—and grateful for it. "Fine, seriously. This is all very superficial. My hands are sore but I'll heal. So what have you heard so far?" Serenity wanted to make sure that Adeline was up to date on everything. She'd been getting updates from Lincoln, who was in contact with the Feds—who had initiated a manhunt for Chloe. Serenity had already been by to see Bianca and had filled her in on everything too.

"Just that she's on the run and that there's an agent keeping watch on my room."

"According to Lincoln, she ditched her vehicle not long after setting the trailer on fire. Well, her neighbor's vehicle, not hers. Anyway, they followed her tracks to another hiding spot where they're certain she got into another vehicle. Looks as if she had this all planned out."

"Jesus, what a psycho."

"No kidding." She was even worse that Black. Chloe had insinuated herself into her victims' lives, had gone after her friends.

"The first day she bragged to me about how smart she was, how she was going to enjoy taunting you." Adeline shuddered, wrapping her arms around herself. Her dark hair was pulled back by a headband, her curls wild and clean again. "Mainly she just liked to watch me and talk about how smart she was." She snorted derisively, then winced slightly.

Serenity jumped up. "Do you need something?"

"No, no, I promise. I have cracked ribs—because she also liked to kick me. Not much anyone can do about that."

She sat back down, guilt eating away at her. "I'm so sorry that—"

Adeline cut her off with a hard look. "You better not be apologizing for any of this. Chloe Thompson is guilty of this. Her alone. Not you, not anyone else. I don't care if she had daddy issues or mommy issues or whatever. She killed people and she was going to kill us. That's not on you."

Serenity blinked. "Well then. You are...very wise."

Adeline's mouth kicked up. "I know. So how's Harper dealing with all this?"

"She's great. She doesn't really know what happened. I'm sure she'll hear things at school but I've downplayed everything. Right now she's with Lucas's mom and dad and they're spoiling the heck out of her. She's safe and happy." Which was all Serenity wanted. Still, she wouldn't rest easy again until Chloe was caught.

"Thank God. I...I still can't believe any of this happened. How did she fool everyone?"

She'd been wondering that too. Going over every interaction with Chloe that she could remember. There had been no signs. "I honestly don't know. I've got little bits and pieces from the Feds. She's really smart apparently, at least when it comes to technology. She spoofed Harper's school's phone number to make me think Harper had been hurt." Serenity fought a chill as she kept talking. "They think she was able to sneak around town because she hadn't been using her own car and that was what the Feds had been keeping an eye on. They're still trying to piece together some things, but she'd been planning at least some of this for a while. She...she had all of the jewelry that Black had taken from his victims. Not in her house, but in her neighbor's. She either left it behind because she didn't care, or didn't have time to come back and get it."

Adeline shut her eyes for a long moment before looking at Serenity again. "They'll get her. Now that they know who she is."

She wouldn't be able to rest easy until that happened. "That's what I keep telling myself. Supposedly someone spotted her up in Georgia a few hours ago so…" She lifted a shoulder. "I'm going to be vigilant until they do."

"You and me both." Adeline yawned, her eyes drooping slightly. "Hey, how'd you get scrubs instead of this?" She picked at her white and blue gown.

"I simply asked." Serenity grinned as she stood. "Go ahead and eat your breakfast. I know you probably want to get some more sleep."

"I'm fine," Adeline said, even as she yawned again.

"Uh huh. I'll be hanging around for a while. They're releasing me soon, so I'll come check on you again in a little bit."

"Okay. I am kinda tired." She gave a grateful smile and Serenity hugged her again, tighter this time.

As she stepped outside the hospital room, Lucas was still standing there like a sentry. Some of her tension lifted to see him standing guard. The man was a force of nature, risking his life by running into that fire to save her.

He pushed up from the wall immediately. "Hey, everything okay?"

"Yeah, she's doing good. Tired but good." Serenity nodded politely at the Federal agent who was standing across the hall, keeping watch.

She linked her hand through Lucas's as they headed back down the hallway. She and Adeline were on the same floor and only five doors separated them.

Her slippers were silent against the floor as she laid her head on his shoulder. Being with him grounded her, made her feel steady in an unsteady world. "I feel better after talking to her, seeing her. She's going to be fine."

"So are you." He kissed the top of her head.

Warmth spread through Serenity at the chaste kiss. She loved this man so much and was so damn grateful for how much he'd stepped up, how he'd been by her side this entire time.

"I got a call from Lincoln when you were in with her," he said as they neared her room's door. "There was a spotting of Chloe up in South Carolina, so she's going north at least."

"Hopefully she'll be too busy trying to stay alive to worry about killing more people." Serenity shuddered. The woman had been smart enough to cover that she was the true owner of various properties, and the Feds had found records of fake IDs she'd made—so they were running those in all databases right now. But who knew what else she'd done to facilitate her escape? The only thing they thought they knew was that Black hadn't been behind any of this. He'd been in contact with Chloe, yes, but he hadn't been urging her to kill. Or at least he didn't appear to be, given the notes the guard had read. Nothing was certain though.

Not that it would have mattered. Chloe was guilty as hell, and as soon as she was captured she'd be locked up forever.

Serenity wasn't going to try to figure out the whys of it all. Because some people were just born bad. And she sure wasn't going to feel sorry for Chloe, who by all accounts had been raised in a decent home by her maternal grandparents. And at the end of the day, the bitch had helped murder Savannah. Serenity would never forgive that.

As they reached her room, a loud siren went off, piercing the hallway. She tensed even as the Federal agent pulled his phone out and began quickly talking into it.

"Go in your room, now!" he ordered. "One of the hospital guards has been found bleeding out."

"Is it her?" she demanded, fighting a fresh wave of terror.

"We don't know. Inside, don't open the door."

"I'm armed," Lucas reminded the agent. The Feds had approved it earlier.

The man nodded and looked down the hallway, motioning to the other guard. "Stay put inside. One of us is going to be watching both your rooms."

She wanted to ask more questions but Lucas ushered her inside, shutting the door behind them. The siren continued, but was slightly quieter in the room. It didn't do anything to stop the jagged streaks of terror slashing through her. "Why the hell would she come back? It's got to be something else." Though Chloe was freaking unbalanced so maybe that was reason enough for her to return.

Holding up a finger, Lucas drew his weapon and pointed to the bathroom door, indicating he was going to do a sweep.

Heart in her throat, she leaned against the wall for support as he stepped back out of the bathroom and ducked behind the curtain, likely checking under the bed. She shuddered, thinking about a monster like Chloe hiding under the bed. She couldn't see how anyone could have gotten past the agent who'd been keeping guard, but she was glad he was being vigilant.

Pulling her phone out, she planned to call Louise to check on Harper and ease her mind. Before she could dial, the hospital room door opened and a nurse in the standard pale green scrubs walked in. A name badge hung around her neck and a waterfall of her platinum blonde bob hung down over her face as she read something on her chart. It was time to be released—though she was sure she wouldn't be leaving the room any time soon. Not until whatever was going on was settled.

She frowned when the woman looked up, revealing her face. She gasped, then froze as Chloe whipped up a gun, pointing it right at her.

Chloe stood before her, looking nothing like the picture the Feds had blasted out to the news. The wig covered her ears, her bangs fell over her eyebrows and she had on big round glasses. And she must have on some kind of padding because she looked about thirty pounds heavier than before.

"Chloe," she rasped out, hoping she didn't know Lucas was in here.

Raw shock stole through her. What the hell was she doing here? She'd escaped—she could have gotten away. She really was out of her mind.

As if she read Serenity's mind, Chloe stepped forward, gun in hand, the bitterness in her eyes clear. "I'm not going to live in a world where you're alive," she hissed.

"You could have gotten away." Numbness stole through Serenity as she focused on Chloe's face, forcing herself not to stare at the gun. Lucas was behind the curtain, behind her. There was no way for him to sneak up on Chloe but if she could distract her or knock her off-balance or...something. She was going to.

"I'm not going to run for the rest of my life," Chloe said. She took another step forward, dropping the chart to the ground. Barely two feet separated them now. She could pull the trigger and that would be it. "And I'm killing you before they take me down." Chloe's hand wavered slightly as she glanced around the quiet room.

Serenity knew she might never get another chance. And she wasn't going down without a fight. She rushed forward the few feet separating them, glimpsed the shock in Chloe's eyes as she ducked low, ramming into the woman's middle.

She heard a faint sound behind her, knew it was Lucas making his move, but she slammed Chloe to the ground.

Pain exploded in the side of her head as Chloe bashed the gun against her skull. She fell back just as a wild shot went off.

Plaster rained down on them from the ceiling tiles. Rolling to her knees, Serenity saw a blur of movement as Lucas kicked the gun out of Chloe's hand.

"Don't move!" he shouted, holding his own gun on Chloe with precision.

Chloe twisted underneath him, kicking at his ankles, her face contorted with frustration and fury. He stumbled slightly and she pulled out a knife.

Serenity didn't think, she reacted. "No!" She dove for Chloe, grabbing the woman's wrist and twisting hard as she tried to pin it to the floor.

Everything seemed to happen in slow motion as they rolled on top of each other, Chloe wrenching her arm free.

Serenity grabbed the knife wrist again, slamming it down—into Chloe's chest.

Chloe's eyes widened in shock and pain, her fake glasses fallen beside her. Serenity stared as blood spread across the front of Chloe's stolen scrubs. She was vaguely aware of Lucas lifting her off the ground and moving her out of the way.

Her feet felt rooted to the spot as she continued to stare but Lucas kicked the gun out of Chloe's reach and hurried her out of the room, taking her with him.

"We need to—" She was cut off as two armed Federal agents raced past them.

Lucas simply pulled Serenity close to him and hurried down the hallway as more law enforcement rushed by.

"I wish you'd let me shoot her," he bit out, pulling her close as they stopped a few doors down.

"I didn't think, I just reacted." Lucas hadn't been in real danger. He could have just shot Chloe. But Serenity had seen that knife and something primal had snapped inside her. She'd needed to stop her. To fight back. To end this.

"I can say I stabbed her," he murmured, holding her close. "For the official report."

She stared up at him in shock. "No. No way. I want only the truth on the record. We did nothing wrong." She threw herself at him, wrapping her arms tight around his middle. The shakes had her now, her chest tight, lungs struggling for air.

"Staying behind that curtain was the hardest thing I've ever had to do." His words were rough and unsteady as he gripped her tight. "I tried to get a clean shot but you were in the way. I've never felt so helpless in my life. I was so afraid she would just shoot you point blank if I revealed myself. Those ten seconds felt like...an eternity." He shuddered, his pain almost palpable.

Pulling back she looked up at him, but didn't let go. She was vaguely aware of the agents coming out of the room and the rush of activity in the hallway but right now the only thing that mattered was Lucas. "You're not superhuman. If you could have taken her out, I know you would have. I trusted you to have my back. And I know I said this before, but I'm making it crystal clear that I want a future with you. I'm laying it out there again because..." She swallowed hard, fighting back tears. Because she could have died. Twice. So could have he. "Deep down I'm still scared that things won't work out and I'll lose a best friend. But it's worth it. You're worth it. I love you, Lucas."

A shudder rolled through his big body as his grip tightened and he swallowed hard. "I love you too."

Hearing those words from his lips set something free inside her. She was tired of living a muted life, tired of being afraid. And she was questioning why on earth she'd been fighting this, been fighting a relationship with Lucas. Feeling like a fool, all she could do was smile up at him.

Crashing into their reality, one of the agents rushed up to them, telling them Chloe was dead and that they needed to come with him. As long as she was with Lucas she'd go anywhere. And hearing that Chloe was dead was all she needed to know.

This nightmare was finally over.

## CHAPTER FORTY

*Four months later*

"This was such a great idea," Serenity said, wiping her soil-covered gardening gloves on her shorts as she stood up, surveying the handiwork in her own front yard.

"They'll bloom every year around this time. According to my mom, anyway." He grinned at her, looking handsome and adorable at the same time.

She seriously loved this man and probably told him too many times every day. But after dealing with the aftermath of four months ago—all the media that had descended on their town, the regurgitation of Black's serial killing spree on crime shows and on social media, and her own personal demons—she finally felt almost normal. Or as normal as she could get.

She looked down at the three small hydrangea bushes they'd just planted. Summer was here and there had been a perfect area in her yard to plant them. She loved the idea of the splash of color here, and the simple act of planting something living made her feel good inside. Every time she looked at them, she would remember doing this with him.

She was still dealing with the loss of her friends, of the horror that had visited Verona Bay, and this was such a simple, freeing act. The whole town was grieving, but they'd held a vigil for Carol and Paisley, and Serenity had started working on setting up a scholarship in their memory. It was a lot more work than she'd imagined, but it was worth it. The guard that Chloe had stabbed at the hospital and whose gun she'd stolen had survived, and the town had rallied around him as well.

Thankfully Bianca and Adeline were both thriving. Serenity had made Adeline an official partner at work and now they ran the business together. It was getting less and less weird to depend on someone. That was mainly thanks to Lucas.

Now she understood that no one ever truly made it on their own. You needed friends, family, a community to help. And there was nothing wrong with that. Hell, there was beauty in it.

Next to them, Daisy was lying in the sun, lazily batting her paws at butterflies who were intently teasing her. She wasn't eager to get up and chase them like usual—not that she ever caught them. And she loved coming over here with Lucas—which was pretty much daily. He hadn't technically moved in but it was close enough. She'd worried about how things would work with her and Harper but he'd blended into their little family seamlessly. And the man could cook—better than her, which was icing on the cake.

"How soon until Harper gets back?" Lucas asked.

She frowned, pulling her cell phone out to look at the time. "About—" Serenity stared as Lucas went down on one knee in front of her in a quick, fluid movement.

She shoved her phone back in her pocket and stared as he opened up a pretty little blue box. Blood rushed in her ears as she stared at the solitaire ring glittering in the sunlight. She opened her mouth to say something but nothing would come out.

"Serenity, will you marry me?" Beads of sweat formed on his forehead and she knew they had nothing to do with the temperature outside.

She couldn't believe he was actually nervous though. Unbidden tears stung her eyes as she shouted, "Yes!" It seemed far too soon but she knew the answer was always going to be yes, whether it was now or two years from now. This man was one in a million. "Oh my God, yes!" She shouted it again, even as he slipped the ring on her finger.

She threw her arms around his neck, practically tackling him as he stood.

Laughing, he held her close, nuzzling her neck and sending tingles of pleasure shooting down her nerve endings.

"I thought of a bunch of different scenarios but all of them seemed wrong," he said, pulling back but not loosening his grip one bit. "I knew you would hate something showy or public. And I couldn't wait any longer to come up with the perfect place. I just want to marry you, Serenity."

Wiping tears of joy away, she cupped his cheek gently. "I love you so much. I'll get married anytime, anywhere. I don't need a big wedding. Not unless you want one."

"We've got time to worry about that later." His possessive grip on her hip tightened, and when his eyes turned all heated she knew what was coming next. "We've got an hour before Harper gets back."

Lucas's mom had offered to babysit today and now Serenity knew why. "Let's make it count, then."

Daisy jumped up, racing in between them as they hurried back inside—though she wouldn't be following them into the bedroom.

Despite all the horror that had come before this, Serenity felt like she was exactly where she was supposed to be. She hated everything that had happened because of a monster—two of them—but she was no longer afraid of everything anymore.

No matter what life threw at her and Lucas, they would face it head-on. Together.

Thank you for reading Dark Memento. If you'd like to stay in touch with Katie and be the first to learn about new releases, sign up for her newsletter at https://katiereus.com

## ACKNOWLEDGMENTS

As always, I'm incredibly grateful to Kaylea Cross for being the best critique partner and sounding board a writer could ask for. I'm also thankful to Julia for such thorough edits, to Sarah for all the behind-the-scenes things she does, and to Jaycee for a stellar cover (I'm so in love with this one!). Of course, I'm thankful to my family for their continuing emotional support. And I owe so much gratitude to God for opportunities. Last but not least, thank you readers!

**Darkness Series**
Darkness Awakened
Taste of Darkness
Beyond the Darkness
Hunted by Darkness
Into the Darkness
Saved by Darkness
Guardian of Darkness
Sentinel of Darkness
A Very Dragon Christmas
Darkness Rising

**Deadly Ops Series**
Targeted
Bound to Danger
Chasing Danger (novella)
Shattered Duty
Edge of Danger
A Covert Affair

**Endgame Trilogy**
Bishop's Knight
Bishop's Queen
Bishop's Endgame

### Moon Shifter Series
Alpha Instinct

Lover's Instinct

Primal Possession

Mating Instinct

His Untamed Desire

Avenger's Heat

Hunter Reborn

Protective Instinct

Dark Protector

A Mate for Christmas

### O'Connor Family Series
Merry Christmas, Baby

Tease Me, Baby

It's Me Again, Baby

Mistletoe Me, Baby

### Red Stone Security Series
No One to Trust

Danger Next Door

Fatal Deception

Miami, Mistletoe & Murder

His to Protect

Breaking Her Rules

Protecting His Witness

Sinful Seduction

Under His Protection

Deadly Fallout

Sworn to Protect

Secret Obsession

Love Thy Enemy

Dangerous Protector

Lethal Game

***Paranormal Romance***
Destined Mate
Protector's Mate
A Jaguar's Kiss
Tempting the Jaguar
Enemy Mine
Heart of the Jaguar

# ABOUT THE AUTHOR

Katie Reus is the *New York Times* and *USA Today* bestselling author of the Red Stone Security series, the Darkness series and the Deadly Ops series. She fell in love with romance at a young age thanks to books she pilfered from her mom's stash. Years later she loves reading romance almost as much as she loves writing it.

However, she didn't always know she wanted to be a writer. After changing majors many times, she finally graduated summa cum laude with a degree in psychology. Not long after that she discovered a new love. Writing. She now spends her days writing dark paranormal romance and sexy romantic suspense.

For more information on Katie please visit her website: https://katiereus.com

Made in the USA
Middletown, DE
17 February 2020